"I'm the one you married.

"By proxy, I mean. I never deliberately set out to deceive you," Rose said, "but what's important is that I'd like to stay. That is, if you'll have me."

Matt steepled his hands before him, his eyes never leaving her face. He'd set grown men to trembling in their boots with just such a look. "Go on," he prompted.

She caught her breath, prepared to plunge on. He had to admire the way she looked him straight in the eye, even knowing she'd been lying through her pretty teeth ever since she'd tumbled out of the wagon onto his doorstep.

"Well, the lawyer said I could behest my way out of it any time I wanted to as long as the marriage was never—that is, as long as we didn't— And of course, we didn't, so..."

We didn't, but we will before this farce is ended, madam. We owe each other that much.

Dear Reader,

Have you ever been tempted to turn Mr. Wrong into Mr. Right? In each of our books this month, you'll delight in the ways these least-likely-to-marry men change their tune for the right woman!

Mainstream historical author Bronwyn Williams returns to Harlequin Historicals—after nearly eight years—with a wonderful Americana book, *The Paper Marriage*. This is the second title in THE PASSIONATE POWERS miniseries, which begins and ends in Silhouette Desire. Here, you'll meet sea captain Matthew Powers, the intrepid forefather to Jackson and Curt. After adopting an orphaned infant girl, Matt soon realizes he needs help—even if it means marrying. But the woman he weds by proxy—thanks to his matchmaking aunt Bess—never shows up. Instead, a friend of Bess's arrives—a young widow who steals his daughter's heart…and his own!

In *Prince of Hearts,* a medieval novel by debut author Katy Cooper, Edmund Tudor, the king of England's youngest brother, must choose between the woman he has fallen in love with and his duty to his brother's kingdom. Another talented first-time author is Julianne MacLean, who brings us *Prairie Bride,* a sexy Western about a recently jilted—and angry—Kansas farmer who advertises for a mail-order bride and finds himself falling in love with her despite her secretive past.

And don't miss *The Sea Witch*, book one of Ruth Langan's medieval miniseries SIRENS OF THE SEA. When a female privateer and a dashing sea captain team up to thwart a villain's plot against the king, they must learn that their love can overcome even the greatest dangers.…

Enjoy! And come back again next month for four more choices of the best in historical romance.

Sincerely,

Tracy Farrell,
Senior Editor

Bronwyn Williams

THE PAPER MARRIAGE

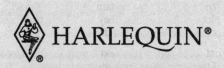

HARLEQUIN®

TORONTO • NEW YORK • LONDON
AMSTERDAM • PARIS • SYDNEY • HAMBURG
STOCKHOLM • ATHENS • TOKYO • MILAN • MADRID
PRAGUE • WARSAW • BUDAPEST • AUCKLAND

ISBN 0-373-29124-8

THE PAPER MARRIAGE

Visit us at www.eHarlequin.com

Printed in U.S.A.

To Rebecca Burrus
and all her friends at *Carolina Living*.
You've added a whole new dimension to our lives.
Becky's Brats

Prologue

February 27, 1898
The Outer Banks of North Carolina

The sound of rain drumming on the roof almost drowned out the sound of the crying baby. Matt wished it could drown out the memory of this infamous day. Wipe it clean from all their minds. They were still stunned, speaking in whispers, staring in horror at the squalling mite bound up in a blanket in the middle of the bed.

Billy was dead. Handsome Billy, with a slew of sweethearts in every port. Billy, who could win at cards and leave the losers laughing. Billy, who had gone to sea as a cabin boy when his family had died of the influenza and worked his way up to chief mate.

As captain, Matt was responsible for his crew, whether on land or at sea. He had warned the lad, but without following him every time he rode into the village, how could he know the boy would dally with a married woman and get her with child?

Hadn't he carefully explained to both Billy and Luther that the village women were to be treated with respect?

He should have found himself another ship immediately after he'd lost the *Black Swan*. At sea, or in any port in the world, a man might get himself knifed in a brawl, but he was unlikely to be murdered by a maddened seaman who had been away from home for eleven months, only to come home and find that his wife had just given birth to a daughter.

"Cap'n, we'll have to shovel more sand on Billy's grave once this rain stops. It's sinking in." Luther, the youngest member of his crew now that Billy was dead, was pale as raw dough, his eyes still dark with the shock of it all.

Matt nodded. Every one of them, even old Crank, whose rheumatism scarcely allowed him to get out of bed on days like this, had gone out again and again to stand in the rain and stare down at the fresh grave, as if to convince themselves that it had actually happened. That some poor, wretched creature had shot his unfaithful wife, then come storming after Billy to put a bullet in his chest and, before anyone could stop him, turned the gun on himself, leaving a screaming newborn infant lying on the ground between the two bodies.

Hearing the first shot, Matt had rushed outside in time to see Billy fall. He'd yelled for Crank, leaped off the porch and reached the boy just as the wild-haired stranger had flung down a bundle and turned the gun on himself.

Billy had struggled to lift his head. "Dammit, boy,

lie still! Crank, get me a rag—get help from the village!''

Without waiting for a response he had torn Billy's shirt open, muttering curses and prayers in the same breath. ''Get the midwife, dammit! Luther, go!''

There was no doctor on the island. The midwife was the best they could do. ''Hang on, son, help's on the way,'' he said, wanting to believe it was true. Wanting even more to make Billy believe it.

''Cap'n, promise me—''

''Hush, now, it'll be all right. Just lie still.''

''You gotta promise me—my baby—it—it—''

''Shh, the baby'll be just fine, it's you we've got to take care of now.''

But he knew even as he said the words that it was too late. They both knew it, yet Billy still struggled to get the words out, his blue eyes pleading desperately. ''My baby—you gotta promise me, Cap'n—''

''Anything, boy, just hang on.''

''Didn't mean no harm—her man couldn't—he weren't—able…''

''Ah, Billy, don't die on me, dammit. Don't do it, son!'' Matt swore because he couldn't weep. A moment later he stood and turned away until he got himself under control. Then, kneeling again, he examined both bodies and pronounced them dead.

It was Crank who rescued the squalling babe, wrapped it in one of his own shirts and carried it inside as gingerly as if it had been a basket of eggs. Luther brought the midwife, who did what was necessary for the infant with angry old eyes and a pinched, disapproving mouth.

"She'll likely not live out the night. If she's still here by sunup, you can sop a rag in water and give her a suck."

It was all the advice the old woman offered before she climbed up into her cart and headed back to the village. The four remaining men stood helplessly and watched her ride off. Matt swore. Crank misquoted a Bible verse about the sins of the fathers. Peg, the ship's carpenter, got to work on a casket while Luther rode back to the village, this time to fetch the magistrate.

It had taken the rest of day to untangle the wreckage. To cart the man's body back to the village, to bury poor Billy, and to learn that the unfaithful wife had been from "away"—the native's way of calling anyone not island-born.

"Not to put too fine a point on it," Dick Dixon, the lawman, had said, "but she weren't one of ours, so don't look for help from that quarter."

"What about the husband's family? Surely one of them—"

"The poor bastard weren't his. They'll not take it."

"Don't call her that, none of this is her fault." Even before the midwife had come, they'd discovered that the tiny thing wrapped in Crank's shirt was a newborn baby girl.

"If I was you, I'd write to the boy's family. Might be one o' them'll take it off your hands."

"No help there. Billy is—was an orphan."

"Well, I don't know where the woman came from. Like I said, she was from away, been here about two years, I believe.'' He stood, settled his hat on his bald head and turned to go. "Looks like you just became a father, Powers."

"No, sir, that I did not." Matt said quickly. He had promised Billy to take care of the baby, but he hadn't promised to do it personally…had he?

On the other hand, until he could find someone to take the child off his hands, he was responsible for its—for her welfare. She was Billy's, and Billy had been a member of his crew.

Before he left, the magistrate had sympathized but warned him again not to look for help from the village. "Meaning no disrespect, Powers, but after what happened, none of our women are going to come anywhere near your men."

Which struck Matt as grossly unfair, but then, when had life ever been fair? Come a hard blow, a smart man trimmed sail, headed into the wind and rode it out.

Matt did the only thing he could think of to do: he reluctantly began a letter to his only remaining relative. Bess Powers was a meddlesome busybody who would never tell the truth when a lie would serve as well, but she'd always been honest in their dealings.

So far as he knew, he amended.

Chapter One

March 3, 1898
Norfolk, Virginia

Most of the mourners had already left. A raw, wet northeast wind whipped the black skirts of the lone woman who lingered, her veiled head bowed, beside the open grave. Nearby, the preacher eyed the lowering clouds as he waited patiently for Rose Magruder to pay her last respects to her grandmother's mortal remains. He took out his pocket watch, glanced down quickly, then looked up at the sky again, and at the grave diggers waiting to finish their work.

Some distance away, a handful of servants huddled uncertainly, hoping the rain would hold off for another few minutes. Hoping Miss Rose would land on her feet, because the poor girl deserved better than she'd had these past few years.

Hoping even more that Mrs. Littlefield had left them the back wages she'd died owing.

On the other side of the plot, under the shelter of

a massive magnolia, an elderly couple lingered, their heads close together as they carried on a low-voiced conversation. Bess Powers had been Augusta Littlefield's friend for more than forty years. Horace Bagby had been her lawyer for at least that long.

"Gussy would've told us all to get inside before we catch our deaths," murmured the plump woman with the suspiciously red hair. "Poor Gussy, she was a tartar, but I loved her like a sister."

"Gussy was always proud of what you've accomplished, you know. Used to read me every one of your letters while you were off on one of your travels." The two longtime friends were among the few who had been allowed to call the late Mrs. Littlefield "Gussy."

"Well, I'm home for a few weeks, at any rate. Horace, what are we going to do about that poor child?" She nodded toward the deceased's only relative. "I suppose I could invite her to move in with me as a sort of secretary-companion, but you know how small my cottage is."

Horace removed his derby, smoothed the few strands of hair laid carefully across his dome, and carefully replaced his hat. They both studied the lone figure dressed in black. Tall as a beanpole, Bess was thinking.

Slender as a willow, Horace mused, a romantic in spite of his elderly bachelor status. "Bess, I just don't know. Right now all I can think of is how I'm going to break the news to her. I'd rather take a licking, and that's a fact."

"Poor child, you'd think she'd have earned a little

peace after all she's had to put up with. Never had a
beau in her life, far as anybody knows. Gussy said
she married the first jack out of the box after her folks
died. Nobody had ever heard of the fellow. Then, less
than two years later, the fellow up and died on her.

"Drowned, I believe Gussy said." They stood in
silent sympathy for the tall, plain woman who lingered beside the grave.

The handful of acquaintances who had braved the
weather to attend the funeral had already left, eager
to exchange this dismal place for a warm, food-laden
parlor where they could enjoy a good meal while they
speculated on how much the old girl had left her only
granddaughter.

Not until the preacher finally led the chief mourner
away did Horace tuck Bess's hand under his arm and
steer her toward the one remaining carriage. "Waiting hand and foot on Gussy couldn't have been any
picnic, either," Bess remarked as she picked her way
carefully around the puddles. "By the time Rose
came to live with her, Gussy's mind was already ad-
dled. Never was much to brag about, poor soul."

Horace nodded. "Came on her so gradually, I kept
telling myself she was just having another bad spell,
but you're right. She never was what you might call
quick-witted. I tried to warn her about those funds,
but by the time I found out what she was up to, it
was already too late." He sighed heavily. "And now
there's that poor girl yonder...."

"I know. I didn't want to believe it, either."

They followed the lead carriage, bearing the
preacher and Augusta Rose Littlefield Magruder,

granddaughter and sole heir to the late Augusta Littlefield, back to the Littlefield mansion.

Bess patted Horace's black-gloved hand. ''Never mind, we'll think of something.''

The house was overheated. It smelled of wet wool. There'd be an enormous coal bill to pay once Rose had time to tackle her grandmother's messy desk. Right to the end Gussy had insisted on keeping her own accounts. She'd allowed no one in what she called her office, a converted sitting room off the master bedroom that was kept locked, with the key hidden in one of Gussy's bedroom slippers.

Rose had known where it was, of course, but neither she nor any of the few remaining servants would have dreamed of using it. A calm and contented Gussy had been difficult enough to deal with; an angry Gussy utterly impossible.

Now Rose sat numbly, half hidden behind a Chinese screen, waiting for this endless day to end. She would have given anything she possessed, which wasn't all that much, to be able to close her eyes and sleep for a solid week.

Unfortunately, even if she'd had the chance, her mind would have refused to cooperate. She had grown up in a house nearly as grand as this one, but the thought of being solely responsible for her grandmother's entire estate was overwhelming.

Gradually, she became aware of a whispered conversation on the other side of the screen. She honestly didn't mean to listen, but without revealing her presence it was impossible not to hear.

"...finally gone, I guess her granddaughter's set for life, the lucky woman."

"Lucky? If you ask me, the poor thing's earned every dollar the old biddy hoarded all these years. Didn't pay her servants worth diddly. Her upstairs maid came to work for me last fall, and she said—"

"Yes, but they say the granddaughter's had a hard row to hoe. I heard her folks were killed in that awful train wreck near Suffolk, and a few years later her husband was murdered."

"He wasn't murdered, silly, he drowned. The way I heard it, he—"

"Black don't become her at all, does it? If I was her, I'd use a touch of rouge."

"For shame, Ida Lee, she's a decent woman, for all she's plain as a fence post."

"The poor thing, they say she's still grieving for her husband, too."

What was that old saying about eavesdroppers? Rose wondered, amused in spite of herself. Black did indeed make her look sallow, but then so did everything else. Some kind soul had once called her unfashionable complexion "olive," and she'd latched onto it because it sounded better than sallow—even faintly exotic—but fancy words couldn't change the truth.

And she *was* grieving. She would grieve for the rest of her life, but not for the lout she had married.

Rose Magruder had never been one to display her emotions. She had come to her grandmother a penniless widow. Since then she had been far too busy trying to keep up with the constant, confusing and often conflicting demands of her only remaining relative to do more than fall into bed each night, exhausted.

Of the staff required to maintain an eighteen-room mansion and the acres surrounding it, only three had stayed on until the end.

Rose fully intended to see that those three were amply rewarded for their faithfulness.

But first she had to find time to go through the mountain of papers her grandmother had left crammed into shoeboxes, hatboxes and goodness knows where else. She knew for a fact that the household accounts were in arrears, because several of the merchants with whom they did business had brought it to her attention.

Thank goodness for Horace Bagby. She didn't know the man well, but he seemed both kind and competent. With the help of an accountant, which Mr. Bagby could probably recommend, they should be able to sort things out. Sallow or not, she had always had a good head for figures.

Not until the last of the mourners had gone did Rose discover that she might have saved herself the worry. Horace Bagby had stayed behind when the others left. He wished he'd thought to ask Bess to stay and help him with the unpleasant task. He hated tears, never had learned how to deal with them.

"As to the, ah—the will, I'm afraid the news is not good, my dear. Your grandmother's estate is...well, the truth is, it's mortgaged to the hilt and will have to be sold immediately to pay off creditors.''

He braced himself to deal with anything up to and including an outburst of hysteria. Mrs. Magruder fooled him. She shed not so much as a single tear. There in the gloomy front parlor, its windows shrouded in respect for the deceased, she sat quietly, her hands folded on her lap, her eyes somewhat swollen, somewhat pink, but quite dry.

''There now, we'll come through this, my dear,'' he said without the least notion of how he would bring about such a miracle. As the poor girl didn't seem inclined to question him, he hurried to fill the silence with all the information he had at hand.

Rose sat quietly as the words droned on and on and on. Now and then a phrase would snag her attention.

Nothing left?

''—gambled away—risky investments—warned her, but you know Gussy, she was headstrong right to the end.''

Sold immediately?

''—lock, stock and barrel, I'm afraid. I'm sure we can think of something. That is, there's bound to be a way—''

Rose took a deep, steadying breath. ''Would it be possible,'' she asked, her voice unnaturally composed, ''to sell several pieces of my own jewelry? They were given to me by my grandmother, but legally, I believe they're mine to do with as I wish.''

''Of course, of course, my dear, you're quite right. I'll handle it this very day, if you'd like.''

   Technically, the jewelry, especially if it consisted of family pieces, could be considered a part of the estate, but Horace wasn't about to let this young lady suffer for the mistakes of a weak-minded old woman. After asking her once again if she wouldn't prefer to go and stay with friends, he reluctantly took his leave. Rose saw him to the door. Mentally she was numb. Physically, she was too exhausted to think about dragging her trunks down from the attic to begin the arduous task of packing. After a night's sleep, she might be better able to think clearly.

   Horace drove directly to Granby Street, where he sold the five pieces of jewelry, none of them particularly valuable. "It should keep her for at least a month, providing she's frugal," he confided to Bess that evening over teacups of fine, aged brandy. "Seems a sensible sort, but you never know. At least now she'll be able to set herself up in a decent rooming house until she can find herself another husband. Shouldn't take too long, even with mourning and all. She's a bit long in the shank, but a widower with children might not be so particular."

   "If marriage was the answer to every maiden's prayer," his companion observed dryly, "the two of us wouldn't be sitting here drinking brandy and smoking cigars."

   Horace lifted his teacup in silent acknowledgement.

   Unable to sleep after all, Rose dragged her trunk down from the attic and began emptying the wardrobe, folding and packing layers on top of the layers she'd never even got around to unpacking. Most were black, except for a few old summer things and the wedding gown she'd saved as a bitter reminder of what could happen when a woman made the wrong choice. She'd been in mourning for so long, she'd almost forgotten what it was like to wear colors.

The next afternoon she divided the proceeds from the sale of her jewelry among the three remaining servants, thanking them again for their support. "I'm sorry it isn't more. Goodness knows you deserve far more, this hardly even covers your salary, but it's the best I can do, I'm afraid."

They seemed to understand, to appreciate her appreciation, and they wished each other well.

Not until the last one had left did Rose allow her guard to drop. And then the tears came. She wept until her eyes were swollen, her throat clogged, her handkerchief a sodden lump. "Oh, Lord, this is a waste of time," she muttered, and then cried some more. On the rare occasions when she allowed herself the luxury of tears, she made a fine job of it, weeping noisily until every last dreg of emotion was spent.

She cried for her parents—the charming rascal of a father she'd adored, her dainty, beautiful mother who had never quite known what to make of her gawky misfit of a daughter—and for the grandmother who had changed so drastically from the woman she dimly remembered from her childhood.

But most of all, she wept for her baby, who had never even had a chance to live.

Eventually she mopped her face, smoothed her

skirt and stood before the heavy hall mirror, recalling the words her grandmother's housekeeper had spoken when she'd tucked her share of the money in her purse. "There now, you'll land on your feet, Miss Rose, you see if you don't. You might not be much to look at, but you've got backbone aplenty."

Not much to look at, she thought ruefully. Never have been. Never would be. At least she would never have to worry about aging and losing her beauty, which had been her mother's greatest fear.

At thirteen Rose had been tall and painfully shy. At eighteen she'd still been shy, and even taller, but she could walk without tripping over her feet. She'd even learned to dance so that on those rare occasions when some poor boy had been forced to do his duty, she wouldn't disgrace herself.

"No, you're not much to look at," she told her mirror image. Given the choice between beauty and backbone, she would have chosen beauty, which just went to show she still hadn't learned anything.

Fortunately, the choice wasn't hers to make. She'd been stuck with backbone, which was a good thing, because backbone was just what she would need until she could find a position and establish herself in a decent neighborhood.

With the house empty and her luggage stacked beside her, Rose sat on one of the delicate chairs that flanked the inlaid hall table and waited for her grandmother's friend, Bess Powers, who had located a suitable rooming house and offered to drive her there, as her grandmother's horse and buggy had already been claimed by a creditor.

Limp with exhaustion, she was afraid to relax for fear she might fall asleep. Afraid the few dollars in her purse would not be enough. Perhaps she should have kept back part of the proceeds from the sale of her jewelry in case the landlord insisted on being paid in advance.

What if she couldn't find a position right away?

And even if she could, it would be weeks, perhaps months, before she could expect to be paid.

Choices. It came down to making the right one. Unfortunately, women were rarely given a chance to learn, their choices being made for them, first by parents and then by husbands. The first time she'd had to make a choice, she'd made a disastrous one. After suffering the consequences, she'd had no choice but to turn to her grandmother.

This time she was fresh out of relatives. It was a criminal shame, she told herself, that well-bred young women were never trained to be self-supporting.

Bess arrived on the dot of four. "There you are," she declared, as if she'd been searching everywhere. Parking her umbrella in the stand, she stood before the mirror and re-skewered her hat atop her freshly hennaed hair with a lethal-looking hatpin. "Shame about the house, but I've been telling Gussy for years that this was too much house for one lone woman. Don't be possessed by your possessions, I always say."

Which was all very well, Rose thought, as long as

one possessed a roof over one's head. A bed in hand was worth two in the bush.

Giddy, that's what you are. Good thing your feet are as long as they are, my girl, because you're going to have to stand on them from now on. "Grandmother's housekeeper gave me the name of a reliable agency where I might look for work."

"What kind of work can you do?" Bess didn't believe in mincing words. As a woman who supported herself with words, she valued them too highly. "Can you take shorthand? Can you cook? Not that I'd recommend it, but better to lord it over a kitchen than to have to wait on every oaf with the price of a meal."

Rose had never even considered serving as a waitress, but it might well come to that. "I've never tried it, but I'm sure I could learn. I'm good with invalids, too."

"You want to be a doormat all your life? I haven't known you long, child, because I've been away so much these past few years, but we both know Gussy was no invalid. What she was, poor soul, was crazy as a bedbug, not to put too fine a point on it. Now, don't tell me you want to go to work in one of those asylums, you wouldn't last out a day."

Rose knew the woman meant well. And after all, she was one of those rare creatures, a truly independent woman. "All right, then what do you suggest? Governess? Companion? Surely I could qualify for either of those positions."

"I thought about hiring you as a secretary-companion."

Rose waited for the catch. She was certain there would be one.

"Trouble is, I couldn't afford to pay you enough to live on. My publisher pays my expenses when I'm traveling, but I doubt if he'd pay for a secretary."

On her good days, her grandmother used to talk about her friend, Bess Powers, who was considered a minor celebrity after the diaries she had written while growing up aboard her father's ship had been published. Rose envied Miss Powers her freedom and independence but, celebrity or not, she wasn't at all sure she could abide the woman for any length of time.

"I'm afraid I don't take shorthand. I'm sure I could learn, though, and my penmanship is excellent."

"'T'wouldn't work. I've traveled in single harness too long. As it happens, though, I have another problem on my hands. You might be just the one to tackle it. I don't suppose you've got a drop of brandy in the house, do you? This miserable weather goes right to my knees."

"I'm sorry. Knowing I'd be leaving today, I let the servants take home all the food and drink, but I'm sure there's some tea left in the caddy."

"Never mind. Now, where was I? Oh, yes, Matt. My nephew. Poor boy, he was desperate enough to write to me for help, which means he's at his wit's end. Last time I saw him he called me a meddling old busybody." She chuckled. "I'll not deny it, either."

Rose murmured a polite disclaimer. She scarcely

knew the woman, after all, but if she had indeed spent her formative years at sea in a man's world, as she claimed to have done, then it was no wonder she tended to be outspoken.

Rose appreciated plain speaking. It saved time in the long run, even if the truth did happen to tread on a few tender toes.

"Well anyhow, as I told Horace, you're a tad on the scrawny side, but then Gussy was always frail, too. Still, it takes a strong woman to look after a child."

"A child?" Rose repeated, frowning. Perhaps she was more like her grandmother than she'd thought, for she was having trouble following the conversation. "I'm sorry—did I miss something?"

"Child, baby, I'm not sure of her age, but I do know I'm too old to tackle the job, even if I had the time. Still, I expect you're stronger than you look, else you'd never have been able to put up with Gussy. I know, I know, she was my dearest friend, even though we didn't see much of one another once I started traveling professionally, so to speak. But Gussy was always a bit light under the bonnet, if you take my meaning. Old age struck me in the knees. It struck Gussy's head. I guess it hits us all in our weakest parts."

Rose couldn't think of a single word to say. If this tale had a logical conclusion, she couldn't imagine what it would be.

"Still, it'd be killing two birds with one stone, wouldn't it?"

* * *

That night, as was their habit, Bess and Horace shared tea, brandy, cigars and an assessment of the day's events. They'd lived for years in the same neighborhood, three blocks apart. "So you see," Bess was saying, "if Rose agrees to it, Matt won't have much choice, he'll have to go along. By this time he'll be too desperate to stand on his high horse."

"What if he's found someone from the village to take the baby off his hands?"

"If he could've, he would've by now."

"Speaking of Rose, how is she settling in?"

"I put her in that women's boarding place just off Dominion. The rooms are small, but it's clean, decent and cheap."

"She'll be out first thing tomorrow looking for work," Horace reminded her. "If she finds it, what happens to your plan to pair her up with your nephew?"

"Finding work won't be easy. She's feeling her way right now, but she's got pride and backbone. Women wanting a maid or a governess won't like it, it throws off the natural pecking order."

"What makes you think your nephew will hire her?"

"Like I said, the boy's got no choice. If he did, he'd never have asked for my help." She chuckled. Lifting her left foot to the ottoman, she gently massaged her knee through layers of serge, taffeta and muslin. "Can you picture me with a leaky, squalling babe in my lap? The good Lord knew what He was doing when He gave babies to young folks. We old folks don't have the patience, much less the energy.''

Horace nursed his brandy and stared into the fireplace. "Now why," he mused, "do I get the feeling you're up to something more than just finding a nursemaid for young Captain Powers?''

Chapter Two

They called her Annie, after Billy's mother. At the moment she was shrieking, stinking and kicking. For all of ten seconds Matt stood in the doorway and thought about walking away. Walking until he could no longer smell the stench or hear the ear-splitting wails.

"You write to that aunt of yours again?" Crankshaw Higgins, the eldest member of the unorthodox household, set down the half-empty nursing bottle. With a harried look, he handed over the baby, along with a clean huck towel.

"Third letter went out last week," Matt replied.

"She going to take her off your hands?"

"Hasn't said yet."

Crank swore. A ship's cook by trade, he had better things to do, but like the rest, he valiantly stood his watch.

Could the captain do any less?

Resigned to his fate, Matt poured water from the

kettle into a basin, dropped in a bar of lye soap and prepared to do his duty.

Some thirty minutes later, his sleeves and the front of his shirt soaked, he stood back and admired his handiwork. "There now, you're all squared away, mate. You know, you're not all that homely with your mouth shut."

The infant gazed up at him, her large blue eyes slightly unfocused. She was bald as an egg, but at least she had some heft to her now. She'd been little more than skin and bones when he'd inherited her, but these last few weeks, thanks largely to Crank's efforts, she had begun to flesh out.

"Yeah, you heard me right," he murmured softly in a voice that none of his men would have recognized. The cords of tension that recently had tightened his shoulders until he could scarce turn his head from east to west were beginning to ease off now that he was getting used to handling something this fragile.

Luther poked his head into the room, his beardless cheeks reddened by the cold northwest wind. He'd been out fishing the net, dressing the catch and salting down those fish not needed for the day's meals. "Let me clean up first and I'll stand the next watch. Think she'll be sleeping by then?"

"More likely she'll be squalling again."

Because his grandfather had been one of them, Matt had been guardedly accepted by the villagers when, along with the two youngest and the two eldest members of his crew, he had returned to Powers Point, the land his grandfather had purchased soon after he'd sold his ship and retired. After standing empty for years, most of the buildings had been storm-damaged, a few of them washed clean away, but the main house was still sound. With the help of Peg, his ship's carpenter, and a few of the local builders, they had brought it up to standard, adding on whatever rooms were deemed necessary.

In Matt's estimation, it was as fine a place as any man could want, still he counted the days until he could leave. Crank and Peg would stay on as caretakers once he got his ship back. Neither of them was young or nimble enough to return to their old way of life.

The five men had quickly settled into a comfortable routine, fishing, repairing the outbuildings, working with the half-wild horses they'd bought on the mainland and had shipped across the sound—riding into the village for supplies or to meet the mail-boat.

Billy and Luther had quickly made friends, especially among the young women. The first few times they'd ridden south, Matt had cautioned them as a matter of course against drinking, gambling, fighting and fornicating. "A village like this is different from a port city. If either one of you oversteps the boundaries here, we'll all pay the price."

"I ain't heard no complaints, have you, Lute?" Billy had grinned in the infectious way that had made him a favorite of all, male and female, young and old. Remembering what it had been like to be young and full of juice, Matt hadn't kept too tight a line on them.

Now Billy was lying under six feet of sand.

Not a one of them doubted he'd done what he'd been accused of doing. Luther had as much as admitted he'd suspected what was going on. Evidently, half the village had suspected, but as the woman in question was from away and her much older husband had a reputation for meanness, they had chosen to mind their own affairs.

Hearing the sound of Peg's hammer as he nailed another rafter in place, Matt slowly shook his head. Using wrack collected along the shore, the old man had insisted on building another room for Annie, as if they didn't have rooms going unused in the old two-story frame house.

But then, it made as much sense as Luther's wanting to buy and train a pony for her, and her not even two months old. Crank had even mentioned getting her a puppy.

It amused Matt to watch his crew vie for Annie's favor. If she preferred one over the other, she didn't let on. Bess could sort it all out, if she ever showed up. He had lost his temper and called her a meddling old busybody the last time she'd poked her nose into his personal affairs, but sooner or later she'd be back. Out of curiosity, if nothing else. And once she was here, he could concentrate all his efforts on regaining his ship.

His ship…

Looking back, Matt marveled at the depths of stupidity to which an otherwise intelligent man could sink. Four years ago, at the behest of an old friend of his father's, he'd reluctantly agreed to attend a ball being held to raise funds for the Old Seamen's Retirement Home.

It was there that he'd met Gloria Timmons, daughter of one of the sponsors. She had stood in the receiving line looking like one of those Christmas-tree angels, all white and gold and sparkling.

A large man, used to towering over all women and most men, Matt had been flat-out terror-stricken when she'd placed her small, soft hand in his, gazed up at him with eyes the color of a summer sky, and fanned her eyelashes. With his free hand he'd tugged at his collar. He'd had to clear his throat several times, and she must've felt sorry for him because she'd given him a smile that would melt a cannonball.

Matt could readily hold his own in the company of men, but he was a fish out of water when it came to women. The truth was, he'd never really trusted one, not since his mother had decided she'd rather live ashore than aboard her husband's ship, even if it meant leaving her eight-year-old son behind with his father.

Not that he hadn't enjoyed his share of doxies, but respectable women—especially young, beautiful, dainty, respectable women with soft voices, soft faces and soft hands—those were his downfall.

It had all started that night. Matt had never bothered to learn how to dance. With Gloria, he'd scarcely been able to string two words together without stuttering, but somehow she had made him feel like a regular Prince Charming. By the time that first evening was over, he'd been heart-stricken in the worst way.

They'd spent every day together the entire time his ship was in port. Neglecting appointments with custom officers, shipping agents, brokers and consigners, over the course of seven days he had listened to more music, drunk more tea and sat through more dull lectures than any man should have to endure in one lifetime.

He hadn't uttered a word of complaint. If Gloria had asked him, he would have crawled over a bed of live coals.

The night before he'd sailed she had allowed him to kiss her. Scared stiff he would break her, or at the very least, terrify her by either his size or his tightly leashed passion, he'd been shaking too hard to do the job justice.

"If only you didn't have to leave," she'd whispered after that brief hard, dry kiss. "I could never marry a man who would go off and leave me by myself for months at a time. I would simply die of loneliness."

He hadn't realized it at the time, but she'd hit him in the one place where he was vulnerable. It had been years since he'd last seen his mother. As an adult, he'd seldom even thought about her. The last time they'd met had been at his father's funeral where, like the strangers they were, they had made polite conversation. She'd told him she would be marrying again and moving to Chicago; he'd told her he was off to Honduras at week's end and they'd parted still strangers. Since then she had rarely crossed his mind, but evidently the old scars were still there.

Oh, yeah, he'd been broadsided, all right. By the time he'd left Gloria that last night in port he had promised to finish one last run, then put his ship up for sale and invest the proceeds in her father's ship-building firm in exchange for a seat on the board of directors.

In the end, he got exactly what he deserved. After delivering a cargo of dyewood, mahogany and ba-nanas to Boston only three days behind schedule, he had contracted with a broker to sell the *Black Swan*. With his head still in the clouds, he had bought the biggest diamond ring he could find and headed south with marriage on his mind, only to be informed that Miss Timmons was visiting a friend in West Virginia. Five days later, having partially regained his senses, he'd taken a train to Boston, intent on pulling his ship off the market.

He'd been three days too late. She'd just been sold.

So he'd headed south again, determined to make the best of a bad situation. If he could no longer be captain of the finest three-masted schooner afloat, he would be the finest husband, and make a stab at being a damned good director of Timmons Shipbuilding. He was not without business experience, after all.

That was when he'd discovered that the woman who had stolen his heart was too busy reeling in an-other poor sucker to spare him more than a rueful smile. "But darling, I never actually said I'd marry you, did I? I'm sure I didn't. I'm having far too much fun to settle down yet, but Daddy's still saving you that seat on the board as soon as you've sold your ship.''

For the first time in years he had gone out and gotten howling drunk. Two and a half days later he'd wakened up in a Newport News flophouse with a fistful of busted knuckles and a head the size of New Zealand, both his pockets and his belly turned wrong-side out.

Dammit, he wanted her back.

The *Black Swan,* not Gloria. God knows, any romantic nonsense had been purged from his heart.

After four years, the broker was still working on getting his ship back. The new owner, a consortium of dry-land sailors, was intent on playing games with him, their latest demand, relayed by the broker, being a five-percent cut of the captain's share of the profits for five years and a sale price well above the original purchase price.

He'd been in the process of negotiating for a two-year split and a lower sale price when all hell had broken loose and he'd found himself with a problem no broker could solve.

Annie.

With the tip of his big, booted foot, Matt rocked the cradle Peg had fashioned from a rum barrel and padded with goose down. If Bess didn't soon come through for him, he was going to have to broaden his search. He could hardly take an infant to sea with him.

If she'd been a boy, he might have considered it, but she wasn't. All he had to do was look at Bess to see what that kind of a life would do to a girl. Bossy, meddlesome, conniving, his aunt drank like a man and cursed like a man, and got all huffy when a man did the same thing in her presence.

He sighed and then he swore. He'd done more of both in the short time since he'd become a surrogate father than in all his thirty-one years put together.

Yeah, Annie needed a woman. And so, unfortunately, did he. The trouble with a small, insular village was that everyone knew everything that went on. Without a decent whorehouse, a man could get into serious trouble, a tragic lesson they'd all learned the hard way.

Crank, in his Bible-quoting mode, claimed it was better to marry than to burn, but Matt wasn't about to commit that particular folly. He was old enough that he could wait until he went to the mainland.

It wasn't so easy for a younger man. The first time Luther had ridden in for supplies after the shooting he had come back with his jaw dragging. "Hell sakes, Cap'n, all the girls has disappeared."

They hadn't disappeared, they'd been hidden away, forbidden to associate with the men from Powers Point. Considering what had happened, Matt couldn't much blame any man for trying to protect his womenfolk, but dammit, Annie wasn't at fault. She'd come into this world an innocent victim. Matt refused to allow her to suffer for the sins of her parents, if he had to give up the sea forever.

But it might not come to that. Things were gradually beginning to thaw. The first time Crank had ridden in to lay in a supply of tinned milk, one or two of the older women had offered advice about bringing up a baby's wind in the middle of her dinner, and using lard to clean her tail instead of lye soap.

Another woman had offered them the loan of one of her milk goats, but for the most part, the men of Powers Point had been left alone with a task not a one of them was equipped to handle.

"Bess, you're going to have to help me with this," Matt muttered to the cold, damp night. Unable to sleep, he stood on a wooded ridge overlooking the Pamlico Sound, watching the moon sink behind a cloud bank. "God knows, you're not my idea of a nursemaid, but I don't know where else to turn." He didn't consider it praying, but the same heartfelt sentiment was there.

Watching a shooting star arc across the sky, he wondered how the death of anything in the universe could be so beautiful. So far he'd seen only the ugliness of death. If he'd been of a mystical turn of mind, he might have taken the shooting star for an omen, but Matt was a realist. Always had been. The second generation of Powers men to have been raised at sea, he'd learned from his father, who had learned from his own father, that a fair wind, a sound ship and a good crew were all a man needed to make his own luck.

Rose watched as Bess Powers poured two cups of tea, then added a dose of medicinal brandy to her own. She'd been invited for the afternoon to discuss her plans for the future, a future that was beginning to look increasingly dismal.

She stirred sugar into her tea, which was stronger than she liked, but hot and fortifying. "I should have worked harder on my art and music. Mama warned me I'd live to regret it. The trouble is, I have no sense of rhythm, and as for my watercolors—well, the less said, the better. Bess, how can I even teach a girl to walk properly when I'm apt to trip over my own feet?" Extending her limbs, she gazed dolefully down at her long, narrow kid slippers.

Bess snorted. "Woman your height would look damned silly with feet no bigger than mine."

"Who wants a governess who can't dance, can't play the piano, can't paint and—"

"I heard from Matt again today. Poor boy, he's in sad shape. That's the third letter in two weeks."

"Did you know that no one will even consider hiring a woman accountant? I'm smart as a whip when it comes to figures."

"Didn't do poor Gussy much good, did it?"

Rose looked up quickly, a stricken expression on her face. "I'm afraid not," she admitted. Given a chance, she might have been able to salvage something, but before she could even go through the accounts, it was already far too late.

"Sorry, child, you didn't deserve that."

Perhaps she did, but this was no time to pile guilt onto a feeling of inadequacy. If she could just keep her head level, her feet on the ground and her spirits high, she would come through this just fine.

"I interviewed for a companion's position yesterday. The pay is barely enough to keep a mouse in cheese, and I'd be expected to sleep in an attic room.

The ceiling slopes so that I can't even stand up, but there's a lovely view of the garden.''

"Like I said, poor Matt's in desperate straits.''

Rose surrendered gracefully. She had gone on and on about her own slender prospects while Bess listened; it was only fair that she return the favor.

"You remember I told you about my nephew?''

Rose knew all about Captain Powers, his landlocked crew and his inherited baby. Bess was a gifted storyteller who never missed an opportunity to practice her art. "Can't he send off to one of the employment agencies? I'm sure they can find someone suitable, there are so many women looking for respectable work.''

"And some not so respectable, I shouldn't wonder. Would you take the job if it was offered?''

As tempting as it might sound, Rose wasn't about to leap out of the frying pan into the fire. One thing she'd learned was that she was no good at making quick choices. Another was that positions that sounded lovely on paper weren't always so lovely in fact.

Besides, while her heart might ache for any motherless infant, she wasn't at all certain she wanted to get involved with one of Bess's relatives. "I haven't given up. Just because the ideal opening hasn't presented itself yet, that doesn't mean something won't turn up tomorrow.''

"Thought I'd ask. If it'd been a married couple needing help with a baby, I'd have talked you into it, but I can't see sending a decent young woman into an all-male household. 'T'wouldn't be seemly.''

"He's your nephew. Couldn't you do your writing there as well as here, and look after the baby, too?"

The older woman emptied her teacup and refilled it from the decanter, not bothering to add fresh tea. "I'm a spinster, a traveler and a writer. I have neither the time nor the desire to be a nursemaid. Still, the poor little wretch deserves better than a handful of rough seamen to look after her. Know 'em all, and they're as fine a lot as you'd want to meet, but still…"

Bess had relayed the tale to Rose as it had been told to her by her nephew, about a shooting that had involved three adults. She'd lay odds there was more to it than she'd been told. "Tragic, tragic," she murmured, now frowning at her teacup, which was empty again. She fully intended to sniff out every juicy detail of the whole sordid mess, but that could wait. When it came to plotting a story, she never liked to be hampered by too many facts. Not all the travel pieces she wrote were entirely factual, although most had a basis of truth.

"And there's no family at all on either side?" Rose persisted.

"Not a speck. Matt said he beat the bushes without flushing out so much as a shirttail cousin. Poor Billy. Sweetest boy you'd ever hope to meet, but then, you never know…." She shrugged her plump, silk-clad shoulders. "Billy begged on his deathbed for Matt to look after his daughter, and Matt, bless his tender heart, gave his word. Takes after me, Matt does. My own brother's child, don't you know?"

Rose sighed. "Oh. Well, I guess that settles it, then."

Bess stroked her knee and cursed the weather, which was wet and cold, even for early March. "Settles nothing. Being a man of his word is all very well, but it don't do that poor helpless infant much good."

Now why do I have the feeling I'm being manipulated?

Rose answered her own unspoken question. Because she'd been blindly running in circles for so long.

Bess wouldn't do that…would she?

During all the months she'd been burdened with the constant care of her demanding tyrant of a grandmother, Rose's grief for her own lost child had been pushed aside. Now it was back, as fresh and painful as if it had happened only two days ago instead of two years. Was it better, she wondered now, to have held a child in one's arms and then lost it, or never to have held it at all?

There were no answers, only the familiar aching emptiness.

"I've been thinking," Bess announced, a glint in her eye that Rose was beginning to recognize. "Now, if you were to—"

Suddenly wary for no real reason unless exhaustion and discouragement could be blamed, Rose stood and began collecting her purse and gloves. "Bess, could it possibly wait? If you don't mind, I believe I'd better be getting back to my room. I've an early interview tomorrow."

"Not the housekeeping job?"

"Well, yes. It doesn't pay very well, but it's either that or the attic. I understand the housekeeping position includes a lovely set of rooms off the kitchen."

"Bed in the pantry, no doubt, complete with lecherous butler lurking outside the door."

There were times, Rose told herself, when Bess's creative mind went too far. "I'm sure no respectable butler would dream of—"

"Butlers are male, aren't they? Like I said, I've been thinking of a possible solution. Let me talk it over with Horace and see if it's legal."

See if it's *legal?*

Rose closed her eyes. She didn't even want to know, she really didn't. It was late and she was tired, and she still had her best black twill to sponge and press before she went to bed.

That evening, Bess presented her case to her longtime friend over brandy and cigars. If they'd been half a century younger, she might have thought of him as a beau, but they weren't, and so she didn't.

"Here's the problem as I see it. It started with the boy's mother, a flighty female if ever there was one. The Powers men have all been steady as a rock, but not a one of them ever had a lick of sense when it came to women. First the useless bit of fluff my brother married, then that hussy who trolled her bait in front of Matt, set her hook, landed her fish and then left him there high and dry."

"I take it you mean the young lady who talked your nephew into selling his ship. Shady dealings, if you ask me, her and her father alike. I believe questions are being raised in certain circles about the source of their funding.''

''That's as may be, but right now what that boy needs is a decent, respectable woman with some grit in her craw. Strikes me, Gussy's girl just might fill the bill. Don't have much to say for herself, but she took good care of Gussy. I'll lay you odds she'd do the same thing for Matt's baby. Might not look like much, but buried underneath those meek manners of hers, the girl's got grit.''

''Oh, she's not bad to look at, just not in the usual style. Five men, you say?'' Horace savored his cigar, his gaze resting gently on the small, plump woman seated across from him.

''Four, now that Billy's gone.''

''Still, an older woman might be better.''

''Don't look at me, Horace Bagby, baby-tending is a full time job. I've got commitments. Papa's crew spent half their time keeping me from climbing the ratlines, and me barely out of the cradle. Many's the time he had to send a man overboard to fish me out. I liked to walk the pinrail, to prove I could do it. Tripped on a pin or two and went over the side more times than I can remember.''

Horace's smile was indulgent. He had known Bess for half a century. ''Still proving yourself, too, aren't you? You've not changed all that much, Bessy my girl.''

''Ballocks. Now, back to what I was saying—a woman with my responsibilities don't have time, and a young one, leastwise a decent one, can't be expected to go live among a houseful of men.

'T'wouldn't be seemly. So here's what I have in mind.''

Five minutes later, Horace shook his head admiringly. "It's legal, all right, but I doubt if your nephew would agree to it."

"You leave Matt to me. If a man's drowning, he'll grab aholt of the first thing that floats past."

It took three weeks and any number of wires and letters. In the first letter, Bess laid out the bare bones of her plan. She knew of a young widow, a hard worker, clean, decent, sound of limb and meek of disposition, who stood in desperate need of a home. And while Bess couldn't very well send a respectable young woman to live in an all-male household, if Matt would be willing to marry her for the sake of the baby, his troubles would be over.

Matt would not, he wrote back immediately, with appropriate emphasis.

To which Bess replied that in that case, neither she nor her friend Horace Bagby, the lawyer who represented the young woman in question, could recommend the position to her, which was a shame as she was capable, trustworthy, honest as the day is long, and an excellent hand with children and infants.

"If you can't take over Annie's care yourself, try to find me someone else," Matt wrote back. "I'm not taking on a wife."

Meanwhile, nearing the age of three months, Annie was given her first taste of solid food against the advice of the goat owner, who said a child couldn't take real food until it was at least a year old.

Annie took to what Crank called burgoo, a thin oatmeal mush, like a cat to raw fish. She had a few wisps of colorless hair and had learned to smile. Luther took credit for the smile, said he'd taught her how, but to Matt's way of thinking, her smile was Billy, all over again.

It made him sad. Which was some better than being angry and frustrated, but not a great deal.

Bess wrote that the only women she'd found willing to move so far from civilization were either too decrepit to get a job on the mainland or else they were running away from trouble. She added that she was sorry not to be of any more help.

"Dammit, Bess," Matt wrote back. They had long since dispensed with the formalities, as Bess didn't fit anyone's notion of a maiden aunt, and he detested being called "boy." "Help me out here. It's on your conscience that Annie's stuck here with no proper care."

"Don't see what I can do. You say you don't want a wife. My friend don't want another husband, either, so a proxy wedding would satisfy propriety without committing either of you to more than you're wanting to take on."

Reading Matt's answer to Horace, Bess broke into a broad grin. "There, I told you it'd work. Sneak up on 'em, one step at a time, then spring the trap."

"Bess Powers, you're a wicked woman," Horace said admiringly. "You should've been a lawyer."

"All it takes is a creative mind to come up with the plot and a lawyer to work out the details."

"We're a pair, all right. Now, all we have to do is convince Rose."

Convincing Rose wasn't as difficult as it might've been a month earlier, when Bess had first told her about the motherless infant left in the care of four rough seamen. Rose had been able to see it all too clearly—the barren island, the weathered shack, a helpless infant left to the tender mercies of four rough men who cursed and scratched and bathed once a year, if at all.

Although Bess had mentioned visiting the place a few times....

But then, Bess had also written about crocodile-infested rivers and dugout canoes paddled by men dressed in feather headdresses and small straw baskets to cover their private parts.

Still, the place wasn't all that far away. She'd heard of a few fishermen who lived there with their families. Presumably, they fared well enough.

Probably better than she did at the moment, here in civilized Virginia. Of her two most recent situations, neither had lasted more than a few days. First she had found a position as assistant housekeeper in a girls' boarding school. After wheezing and sneezing for two days she'd discovered she was highly allergic to chalk dust.

Her luck seemed to have changed when she had taken the job of governess to seven children between the ages of five months and eleven years, until the night the children's father had come to her room wearing a silk bathrobe and suggested it was time they had a quiet conference.

Rose had shut the door in his face, packed her bags and left.

After that, she'd been forced to lower her expectations. Hunger did that to a body. Even so, her last job—she no longer thought of them as positions—had lasted less than four hours. Having had her bottom pinched black and blue and her bosom, modest as it was, loudly admired by an oaf who called himself a chef, she had finally whipped off her apron and marched out of the town's finest dining establishment.

She was getting better at making choices.

And now, having reluctantly been forced to borrow funds for her room and board from Bess, she had no choice but to sit quietly and listen as Bess and Mr. Bagby presented their proposal.

She had heard it before. Her answer the first time had been a flat refusal. "Thank you, but I'm not looking for another husband. Things may be a bit discouraging at the moment, but that's only because so many people are looking for work at the same time. I read that in a newspaper recently."

That was yesterday. Today she had agreed to hear the proposition again. Not that she expected to change her mind, because one husband had been more than enough, but Bess had been kind, and she owed her more than she could easily repay.

"It's merely a business arrangement for your own protection," Horace explained. Rose sensed that Bess had the poor man twisted around her little finger.

She opened her mouth to reply, but Bess broke in. "You see, Matt doesn't want marriage any more than you do, but by now, he's desperate enough to wed the devil. That's what makes it so perfect.''

Rose, wondering if she'd just been insulted, tried again. This time it was Horace who shut off her objections before she could voice them. "Happens all the time, this kind of arrangement. Just a convenience, like I said before, done by proxy and properly witnessed, it's as legal as any other contract, which is not to say the whole thing can't be dissolved at the behest of either party."

"Well, I don't know," Rose said hesitantly.

Bess carefully avoided looking at Horace, but they both knew the battle was won.

And what a story it would make, Bess thought gleefully. Of course, she would have to allow a decent interval to pass before she could set it to paper. By then she'd have learned all the gory details of that so-called accident. And naturally she would change the names of all parties involved.

Rose's courage held up until nearly the end. It was when she looked down and saw her own shaky signature, *Augusta R. L. Magruder,* on the marriage certificate, that her knees threatened to buckle and her breakfast threatened to return on her.

Except that she hadn't had any breakfast. She'd been too nervous to eat a bite.

"Oh, my, this is a mistake," she whispered.

"You look lovely, my dear," Horace said, beaming as if it had been a real marriage instead of the mockery it was.

She didn't look lovely, she looked green. Given a choice, she'd prefer even sallow to green.

"Captain Powers will be pleased, I'm sure. You've made a good choice, for Bess assures me that your husband is a man of some substance. I've, uh—taken the liberty of looking into his—"

"No." As they went right on talking, she said it again. "No!"

Three people in the room turned to stare at her. Bess, who had already started celebrating, Horace, who'd worn a rosebud in his lapel in honor of the occasion; and the dentist from the office down the hall, who had stood proxy for her absent bridegroom.

"I'm sorry, but I can't do this. You said I could behest myself out of it. How do I start?"

"Now, Rose," Bess soothed.

"He won't like me. I have a sour disposition, no social graces whatsoever, I'm too tall, and I don't know the first thing about babies."

"Matt's built like a lodgepole pine, he wouldn't know a social grace if it reared up and bit him on the behind, and everybody's tall to a baby. As to your disposition, that's just worry. It'll sweeten up once you quit fretting, and he'll like you just fine. If he don't, he's a fool."

"What if I don't like him?"

"'T'wont make a speck of difference, he'll be gone soon's he sees you settled. Boy's been chafing at the bit to get back to sea ever since he sold his ship."

Seeing the determined glint in Rose's eye, Bess

spoke up quickly. "As it happens, however, I just had another excellent idea."

Rose wasn't sure she could survive another of Bess's excellent ideas, but at the moment she was too weak to do more than sit and listen.

Chapter Three

The last piece of trim had been nailed onto Annie's room just that morning. As Peg had been determined to build it for her, Matt had directed him to add it onto the bedroom at the far end of the hall, privately designating that as Mrs. Powers's room. He had no intention of sharing his own quarters with the woman.

Bess and her companion could work it out between them. Bess had her own favorite room with a corner exposure. He seriously doubted she'd do him much good with Annie. As for her friend, if the woman would fill in until his wife showed up, he'd be forever grateful.

Wife. Some helpmeet she'd turned out to be, Matt told himself bitterly. He'd had her for nearly two weeks now, and had yet to set eyes on the woman, much less benefit from the alliance. According to Bess, she'd been called out of town just after the wedding to look after a sick relative.

And now, instead of one, he had *two* women to

contend with. Bess hadn't come right out and said so, but if he knew his aunt, it would be the Widow Littlefield who got stuck with the job of playing nursemaid. Fancying herself a famous writer, Bess could twist words until plain old black and white might mean any of a hundred shades of gray.

"Mailboat's headed into the channel, Cap'n, want me to hitch up the cart?" Crank had been baking all morning. One thing about it, with company on board, they'd all eat better. Matt, for one, had had his fill of beans, fish and cornbread.

"Tell Luther to see to it." The crew had long since stood down from shipboard protocol, but they still looked to the captain for direction.

Matt returned to the reports he'd been studying all morning. The *Swan* was losing money with every haul. The captain signed on by the consortium that had bought her was obviously an incompetent fool with no more business sense than a slab of bacon. According to Matt's source at the Port Authority's office, the *Swan* had lost cargo from improper stowage, lost money by being consistently late delivering consignments, and suffered considerable damage in a hard blow off Barbados. Damage that hadn't been properly repaired before the turnaround.

Matt swore. The first ship he'd ever owned, the *Black Swan* had been his pride and joy. At the rate she was going, by the time he reclaimed her she'd be fit for little more than hauling coal. He'd be damned before he'd do that to her. He'd give her a decent sea burial himself before he would lower her pride any further.

Briefly, he had even considered buying one of the small, fast schooners and taking up the coastal trade. It would ease the tedium of waiting to get his own ship back. With any luck, on a regular run from Maine to Savannah, he'd not have to see his wife—when and if she ever showed up—more than once or twice a year.

But the proceeds of selling the *Swan* were earmarked for buying her back. As long as he kept his focus on that end, he could wait as long as it took. For better or worse, the *Black Swan* was the one true love of his life, and by damn, he was going to have her back.

"And then you, Mrs. Powers, wherever you are," he said softly, "can have Powers Point with my blessing."

Rose lay on her side on a filthy pad on a bunk that had obviously been built for someone half her length, her eyes tightly shut as she fought down a fresh surge of nausea. Bess had given her gingerroot to chew on, which had helped somewhat, but by the time the miserable little mailboat had wallowed her way in and out of every tiny village with so much as a two-plank wharf, she was praying only to die quickly.

As for Matthew Powers and his baby, she fervently wished she had never heard of either of them.

Bess popped her head through the doorway. "Time to spruce up," she announced cheerfully. A seasoned traveler, she had spent the entire journey in the pilothouse, swapping tales and taking notes.

"Just leave me to die in peace," Rose begged

without opening her eyes. She was as spruced as she would ever be. They could dig a hole and bury her at the next stop for all she cared, just so long as she never had to set foot on a boat again.

"Folks don't die of the seasickness."

"They only wish they could," Rose said. Bracing herself against the constant rolling motion, she waited a moment to see if she would need the bucket again, then struggled to her feet. "You might as well know, I'm never going back. Not unless someone discovers a land route to the Outer Banks."

"Here, chew on this, it'll make you feel fresher." Bess handed her a sprig of wilted mint. "Now, pinch your cheeks and do something with your hair, you don't want your bridegroom to see you looking like the scarecrow's ghost."

"He's not my bridegroom until I say he's my bridegroom," Rose grumbled.

"That can wait. You're here to get the lay of the land before you commit to anything more permanent, remember?"

How could she forget? She didn't know which was more preposterous, marrying a man she'd never met or pretending now that she hadn't. For years she had railed at not being allowed to make her own choices, yet every time she'd been given a choice, she'd made the wrong one. This time she intended to be patient, to look at the situation from all angles and think carefully before reaching a decision.

Using a sliver of her favorite lilac soap, she washed her face, then smoothed her damp palms over her hair. She had taken down her braids because it hurt to sleep on them. Now her hair resembled old, unraveled rope. Her mother had once lamented the fact that everything about her was the color of dead grass, from her hair that was too dark to be called blond and too fair to be called brown, to her eyes that were the color of unpolished brass, to her sallow complexion.

Thank goodness, she rationalized, he won't know who I am. He couldn't possibly care what his aunt's secretary-companion looked like.

Anonymity was small comfort, however, as she stood on the deck a short while later, still rocking and reeling. Warily, she gazed out over the small crowd, searching for someone who looked like Bess—someone short, stout and redheaded, with a stubborn jaw and snapping dark eyes. No matter how unattractive the poor man appeared at first glance, she vowed to withhold judgment. To be thoughtful and deliberate before making a final choice. She could only hope he would be as forbearing.

Bess bustled about cheerfully, gathering up her hand luggage, which consisted mostly of books, notebooks and writing material, while the young mate toted their trunks ashore. If it hadn't required too much energy, Rose could have hated anyone who looked so chipper after enduring an endless journey through the bowels of hell.

"There's Luther come to drive us to the Point." Waving her furled umbrella, Bess marched surefootedly down the narrow bouncing plank. Rose followed cautiously, trying not to look down at the expanse of dark, choppy water between wharf and deck.

The wind caught her hat, which had been anchored, with the only hatpin she could find, onto hastily reconstructed braids. She slapped one hand on top of her head and with the other held down her blowing skirts.

Luther, a handsome young man whose eyes belied his obvious youth, offered her a shy smile as he handed her up onto a crude bench seat. "Welcome, Miss Bess, ma'am."

"Poor Billy. I know you miss him." And without pausing for breath, Bess went on to say, "I thought Matt was going to get a proper cart horse. Don't he know the difference between a mare and a mule?"

"Yes'm, this here's Angel. She swum ashore off'n a barge that went aground back in January. Nobody else wanted her, so we kept her. Even for a mule, she's not real smart, but she took to the harness right off." He turned to grin at Rose. "We got some nice horses if you like to ride."

Rose had never ridden a horse in her life. She'd driven her own gig and ridden behind any number of coachmen, but a mule cart was a new experience.

I can't believe I agreed to this mad scheme, she thought again as they set out along a deeply rutted sand trail for a place called Powers Point. She should've applied for a position at the asylum, it was obviously where she belonged.

Luther asked Bess if there was any news of the captain's bride, and Rose felt her face grow warm.

"She'll turn up directly," Bess replied calmly. "How's Peg mending?" Briefly, she explained to Rose that the ship's carpenter had broken several bones when the jolly boat had fallen on him in the storm of '91, and still suffered for it whenever the weather changed.

"Same's always. Don't slow him down much. He built on a new room for Annie, so you and Miz Littlefield can take your pick of the rest."

Mrs. Littlefield. Merciful heavens, that's me. Not Augusta Rose, not Mrs. Robert Magruder, I'm Rose Littlefield again.

The young driver made a noise with tongue and teeth and slapped the reins across the mule's thick hide. "Git on home, Angel, we've not got all day. I reckon maybe Miz Powers'll have some say in who sleeps where, but so far, she's not showed up."

"Oh, we'll leave as soon as Matt's bride shows up. One woman in a household is aplenty, I always say," Bess chirped.

Do you? I've never heard you say that, but then you say so many things....

Rose knew she was being uncharitable and promised to think kinder thoughts if she ever recovered from this awful journey. Keeping her eyes firmly fixed on her own knotted fingers, she waited cautiously to see if mule travel would affect her the same way boat travel did.

Evidently not. Her head was still reeling, but her stomach no longer threatened rebellion.

Gradually she began to take more notice of her surroundings, reminding herself that she was stuck here until she made up her mind whether or not to accept her paper marriage. Or until she could bring herself to board that awful little mailboat for the journey back home.

Wherever home was.

Her sole impression, once they left the wooded village, was emptiness. Sand, a strip of marsh grass to the left, a single rutted cart track, and a few wind-twisted, vine-covered shrubs.

And water. With the Atlantic on one side, Pamlico Sound on the other and, according to Bess, an inlet on either end, she was completely surrounded, held captive, by water.

She was familiar with Cape Cod and Cape May, having vacationed at both places with her parents. Robert had wanted to build on Cape Cod, but the best he'd been able to do was a small cottage on Smith Creek, on the outskirts of Norfolk.

This barren place had nothing whatsoever in common with either of those fashionable watering holes except for the water. Even the village consisted only of a few unpainted houses scattered haphazardly under enormous, moss-hung live oak trees. No streets, no shops, only the weathered cottages, a few tombstones, a few boats at various stages of repair, and nets strung between sprawling live oaks like giant spiderwebs.

Oh, Lord, you've done it again, haven't you? Leaped before you looked.

As they bumped along over the rutted road along a stretch of open beach, she hung on to her bonnet and wondered why any woman in her right mind would choose to live in such a desolate place. Evidently, she wasn't alone in making bad choices and being forced to live with them.

Powers Point, which according to Bess, had been family land for generations, came into view slowly. *My husband's estate,* Rose thought as she gazed over the backside of the mule at the scattered assortment of buildings, none particularly impressive so far as she could determine.

"You remember Jericho, Miss Bess? Matt's got him to where he can ride him and not even get throwed more'n once or twice a day," Luther said proudly.

"That so? They make a pair, all right. One stubborn as the other." To Rose she explained that Jericho was a wild stallion her nephew had bought in a moment of weakness.

Taking some small comfort in knowing that even men could occasionally make unfortunate choices, Rose gaped at the only thing resembling a residence. Unpainted, it seemed to have come together by accident. Although it might once have been an ordinary two-story frame house, rooms had been added on with no thought as to style or balance. There were random gables, mismatched bay windows, even a widow's walk.

"Humph! Whose idea was that?" Bess pointed to the small railed platform on the highest part of the roof.

"Peg thought now that the captain's married, his wife might want to keep watch for when he passes offshore. He can fly a flag or something when he rounds the Cape so she'll be able to tell the *Swan* from the other ships.''

Oh, my mercy, he means me, Rose mused, picturing herself standing high on the rooftop, frantically waving her scarf at every ship that sailed past.

As far as she was concerned, the sole appeal of her husband's estate was that it stood high and dry on solid ground, each gaunt, weathered building telling the world, ''What you see is what I am. Accept me or not, I'm here to stay.''

Which was more or less her own position. *Here I am,* she announced silently. *This is what I am and who I am, and you can take me or leave me, I'm sure it won't matter to me in the least as long as someone will direct me to a bed and a bucket and leave me alone for the next few years.*

The mule meandered to a halt. Several speckled chickens ran squawking to greet them. Luther reached into one of the sacks in the back of the cart and tossed down a handful of grain. ''Go on inside, ma'am—you, too, Miz Littlefield. I'll fetch in your bags as soon's I feed up and unhitch.''

Bess hopped down as nimbly as someone half her age. Rose followed more cautiously, willing her knees not to buckle. It was bad enough that she was here under false pretenses without landing in an ungainly heap at her husband's feet.

''Matt, we're here! Now where's this baby of yours?''

Trudging through the sand behind the older woman, Rose heard a door open and glanced warily past Bess's portly frame. Her eyes widened.

This was Bess's nephew? This giant of a man?

This was her paper husband?

She swallowed a fresh surge of nausea and wondered if it was too late to catch the mailboat. Being seasick was utterly miserable, but physical violence was far worse. She still had nightmares, especially on stormy nights.

If this man ever lost his temper and struck her, she might not survive. His arms were as thick as tree limbs.

"Rose, come here and meet Matthew. Matt, this is Mrs. Littlefield. She's my secretary and companion, but I'm lending her to you for a spell."

When Bess had said the Powers men bred true, Rose had taken it to mean they were all short, stout and redheaded. This man had hair black as pitch. He stood more than six feet tall, even without the boots. If there was an ounce of spare flesh anywhere on his muscular body, it wasn't evident from this distance. Rose had been around men all her life. Her father, the sons of her parents' friends who had teased her as a child and ignored her thereafter.

And Robert, of course.

Not a one of them had been so utterly, blatantly *male* as the man who stood on the porch, his belt buckle level with her eyes, his close-fitting trousers practically flaunting his masculinity.

Oh, my mercy...

"Rose? What's the matter, are you still sick to your belly?" Bess inquired, and, in an aside to her nephew, added, "She don't travel well. We're working on it, but she'll likely be glad to stay in one place for a spell.''

It took every vestige of courage she possessed, but Rose forced herself to climb the five sandy wooden steps and follow Bess inside, even though it meant brushing past the man who held the door. She was careful not to breathe, but she could feel the heat of his body. The weather outside was cold and damp, yet he was wearing only black serge trousers and a white shirt, open at the throat, with the sleeves turned back to reveal corded, hair-roughened forearms.

''You'll want to freshen up,'' he said. ''I'll tell Crank to boil up some tea. There's cold biscuits left over from dinner if you're hungry. You can have 'em with preserved figs or mustard and ham. They'll hold you off till supper.'' He looked directly at Rose. ''Miz Littlefield? Did you hear me?''

Rose's stomach gave a small lurch, but she managed to nod. Bess said, ''Tell that old seacook to fix my tea the usual way, will you? Come on, Rose, I'll show you where to hang your hat.''

Rose didn't even try to take in her surroundings, other than to give thanks that the rooms smelled clean and fresh and the floor felt steady underfoot.

''Annie's back here in the new room. I've put you in the room next to it, Miz Littlefield. Bess, Crank aired out your usual.''

His voice was like the man himself. Deep, dark and dangerous, his accent impossible to pin down. It was neither southern nor northern, the single identifiable element being the ring of authority. Matthew

Powers was obviously a man accustomed to being obeyed.

He held the paneled door for her to enter, his hand, she couldn't help but notice, the size of a ham for all it was nicely shaped.

Get out while you still can, the voice of caution urged.

But of course, she didn't. That would have required initiative, something she'd never possessed in abundance, but she was working on it.

"Now, isn't this lovely?" Bess inquired of no one in particular.

Lovely was hardly the word Rose would have chosen to describe bare floors, an enormous iron bed, a varnished cane rocking chair and the plain, unpainted washstand. There was a bowl and pitcher, both of undecorated white crockery. The bed was spread with a simple white coverlet, the feather mattress plumped up high as a cloud.

"There's quilts in the locker. Lamp's filled, wick's trimmed, door there leads to Annie's room and the head's through the door at the end of the hall."

"The head?" Rose echoed, her voice weak with horror.

"Means the privy." Bess planted her hands on her hips and addressed her nephew. "You ever hear of indoor plumbing? What about little Annie, you expect her to grow up like a heathen?"

"Now, don't tell me you didn't squat in the bushes out in that Amazon jungle you wrote about last winter."

The man's grin was surprisingly infectious. Fortunately, Rose was immune. She'd traveled that road once before.

Bess snorted. "I'll send you a catalog soon's I get back."

"You do that."

Rose gripped the doorframe, willing them to leave her alone. If only she could sleep for a few weeks she might be ready to deal with that dark, enigmatic gaze, the deep drawl that hinted at amusement, exasperation, and a few other things not so easily identified. Nausea alone was bad enough. Nausea, fear and a guilty conscience was too much. She wasn't sure she could carry out the charade.

"Come meet Annie," the captain commanded.

"Who, me?" Rose inquired inelegantly.

"You."

Swaying only slightly, she followed him, once more pinning her eyes to the horizon. Bess had said it helped to maintain one's equilibrium, only in this case the horizon happened to be the captain's backside, which was even more impressive than his front side. Shoulders broad as an ox, a long back that tapered down to narrow hips and long limbs, both of which functioned with an economy of motion that threatened to unsettle her belly all over again. To think she'd been married for nearly two years without ever noticing how differently men and women walked.

"I had Peg build her quarters through here to make it handy for the woman I sent for."

"The woman you sent for? Matthew Powers, is that any way to speak of your wife?"

"What wife?" he growled, turning so that the late-afternoon sun caught his profile, illuminating a jaw that could have been cast from bronze and a high-arched nose that could only be called proud.

Brushing past him, Rose entered the small room, drawn by the sound of a baby's whimper. Her throat constricted. Tears dimmed her eyes as she stared down at the tiny infant swathed in an unadorned gown of coarse muslin.

"That's Annie." The man had come up silently to stand beside her. The unexpected note of tenderness in his voice threatened to undo her completely. Kneeling, he lifted the tiny bundle from the cradle, growled softly as he rocked her in his arms and said, "Annie, this is Miz Littlefield. She's going to be taking care of you for a spell. She's not much to look at, but at least she's got hair now."

Rose blinked in disbelief. She knew very well she wasn't much to look at, she'd been hearing it all her life, but she had hardly expected to hear it from a stranger. And she certainly *did* have hair, yards and yards of it, even if it was the color of dead grass.

"She eats most anything you give her, but so far we've held her to tinned milk and burgoo. We tried goat's milk, but it didn't set right."

And then, of course, Rose realized that he'd been describing Annie to her, not her to Annie, which made her feel almost charitable. "I'm sure we'll get along just fine, but you might as well know, I haven't had much experience with babies."

"None of us has, but Annie's a right fair teacher."

Bess took one quick look, sniffed dismissively and

disappeared down the hall. Peering down at the wide-eyed infant cradled so tenderly in those massive arms, Rose forgot her misgivings and said softly, "Oh, she's beautiful. Do you think she'd mind if I held her?"

"Annie's not particular, long's she gets to call the shots."

She laughed, but it was a shaky effort. When the captain carefully transferred the small bundle into her waiting arms she felt her eyes film over. Knowing she had to take control of her emotions or risk having to endure all over again the devastating pain that came with the loss of a child, Rose did her best to seal off her heart. In case Captain Powers didn't like her, or she didn't like him, she couldn't afford to let herself get too attached to his baby.

"She feels damp." She glanced up questioningly.

"We've not been able to housebreak her yet," the captain said gravely. "You'll find napkins in the locker over by the window. I'll set Crank to heating her some milk. Um…welcome to Powers Point, Miz Littlefield."

Back in his office, Matt tried and failed to concentrate on the shipping news that had come out on the same boat as the two women. He gave it up, tilted back his chair, clasped his arms behind his head and gazed out the window, to where Venus gleamed like a diamond in a bed of purple velvet.

Bess's Mrs. Littlefield was something of a surprise. He didn't know what he'd expected—maybe another pouter pigeon like Bess, short, bosomy and bossy.

The woman didn't have a lot to say for herself, which was all to the good. Bess could talk the hind legs off a jackass.

She wasn't much to look at except for her eyes. Funny color, he mused. Still, they were steady. The kind of eyes that looked directly back at a man.

Matt was admittedly no expert when it came to women. Having been deserted by one and made a fool of by another, he was unable to form any but the most fleeting commercial relationship with any woman. Since moving to Powers Point, he had done without even that brief convenience.

Which reminded him that he was going to have to tackle Bess about the Magruder female. Bess had described her as down on her luck, plain, but sound of limb and meek of disposition. He should've held out for reliable, but by the time he'd given in, he'd been so damned desperate he wouldn't have cared if she howled at the moon as long as she took good care of Annie.

So far, she hadn't even bothered to show up.

Flexing his shoulders to ease the tension that always seemed to collect there, he settled back in his chair and picked up the shipping reports again.

By the end of the first week, one thing was plain. Bess knew nothing about babies and had no interest in learning. Commandeering his mule and cart, she spent every day in the village collecting stories of early island lore, all the way back, as she informed the table at large, to the first English settlers and the Hattorask Indians who'd been there to meet them.

"Hell, I could've told you that," Matt said. "Pass the biscuits. Please," he added as an afterthought.

"Don't swear," Bess said primly, as if she couldn't cut loose like a stevedore when it suited her purpose. "Mrs. Littlefield don't like it."

"Beg pardon, ma'am," Matt muttered. Rising abruptly, he begged to be excused and stalked out. "Damned house's too small," he grumbled to Peg, who'd chosen to eat with Crank in the kitchen instead of in the seldom-used dining room.

The two old men glanced up, then went back to their fried oysters. Matt stood in the open back door for a long time, letting the chilly air flow past him into the warm kitchen.

Ignoring him, the other men picked up their desultory conversation. "Don't talk much, do she?" Crank observed. He speared another oyster off the platter.

"Good with the young'un, though," the carpenter said after he'd split another biscuit and drowned it in molasses.

"Aye, she is that."

"Peculiar eyes. Seen a cat once with eyes like that." Peg loosened the rope at his waist that held up his canvas trousers.

"Yeller, I'd call 'em, wouldn't you, Cap'n?"

Matt flexed his shoulders, but didn't reply. He was tired of hearing about Mrs. Littlefield. Bess sang her praises enough, without his men jumping on the bandwagon.

"I'll be riding south in the morning," he announced abruptly.

The two old men went on eating. When Matt stepped off the back porch and strode down to the three-plank wharf where the shadboat was tied up, Crank grinned. Peg shook his head. ''All I can say is, that wife o' his better hightail it on down here. Last time the boy had that look about him, he went and sold his ship.''

Chapter Four

Much to her amazement, Rose couldn't remember a time in her life when she had felt so utterly content, not even in the early months of her marriage, before she had learned that she was no more than a means to an end.

Against all her expectations she found herself in the ideal situation of having a baby without having to deal with a husband. No matter how she tried to protect her heart, there was no way she could keep from loving Annie. Her own baby, if she'd lived, would have smacked her lips the same way, would have gazed up at her with the same innocent look— would have fit the curve of her arms the same way. The men obviously doted on her, but they were just as obviously relieved not to have the responsibility.

As for Bess, she spent most of each day in the village, returning in the late afternoon with any mail that had come in on the boat and whatever supplies had been ordered, along with pages of notes to be woven into a series of articles. If anyone thought it strange that her secretary took no part in the process, they didn't bother to mention it.

Luther, still shy, but increasingly friendly, showed her a sheltered place high up on a wooded ridge overlooking the sound where she could sit for hours, gazing out over the water. From a safe distance, the Pamlico Sound looked remarkably benign. The sunsets in particular were spectacular, each color faithfully reflected in the waters below. So far she'd counted several wildflowers she had never before seen and almost as many birds.

Annie loved it, too. Crank had fashioned a carrying basket with sturdy rope handles and padded it with a pillow. With the weather growing warmer each day, Rose had delved into her steamer trunk to find her old summer gowns, most dating from before her marriage. Sometimes it seemed as if she'd been in mourning forever, first for her parents, then for her baby, and even now for her grandmother. But black was not only depressing, it was hot, and here on the Outer Banks the ordinary conventions seemed irrelevant.

Wearing an old blue muslin that was snug across the bosom and loose at the waist, she settled herself on the bench Peg had built and Luther had carried up to what she thought of as her private garden. She'd been warned against snakes, sunburn, sandspurs and prickly pear cactus. Bess had mentioned ticks, and Rose watched diligently to see that no insect, large or small, crawled into the basket.

Adjusting a light spread over Annie's basket, she unfastened another button at the neck of her gown.

"Annie, my sweet, I could get used to this life of indolence, couldn't you?"

Annie kicked and gurgled in agreement.

As was too often the case when she had nothing better to occupy her mind, Rose thought about Matthew Powers. After three weeks, she still didn't know quite what to make of the man, but at least she was no longer intimidated by his size. In fact, she rather enjoyed the novelty of looking up to a man. It made her feel...well, hardly delicate, but still, it was a pleasant feeling.

She had learned at an early age that men couldn't abide tall women. Even her father, once she'd grown a full two inches above his respectable height of five and a half feet, had avoided standing beside her whenever possible. She had understood intuitively, but it had hurt, all the same.

Matthew avoided her, too, but it had nothing to do with her height, or even her lack of looks. According to Bess, he simply didn't care for women. Which suited her just fine, as she wasn't overly fond of men. Once this trial period was over, if she decided to go through with the marriage, at least she wouldn't have to worry about the marriage act.

She hated it. It was painful, demeaning and embarrassing. A friend had once confided that she enjoyed it every bit as much as her husband did, and Rose had thought she must be lying. When, a year into her own marriage, Rose had learned that Robert kept a mistress, she'd been relieved rather than angry, thinking that he might leave her alone.

He hadn't. Especially when he'd been drinking, in

which case he would grab her with no warning at all, shove her down on the bed, even in broad daylight, and do it to her.

She had hoped her pregnancy would end all that, for he'd been eager for a child right from the first. For a while he'd seemed delighted, seldom snapping at her, even paying her some of the same small courtesies he'd shown during their brief courtship.

She'd been nearly five months along when Robert had come home one day in a rage. "Guess where I've been, my dearest little wife." Sarcasm was one of his favorite weapons.

"I can't imagine. At the club?" He reeked of strong drink, and it was barely past noon.

"Right you are. I happened to meet the trust officer who handled your father's estate. Would you care to explain yourself?" His eyes flashed dangerously in his pale, narrow face.

She couldn't think of a single thing to say. "I— I'm afraid I don't remember him very well. I believe he was in Switzerland when Mama and Papa—after they—"

His control snapped. Waving a fist, he shouted, "Why did you lie to me? What in hell did you hope to gain?"

"B-but I've never lied. Why would you think that?" She'd been truly mystified.

"Oh, no? What about your trust fund, what about that?" By that time his face had been fiery red, spittle flying from his thin lips.

"Robert, please don't shout, I don't think it's good

for the baby. I won't be twenty-one until September, you know that.''

"What good will your blasted brat do me, when there's not a damn copper penny left to inherit? All that money, wasted! Blown away!''

That was when she'd learned that he'd married her for the fortune he'd expected her to come into on her twenty-first birthday, insuring it with a son.

"It's gone, I tell you! Every single investment cashed in and wasted by your cheating scoundrel of a father!''

She'd backed away, instinctively holding her hands out to ward off his temper. "I didn't know, Robert, truly I didn't. Father never talked to me about money. He—he always said ladies didn't discuss such things.''

"Don't lie to me, bitch, you had to know! What about your father's will?''

"The will...I don't remember. I must've...but I was ill for weeks after the funeral, you know that. Papa's lawyer was away in Switzerland, and I—by the time he came back, I'd met you and we were getting married, and I never even thought about the money,'' she'd whispered, frightened as he continued to curse and shout.

Actually, it had been Robert who had rushed things along, hardly giving her a chance to think. She'd been in deep mourning, still in shock, and he'd insisted she needed him to take care of her. He'd been so sweet, so convincing, and she had desperately needed someone....

"Why the devil do you think I married you, for

your pretty face? For your stupid female brain?'' he'd shouted.

She'd tried to reason with him, but as usual when he'd been drinking, which was more and more often, he'd refused to listen.

Instead he had struck her across the face. As she'd been cowering in a corner, there was no escape. He'd struck her again, and she'd slid to the floor, and then he'd started kicking her.

By the time he had slammed the door behind him, she'd been too hurt and frightened even to cry for help. Eventually she'd managed to drag herself to her bed, too sick at heart even to weep.

It had stormed that night, the constant lightning and thunder that shook the house merging with her own sick nightmare. Sometime before morning she had started to bleed. Frantic, she'd shouted for help, and eventually the housekeeper had heard her, come to her aid and summoned the doctor.

By then, it had been too late.

Hours later the police had come to tell her that her husband was dead. Robert, it seemed, had left her and gotten himself roaring drunk, fallen off the Smith Creek bridge and drowned. In a single night, still mourning the loss of her parents, she had lost both her baby and her worthless husband.

''But now I have you, Annie, my love.''

The baby looked up, a frown puckering her all-but-invisible eyebrows. ''I know, I know,'' Rose murmured, ''you're hungry again. Why don't we go and see if Crank has supper ready.''

So many things in her life had changed since the

day she had staggered off the mailboat onto this sandy little barrier island. After the first few days, meals were taken in the kitchen. Luncheon had become dinner, dinner was now supper, and an early one, at that. A musical evening was no longer Mozart on the pianoforte, but sea chanties—bawdy ones, she suspected—played on a mouth organ and a pair of tablespoons.

She had learned to launder clothes. She had eaten things she'd never even heard of before, much less tasted. No one yelled at her or made unreasonable, conflicting demands the way her grandmother had done. The men, with the possible exception of Captain Powers, went out of their way to be helpful.

Oh, yes, she could do very well here as Mrs. Littlefield, secretary-who-couldn't-take-shorthand and companion to a darling little girl who filled a place in her heart that had been empty far too long.

As to her other role, that of the captain's wife, she'd as soon go on as she was without being pressed to make a choice.

Tomorrow, perhaps.

Or next week....

After three days of rain that put the entire household out of sorts, the weather turned sunny again, and warmer than ever. Luther, as usual, pitched in to help with all the laundry that had accumulated. "Before you and Miss Bess came down here, me and Billy did the wash," he confided. "It weren't half as much fun."

With the sun shining from a sky so intensely blue

it hurt the eyes, and the lines billowing with baby napkins, men's shirts and ladies' smalls, Rose felt a sense of exhilaration. Here, so far away from civilized society, even the conventions were different. Rules she had lived by all her life seemed unimportant, even silly. She knew for a fact that her grandmother's laundress never washed men's and women's clothing in the same tub.

Here she washed everything together, for rainwater was not to be wasted. Bailed from a cistern by the bucketful, it was heated in a boiler on a wood fire in the backyard. Here she was free to hang as many pairs of drawers and as many petticoats on the clothesline as she wished without ruining her reputation.

And just yesterday, Captain Powers had unpacked a crate of newly arrived books and told her she was welcome to make use of his library. He'd glanced at the yellow dimity she'd been wearing, turned away, then turned back for a second look. She'd been surprised. Except for Robert, who had hardly been motivated by her beauty, no man had ever given her a second look. As a rule, the captain avoided looking at her at all.

"It must be the sunburn I'm collecting," she told Annie. "At this rate, I'll soon be as dark as your captain."

Not that it mattered what she looked like. It hadn't mattered to her first husband; it certainly didn't matter to her second one. When and if she decided to disclose her real identity, it still wouldn't matter. Matt Powers had married her sight unseen, not for her looks but for her usefulness. What difference did it make if she was brown as a berry, if her hands were red and rough, her hair a sun-bleached mass of corkscrew curls?

"What if I decide to stay, Annie?" she whispered, knowing her decision had already been made. She laid a carefully folded stack of napkins in Annie's basket and carried basket, baby, napkins and all to the house. "Do you think he'll have me?"

Annie gurgled cheerfully. From overhead came the maniacal laughter of the ever-present seagulls. Rose pondered her own question without arriving at an answer.

Chapter Five

The air had a stillness about it that made him uneasy. Matt put down the ax and stood for a moment, eyes closed, his head tilted back as he absorbed the keening sound of gulls and the pungent smell of mudflats at low tide. There were bare shoals far out into the sound. Not a breath of wind stirred. The sky held a sulfurish tint, and instead of rising, smoke from the chimney followed the slope of the cypress-shingled roof.

Line squalls. Nothing serious, thank God, unless they spawned a few waterspouts. They'd hit hard and fast and, with any luck, move offshore before any real damage could be sustained. It occurred to him, not for the first time, that here on the island the elements were almost as immediate as they were at sea. He wondered if the first Powers had settled here because of that, or if he'd simply washed ashore from some long-forgotten shipwreck, taken the line of least resistance, and put down roots.

Without dwelling further on the matter, he went

back to splitting kindling, a task he'd willingly taken over after Billy had died. Inactivity made him restless. Always had, even as a young sprout when he'd spent most of his time and energy avoiding the old man's eagle eye.

He needed his ship, dammit. Needed a deck to pace, needed the challenge of getting the best consignments, the best prices, racing the wind to make the best time. At this rate he'd soon grow soft as a striped-suit banker.

All of which meant he was going to have to find a permanent solution for Annie. Mrs. Littlefield was good at babytending—surprisingly good, considering her claim of no experience—but she'd be leaving as soon as Bess had bled the life story from every villager over the age of fourteen.

The quick stab of disappointment that followed the thought was for Annie's sake, he assured himself. It had nothing to do with the fact that she was easy to have around. Or the fact that he would find himself listening for the sound of her laughter, the silly nonsense songs she sang to Annie, the way she encouraged Crank to relate the same old stories he'd told a hundred times or more.

Hell, he'd even found himself watching the way she puckered her lips when she was pegging wash to the line.

Matt blamed his increasing distraction on the novelty of having a young woman in the house. Any woman at all. With the possible exception of Bess, the women in his life could be classified as either available or off-limits. Aside from that, they were either useful or merely decorative.

At this point he hadn't made up his mind about the Widow Littlefield. She was young; far younger, in fact, than she'd first appeared. He had to admit she was useful. As for being decorative, he wouldn't have given her a second look when she'd first shown up, but once he'd got used to her, he'd have to place her in the decorative category.

The one thing she was definitely not was available. Not to him, at any rate. He was supposed to be a married man.

A scowl darkened his face as he considered the last letter he'd written to the lawyer Bagby, demanding to know where the devil his bride was. In it he had reiterated his reluctance to enter into any such irregular connection.

"Having traded room, board and the Powers name for the simple task of raising one small infant," he recalled writing, "I believe I am justified in expecting the woman to live up to her end of the bargain. Please pass along my sentiments to Mrs. Powers and urge all haste."

The reply, when it finally arrived, had been anything but helpful. The lawyer claimed to know nothing about the woman's present whereabouts and suggested he ask his aunt, which Matt had done until he was blue in the face. But as Bess would sooner lie than tell the truth, even if she'd come up with an answer, he'd be hard-pressed to believe her.

"Who the devil takes precedence?" he'd demanded, cornering her when she'd come back from her daily trek to the village. "A malingering relative or a legally contracted spouse?"

Without batting an eye she'd said, "Depends on if it's a blood relative or not. I'd think a parent would take precedence over a husband—but then, there's that 'cleaving unto' business with spouses. I could ask Horace if you're interested."

"It was you and your friend Bagby that got me into this mess in the first place. He's ignored every letter I've written save the first, so you can tell him for me he can damned well untie the knot."

With that he had slammed out and gone back to splitting wood. At the rate he was having to work off his frustrations, they'd soon have enough wood to fire every stove between here and Nova Scotia. If the woman had actually been called to the side of a sick relative, she should have written to explain. More likely, she'd changed her mind and found herself a better mark. It wouldn't be the first time he'd been cast aside when a bigger fish came along.

Leaning on the ax handle, he let his gaze wander over his princely estate: a straggling collection of unpainted buildings, a mule, half a dozen mares, one good stallion and a sail skiff.

God, no wonder she'd had second thoughts. What woman in her right mind would settle for this desolate outpost when she could live in the city and have an unending stream of fancy parties, pretty clothes and smooth-talking gentlemen to dance attendance?

He might even have agreed to set her and Annie up in town, but then what about Crank and Peg? He owed those two old men more than he could ever repay. They'd more or less raised him. He couldn't see either of them settling down in a town where the horizon was hidden behind a bunch of three- and four-story buildings; where you couldn't spit without looking first to see if your neighbor was in range.

At least on a barrier island a man was free to fight the elements, win or lose, unhampered by all the trappings of so-called civilized society. Roots, he was learning, went surprisingly deep in sand.

A patch of blue over on the ridge caught his eye. Damned if she didn't dress to match those little blue flowers she kept digging up and bringing home. If she stayed out much longer she'd be burned to a crisp, that aristocratic nose of hers as red as a boiled crab.

Deliberately turning away, he swung the ax over his head and whacked into another chunk of oak. When the splits fell neatly on either side of the chopping block he kicked them aside for Luther to stack. Chopping wood helped a man work off his natural frustrations. God knows, he had enough of those.

Stacking it did little but give him a backache.

From inside the kitchen he could hear Crank grumbling about something or another. Crank always grumbled on a falling barometer. His cooking was getting more erratic every day. Matt didn't know how to tell him without hurting his feelings, but he didn't know how much more undercooked fish and unsalted bread he could stomach.

Rose, or Primrose as he'd taken to calling her in his mind, never complained. She would pick around the edges of her fish, douse her cornbread with molasses, and praise the plain boiled potatoes. She was considerate, more than he would have expected.

It occurred to him that Gloria, with all her fine foie gras manners, would never have gone out of her way to spare anyone's feelings, much less those of an old man nearing the end of his usefulness.

Out near the shed Peg was mending the gate Jericho had kicked down and cursing the chickens that insisted on pecking around his feet. With his stiff hands, it was slow going, but the gate would eventually get mended, good as new.

Resting the ax between swings, Matt squinted against the brassy glare of the sky at the place where her ladyship lolled about on the sand. He'd lay odds she wasn't near as cool and collected right now as she'd like the world to believe. He was half tempted to quit splitting wood and climb the ridge, just to watch her swatting mosquitoes and sweating like a horse.

But he wouldn't. It had been a year and seven months since he'd had himself a woman. As long as he stayed busy, with enough on his mind to keep him occupied, it didn't bother him overmuch, but lately he'd had trouble falling to sleep.

The time had come to make another trip to the mainland. A man's natural urges, if they went too long unsatisfied, had a way of interfering with the logical workings of his mind. The trouble was, with a wife apt to show up most any day he was afraid to leave.

So he chopped wood.

Chopped wood and thought about the way a

woman looked when she was fresh from her bath of a morning, with her skin all soft and smooth and smelling of lilacs. Or drying her hair on the back porch, with the afternoon sun setting fire to a halo of curls. Or later on, at the supper table, when she'd braided it up so tight it flattened the curls and pulled her eyes aslant, making them look even more like cat eyes.

She was a puzzling woman, all right. For all she seemed to be so prim and proper, she could laugh at two old sailors' crude attempts at humor. She could even laugh at herself, a trait rare enough in anyone, man or woman.

She was unfailingly cheerful. She'd gone out of her way to be helpful right from the first, even though he suspected she'd never done a lick of work before in her life. Strangest of all, though, was her reaction when he came upon her suddenly, catching her by surprise. At first he'd put it down to shyness, but it was more like fear. Just yesterday he had reached out to brush away a green-head fly before it could land on her cheek, and you'd have thought he'd been about to deck her.

Strange woman. Still, she'd promised to look after Annie, and as long as she kept her word, he wasn't about to rock the boat. If she had no better sense than to stay out in the sun until she was burnt to a crisp and speckled with mosquito bites, that was her problem, not his. As long as Annie didn't suffer the same fate. So far, the woman had done what she'd said she would do, which was all he required of any woman.

Not all, perhaps, but it was definitely all he required of Primrose.

Surrounded by swarms of pesky insects attracted to the scent of sweat, Matt stripped off his shirt, used it to wipe his face, then tossed it aside. He wondered how her highness was faring up on her hill, battling ticks and mosquitoes and all the other predators. By the time blackfly season arrived, she'd be long gone. With any luck at all, his wife would be in residence and he'd be outward bound for the West Indies aboard the *Black Swan.*

Rose waved one hand languidly to shoo away the buzzing insects that swarmed by the millions now that the wind had finally stopped blowing. She had covered Annie's basket with a length of wedding veil that she'd ruthlessly hacked free of the headdress. It had been crushed in the bottom of her trunk, kept as a reminder—as if she needed one—of the folly of indulging in romantic dreams.

"No, sugar, you don't want to kick it off," she said when Annie fussed and waved her tiny feet and fists at the lace-encrusted netting. "I know it's a nuisance, but some of these wretched bugs are big enough to carry you off." If she'd thought of it, she might have draped the rest of the veil over her own face. As it was, she'd be scratching for days, even after bathing in baking soda and oatmeal water. But even with the heat, the humidity and hordes of mosquitoes, she felt more at peace than she ever remembered feeling in her entire life.

Part of it, she'd finally concluded, was the constant

sound of water lapping against the shore. Even on the calmest day she could hear it, soothing as any lullaby. To think that not long ago being on that very same water had made her so miserably ill she hadn't cared whether she lived or died.

Wonders never ceased, she thought idly, digging a finger under the neckline of her gown to scratch at a heat rash. She'd left off her corset and all but the bare minimum of undergarments, but that didn't keep her from perspiring. Of course, summer in town had been even warmer, especially as ladies had to be swaddled to within an inch of their lives before they dared set foot out the door.

"You know what, Annie? Nine-tenths of the rules society lives by, I'm firmly convinced, are pure balderdash. Whoever decreed any such nonsense has no more brains than a bowl of suet."

From her lofty perch on a hill that was no more than ten feet above sea level, she gazed around her. Having come from a society where rules were strictly imposed on every blessed thing, right down to the garden plants, she had come to appreciate this wild, unplanned beauty. Here it was nature and not the lopping pruners of some landscape artist that sculpted the trees. Here, nature decreed where each flower grew, and did a better job of it than any gardener.

She caught sight of Luther, who had gone from working with the horses to doing something with the net. A nice-looking young man, he was always busy, always cheerful, fishing or helping out with the wash, stacking firewood or tickling Annie's feet with a feather—or trying to talk Matthew into letting him ride into the village.

Matthew. The harder she tried not to think of the man, the more impossible it was not to. Impossible to believe he was her husband. Even more impossible to imagine telling him so. There was no way on earth she could pass it off as a joke, not after all this time. *Oops, I forgot to tell you, I'm the woman you married.*

Merciful heavens, he would eat her alive.

He was always scowling, as if he bore the weight of the world on his back. From this distance she couldn't make out his expression, but he was probably scowling even now as he chopped firewood out behind the house. She didn't have to see him to imagine the sheen of sweat on his naked back and the way those tight-fitting trousers cupped him in a thoroughly indecent manner. In any civilized society, a man would be arrested for going about half naked in public.

And a woman, she admitted with wry amusement, could probably get herself arrested for thinking the things she was thinking. She of all people should know better.

But even knowing better, she couldn't halt her wayward thoughts. She'd never been exposed to such blatant masculinity. Yet there was so much more to the man.

She never should have married him in the first place, much less come here under false pretenses. But she'd been fresh out of options, and Bess had convinced her it would all work out for the best, even the trial period.

Rose had squared it with her own conscience by telling herself that as Mrs. Littlefield, she would uphold her end of the bargain by looking after his baby. Once she was certain she hadn't made another mistake, she and the captain could discuss an arrangement whereby she would stay on and he could go back to sea and they could both ignore the silly marriage thing.

But no matter how reasonable it had seemed at the time—and to tell the truth, it hadn't seemed all that reasonable, even then—it simply wasn't working. She loved Annie—who wouldn't love a baby?

The trouble was Matt. She couldn't seem to talk to him, and he couldn't, or wouldn't, talk to her. The man had once commanded his own ship, which meant he couldn't be entirely brainless, so the fault must lie with her.

On the other hand, she mused, Bess said he'd sold his ship and had been trying ever since to buy it back, which didn't seem particularly intelligent, so perhaps they were equally to blame.

But she was the one with a guilty conscience, and before they could come to any sort of an agreement, she was going to have to confess. The trouble was, every time she plucked up her nerve to do it, he walked away. He had a way of looking at her as if he could read the thoughts in her head. Then, without a word, he would turn and walk off.

As often as not he would whistle up that half-wild stallion of his, leaving her to stew in her own guilty feelings. She would watch him racing bareback over the dunes, his crow-black hair flying in the wind. And heaven help her, she envied him his freedom.

She had gone over and over the words in her mind, preparing for the time when courage and opportunity coincided. *Captain Powers, sir, I believe I might have unintentionally—*

There was nothing unintentional about it. She had deliberately deceived the man.

Matthew, if you could spare me a moment, I would like to clear my conscience by admitting to a small deception.

No matter how many times she rehearsed the words there was no easy way to tell a man that the woman he'd married in good faith was too cowardly to confess her own identity for fear he wouldn't like her, for fear he would be angry enough to hurt her, for fear she had finally burned one bridge too many behind her.

"I'm going to tell him, Annie, you just see if I don't. Today or tomorrow—definitely by the end of the week. Definitely."

He wasn't a violent man, else she would've seen signs of it before now.

But then, Robert had given her no hint of his true nature in the first months of their marriage. Or perhaps the signs had been there, but she'd been too inexperienced to recognize them, too grateful that any man had wanted her.

Matt hadn't wanted her. He'd made no bones about that. But he needed her, and that was a beginning. "He loves you, sugar," she murmured. "He might not realize it, but I've seen the way he looks at you when he thinks no one's around. Did you know he tiptoes through my bedroom when he thinks I'm asleep to go and stand over your cradle?''

Rose had fallen into the habit of talking to Annie because there were matters she couldn't discuss with the men and she didn't quite trust Bess not to use her confidences in one of her essays. Annie was the perfect listener.

Jiggling the basket, she said, ''So whatever he might think of me, he needs me to take care of you.'' She plucked the thin fabric of her shirtwaist away from her throat, torn between doubts and determination. ''The trouble is, he doesn't trust women any more than I trust men, and that's hardly a promising basis for any relationship, even a paper one.'' She broke off to dig a thumb into the small of her back. ''The truth is, it's my own judgment I don't trust. If there's a choice to be made, I'll invariably make the wrong one. Know what? The first thing I'm going to teach you, Annie dumpling, is to make smart choices. With a brand-new century right around the corner, women are going to be allowed all sorts of freedoms my generation was never permitted. We're going to teach you to think things through before you reach a decision.''

Gathering up the shoes and stockings she'd removed so as to curl her toes into the soft sand, Rose continued the one-sided conversation. ''I was taught how to dress properly for the occasion, never mind that I looked awful in ruffles and pastels. I was taught to use the proper fork, to smile and utter the appropriate inanities at the appropriate time, but you see, no one ever thought to teach me to use my brain. When my world came crashing down, I was left to fend for myself, and a wretched job I made of it, I assure you."

In her basket, Annie blinked sleepily and blew a bubble. Rose picked a sandspur from her stocking, shook out the sand, and began putting herself together for the return home.

"Thinks he hung the moon," she grunted, leaning over to lace her high-tops. "Know what I think? I don't think he hung the moon at all. And do you know what else I think? I think your father is too— he's too *everything*. Too big, too stern, too masculine. Of course you're in no position to realize it, but he's also entirely too attractive. And if you ever tell a living soul I said that, I'll deny it."

Annie was sound asleep. Without even feeling the least bit foolish—another freedom she had recently discovered—Rose stood, brushed the sand from her skirt and her hands, gathered up the heavy basket and began picking her way carefully across the sand. Luther had carried it up the hill for her. He'd been so sweet lately she was afraid he was getting a crush on her, which was flattering even though she knew it was only because he missed his friend, Billy, and missed being able to socialize with the young ladies in the village.

"I'll tell you something else, Annie. In spite of the pesky bugs and the grit that gets into everything, I love it here. I feel like a new woman. I don't have to live up to anyone's expectations, because I'm not

Marcus and Aurelia Littlefield's daughter, I'm not Robert Magruder's wife—I'm not even Granny's granddaughter. I'm just me. Annie's friend Rose.''

Annie's sleepy response was predictably ambiguous, but Rose nodded complacently. "I knew you'd understand.''

Castles in the air, her father had called the elaborate fantasies she'd constructed as a child. Evidently, she hadn't lost the knack. "So what do you think, should I stay? I'm not eager to go back to boarding houses that smell of cabbage, or job interviews where I'm always found wanting. Most particularly, I'm not at all eager to set foot on another boat. If I stay here, your father can get his ship back and go to sea again, you and I can have the place to ourselves and I'll teach you everything I know about being an independent woman.''

Sliding downhill through the soft sand was almost as strenuous as climbing. Rose was puffing by the time she reached the bottom of the ridge. Shifting the basket to the other hand, she set out for the house, thinking of the cool, shadowy rooms and a tall tumbler of cold lemonade.

That was when she caught sight of the barechested giant, swinging the ax with a strength that should have frightened her, yet, oddly enough, didn't. "We're going to have to tell him soon, Annie. I'll do it, I promise you, but not just yet.''

She'd come a long way from the timid creature who had accepted the very first marriage proposal she'd ever received little more than a month after both her parents had been killed. Like a vine whose tree had suddenly been chopped down, she'd desperately needed something to cling to when Robert had appeared on the scene.

Bess greeted her at the front door. "Well? Have you decided yet? I can't stay here forever, you know."

"Shh, Annie's sleeping. Let me change her and get her settled."

Bess followed her down the hall, and Rose said, "Bess, I haven't quite made up my mind. I'm almost sure I want to stay, but I need to discuss it with Matt. Things have gone on so long now that I don't quite know how to tell him. Why don't you tell him for me?" Now that Bess was ready to leave, it was rush, rush, rush. The least she could do, Rose thought, was help her out of the mess they'd created between them.

"Not my place to tell him. Want to know how I learned to swim?"

"Not particularly." Rose had long since ceased to wonder at the twists and turns of a writer's mind.

"Sink or swim, that's how. Papa tossed me over the side and I started kicking and paddling. I was four years old at the time."

A likely story, Rose thought. "I need to put Annie to bed and tend to my bites. We'll talk later."

Matt couldn't sleep. He read far into the night and couldn't have said what it was he'd read. It wasn't the woman, although for reasons he couldn't fathom he wasted far too many hours thinking about her. Because she was here, was all he could figure. Having a woman in his house was disrupting.

Crank's cooking had improved slightly since she'd
been here. Despite his stiff fingers, Peg built things
for her. Luther followed her around like a lovesick
hound. If it hadn't been so damned disgusting, it
would've been funny. The woman wasn't even good-
looking.

Not downright homely, just plain as a cold biscuit.

And prissy. Prim as a Sunday school teacher. Always bringing in jars full of weeds, plunking them
down on tables and windowsills. Next thing, she'd
be wanting to hang lace curtains on his windows.

But tonight, it was neither the woman nor the jug
of flowers on the table at supper, nor even the sound
of her singing to Annie. It was the weather. The air
was too still. The seas were no heavier than usual,
but now and then a hollow wave cracked down with
a report sharp as gunfire. Thunder rumbled sullenly
in the distance, like an angry beast circling the island.

Even as he watched, lightning lit up the bank of
clouds that had obscured the sunset, like glowing
coals seen through thick smoke. Soon, the flashes
grew sharper, the intervals between them shorter.
When a jagged bolt streaked through the sky, he
counted off three seconds before thunder rattled the
windows in their frames.

God, he loved it. The smell of it in the air, the feel
of it in the very marrow of his bones. Hurricanes
meant hard work, ashore or at sea. In an electrical
storm there was little a man could do except savor
being alive.

He wondered if she felt it, too.

By now she was probably cowering under her bed.

When a hard gust of wind hit the side of the house, Matt closed his book and gave up all pretense of reading. Rising, he made his way silently through the dark house. He opened Peg's door, nodded to the old man, and asked quietly, "All secure?"

"All secure, Cap'n."

Luther was snoring. The boy had worn himself out today, what with hauling out the boat, taking up the net and waiting hand and foot on Her Highness. For all his youth, he was a sound man, surprisingly mature in some ways.

As for Crank, after downing enough rheumatism medicine to take the edge off his various aches, he would sleep through anything.

Still with that restless feeling, Matt hesitated outside Bess's door, wondering if he should go in and shut her window. By now she'd be too brandied up to notice if her bed floated off down the sound. Did she think he didn't know about her nightly cigar and her two or three teacups of brandy?

More likely, she knew he knew and simply didn't give a damn.

He went in and lowered her window, leaving only a strip at the top for air, then silently moved to the next door down the hall. Annie didn't like loud noises. If she was awake, he would take her into his own room. He didn't mind holding her until she fell asleep again, as long as no one was around. When a man made a fool of himself over a female, even a pint-sized female like Annie, the last thing he needed was an audience.

She was sound asleep, belly down, butt in the air.

For a long time he stood and gazed down at the small mortal who had so unexpectedly come into his life. He felt a stirring deep in his gut that no amount of baking soda could ease.

After carefully removing a jug of yellow flowers from her windowsill, he shut her window. "Sleep tight, little princess. Uncle Matthew won't let anything hurt you."

To get to Annie he'd had to go through Rose's bedroom. He'd tried not to look. On the way back, tiptoeing through the darkness, he made the mistake of looking. He had almost reached the door when lightning flashed, followed almost immediately by a blast of thunder. Hearing a sound from the bed, he glanced over his shoulder, then wished he hadn't.

She was sitting bolt upright in her bed, staring blindly ahead. It took him a moment to find his voice. "Sorry, I didn't mean to disturb you, I was just checking on Annie. Are you all right?"

She uttered the kind of sound a cornered mouse might make. "Is that a yes?" he queried, not moving from where he stood.

"Yes?" she squeaked.

He waited. Yes, what? Yes, he shouldn't have disturbed her, or yes, she was all right? In the harsh flickering light he could see her hair, freed of its usual restraints, curling around her face like unraveled hemp.

"Mrs. Littlefield—Rose, are you afraid? It's only a thunder squall. It'll move offshore before you know it."

No response. Her eyes were wide open, but there

was no way of knowing whether or not she saw him, much less heard his reassurances. "Oh, hell," he muttered. Moving swiftly, silently to her bed, he leaned over and peered directly into her eyes, careful not to touch her.

He'd seen this same look on the face of a sleep-walking deckhand once. He'd seen it the day Billy had died. They'd all been in shock for days after that. "Rose, listen to me, it's all right. It's only a thunder squall, it won't hurt you."

He waited. No response. "Listen, Peg's got this place wired up with enough lightning rods to ward off an army."

He didn't mention the two waterspouts he'd seen offshore just before dark. No lightning rod ever made was going to protect them if one of those devils twisted its way ashore, but he didn't think she'd appreciate being told that.

"Rose, listen to me—" He wasn't in the habit of calling her by her given name—wasn't in the habit of calling her anything at all, but this was no time to stand on ceremony. "If Annie wakes up scared, she's going to need you. Rose? Are you listening?"

He'd said the magic word. Annie. The woman doted on his baby, and he played on it for all it was worth. "You might have to hold her, maybe rock her a spell if she wakes up scared. Can you do it? Want me to get your wrapper?"

It broke the spell. She nodded, gulped, then shook her head. Matt became aware that he was staring at the front of her thin cotton gown, where her nipples stood out like twin cartridges.

Sucking his breath in sharply, he stepped back, but not before he'd caught a whiff of the clean, flowery scent of her skin. Before he knew what was happening, he was hard as a hickory limb. All it took was the sight of her, the scent of her, warm and still half asleep.

He began backing away before he did something criminally stupid. Safely back at the door, he took one last look and reminded himself that he had no business lusting after a woman not his wife. Not only was his aunt sleeping just down the hall, Annie only a few feet away in the next room, but he was a married man. On paper, at least.

Closing the door, he told himself he had to get out of here. The sooner and the farther away, the better. He needed his ship, not a woman. If his wife ever showed up, she and Rose could fight it out.

If not, then Primrose could have the whole works, with his blessing.

Chapter Six

As if to reassure himself that last night's brief interval had been a product of his own fevered imagination, Matt forced himself to linger at the breakfast table until Rose came in with Annie. One quick look was all it took to convince him that she hadn't turned into a siren overnight. She was still the same starchy, tight lipped Primrose.

Although not quite so starchy as she'd been when she'd first arrived. A little more sun-flushed now. A little more windblown. Thank God she'd given up those hideous black dresses.

Rising, he held her chair and then took one of Annie's feet in his palm. "Slept through the fireworks, did you, mate? At the rate you're shaping up, we'll soon have you climbing the ratlines."

Rose stared at him as if she thought he'd lost his mind. Frowning, he said, "I'm not serious. I'm not much of a hand when it comes to talking to babies."

"Obviously not," she said, straining the words through tight lips. But she wouldn't quite meet his eyes, a clear indication that he wasn't the only one who'd been affected by all the electricity in the air last night.

It occurred to him that as a widow, the lady would hardly have remained ignorant of what went on between a man and a woman. Could it be that she missed it? That she would welcome a bit of relief?

Not from the looks of her now, yet he'd known sluts who could pass as preacher's wives, seemingly respectable women who weren't. Having never before met a woman like Rose Littlefield, he didn't quite know how to size her up. That bothered him.

"Some blow we had last night." He addressed the neutral observation to no one in particular.

"Indeed," Rose said, spooning sugar into her coffee.

Three spoons full? "Not much rain, though. Still, I guess lightning makes some folks edgy."

"Indeed," she murmured again, her gaze fixed on the wilted bouquet she'd set on the table just yesterday. He could've told her that wild things didn't do well in captivity. There was always the challenge, though. A man needed a challenge to feel alive. Maybe a woman did, too.

Bess marched in, looking a bit under the weather. She'd never actually confessed to a hangover, but then, she'd never exactly admitted to putting away a pint of brandy in one sitting, either.

"'Morning, Bess. Got a headache?" He stood and held her chair.

Ignoring the gesture, she stared in revulsion at the platters of fried fish, fried potatoes, fried bacon and fried eggs Crank had just set on the table. "I believe I'll stay in my room and work on my notes today."

"If you need Mrs. Littlefield, Luther can look after Annie."

"No, no, no, 't'won't be necessary. Just send Crank in with a pot of coffee, will you?" She turned and lurched from the room.

Rose looked after her, obviously concerned, then glanced at Matt. "Do you think I should go after her?"

He shook his head. "Leave her be, she'll come around."

From Rose's lap, Annie lunged for a jar of Crank's pickled peppers. The old cook beamed as if she'd just paid him a great compliment, then watched in satisfaction as Rose mashed up a bit of bluefish and poked it into Annie's eager mouth.

With a few words to Peg about checking out any wind damage, he excused himself and left the room. He had better things to do than watch grown men make fools of themselves.

Some half an hour later, through the open window of his office, he heard the murmur of Rose's voice as she carried Annie out for her morning airing. He knew the drill by now. Leaving Annie on the porch, out of the direct sun, Rose would spend the morning baling water onto the weeds she'd planted the day before, and digging more holes for those she planned to sacrifice later.

The woman was stubborn, he'd give her that much. He'd as good as told her not to bother, but she insisted on hauling weeds down from the ridge and burying them in holes around his house. Called it landscaping. Fancy word for littering his neat yard with dead weeds, but he guessed there was no harm in it as long as she looked after Annie. He'd watched her a time or two, her sleeves rolled back, grimy up to her elbows, with patches of sweat on her back and under her arms. Damned if she didn't look almost pretty with her cheeks all flushed and her hair blowing around her face.

So he stopped watching her. Stubborn female, he told himself. Another week and she'd have his crew calling her Captain Rose, the way they all hopped to do her bidding.

A fair and reasonable man, Matt admitted that it was hardly her fault she affected him the way she did. She had never once batted her eyelashes at him the way Gloria had, or placed his hands on her body and called it dancing, or leaned forward, offering him a view of her bosoms.

With Rose, all he had to do was hear her laughter, see her with her sleeves rolled back and a single button unfastened at her collar, or catch a whiff of that flowery soap she used and he'd be forced to either chop wood or ride the devil out of Jericho. Dammit, he was too old to be ruled by his loins.

Six brand-new books yet to be read. A desk piled high with correspondence waiting to be answered; shipping reports and commodity prices to be reviewed. Being in command of a ship took more than seamanship, it required a thorough knowledge of business trends. He needed to be prepared for when he got his ship back.

Trouble was, he couldn't concentrate. Not that he blamed his present distraction entirely on unslaked lust, but lust didn't help. At the rate he was going, he wouldn't be fit to command a bathtub.

It was neither lust nor negligence that had driven him to marry a woman and misplace her before he could claim her. That had been an act of sheer stupidity. And even now, he hadn't learned his lesson.

Oh, yes, he'd had a lot to answer for, even before Bess had shown up with the Littlefield woman. That, too, had been his fault, for he'd practically begged her to come help out with Annie. Bess was all the family he had left, and while she could drive him wall-climbing, nail-spitting mad, he knew what to expect from her by now. Bess never changed, she only grew more devious with age.

It was the Littlefield woman who was turning out to be a problem. There was no reason he could fathom why she should get under his skin worse than a sackful of ticks. If Annie didn't need her so much—

But Annie did. Which meant that Matt did, too. Because once he got word from Boston, he was going to have to take the next boat out of here, and he could hardly leave Annie alone with only Crank and Peg. Willing or not, neither of them was in the best of health.

To make matters worse, Bess was showing signs of wanting to get back to Norfolk. She'd already stayed far longer than he'd expected. Not that he couldn't do without her, but when Bess went, her woman would go with her, which meant that unless his wandering bride turned up in the next few days, he was going to be in one hell of a fix.

Seated at his untidy desk, he massaged the knotted muscles at the back of his neck. The sound of Rose's laughter wafting through the open window only served to deepen his scowl.

"Watch me, Rose! Keep looking!" Luther was out there showing off again. Damned young fool. Probably walking the fence again, telling her all about how he could walk a bowsprit, turn and come back without once looking down or holding on.

Turning his attention to the letter on top of the stack, Matt took a sheet of clean paper from a drawer and uncapped his ink jar. His pen was poised over the square crystal bottle when he heard the first scream.

Rose.

Annie!

Flinging down the pen, he was at the door before the second scream sounded.

Annie was in her basket on the porch. A single glance told him she was quietly gnawing on her fist, safe and sound. Not Annie, then. Thank God!

It took only an instant to absorb the scene before him. The shouts, the snorts, the sound of pounding hooves. The woman standing in front of the porch between Annie and disaster, both arms flung out as if her slender body alone could protect them.

Luther, off-balance, clinging to Jericho's mane. The maddened stallion kicking and bucking his way toward the house, doing his damnedest to throw off the dead weight that was flopping like a sack of meal on his bare back.

Rose shouted something that sounded like "Shoo, shoo!" She waved her apron the way she did when the chickens came pecking at her weeds.

"Quit flapping," he commanded quietly. Moving to stand between the woman and the horse, he continued to speak in a calm voice.

"Easy, boy…steady now, nobody's going to hurt you."

To Luther he said tersely, "Turn loose, jump free and roll under the fence." Keeping his eye on the horse, he turned, swept Rose up in his arms and tossed her back onto the porch. "Get Annie inside," he ordered softly.

Rose landed on her backside and one elbow, then rolled onto her hands and knees. In a shrill voice, she cried, "Help him—he'll be killed!"

"Get inside." Matt repeated the command, his voice quiet, his authority unmistakable. He stood his ground, carefully gauging the situation.

Luther let out a single yelp, released his precarious hold, and jumped, landing flat on his back. Jericho's flying hooves barely missed the prostrate form as he corkscrewed his way across the hot sand. The wild-eyed stallion had the bit in his teeth by now, the bridle tangled in his flowing mane.

"Easy there, boy, no one's going to hurt you," Matt crooned.

He moved slowly away from the porch, his voice a soft drone, his stance non-threatening. His eyes were focused on the horse, yet his arms still felt the impression of the woman he'd held just long enough to throw her out of danger. In no more than the few seconds it had taken, his senses had registered the heat, the feel of her fragile body, the scent of her lilac soap.

Dammit, she was still there, on her hands and knees at the very edge of the porch. "Don't scream again. Don't make a sound," he warned without turning his head.

Moving forward at a steady pace, he murmured, "Luther, you dumb son of a bitch, roll under the fence and don't move. I'll take care of you later." The tone was gentle, the threat unmistakable.

For long moments Matt continued to reassure the horse until Jericho, still skittish, allowed himself to be herded through the open gate of the horse-pen. A few of the mares, kept in a separate section, were uneasy, but most had gone back to grazing on the sparse beach grass.

Luther quickly rolled out from under the fence, but made no effort to get to his feet. Matt didn't know if he was hurt or not. At the moment, he didn't much give a damn. He took time to glance toward the porch where Crank and Peg, drawn no doubt by Rose's screams, hovered in the doorway. Crank held Annie in his arms.

Matt turned back to the shuddering stallion. "All right, boy, we'll walk on the shore directly, have ourselves a long swim. Cool down now, that's a good fellow," he droned. Reaching out slowly, he stroked Jericho's sweaty flank. He was no great hand with horses, but he was learning. Handling an animal wasn't too different from handling a green crew. Firmness, fairness and consistency. Jericho was the one thing he would miss when he got his ship back. Jericho and Annie.

Annie and Jericho.

And Rose.

"Luther, if I had a whip, I'd flog the hide off your worthless carcass." He spoke softly, but in a carrying tone as he made his way to where the hapless young mate lay, still winded, on the ground.

Reaching down, Matt jerked him to his feet and held him there by a fistful of damp, sandy shirt. Both men were shaking, Matt with a combination of rage and relief, Luther with fear.

"Do you have the least notion what you nearly did? You and your damn-fool showing off, you could've killed Rose and Annie!" He kept his voice down so as not to frighten Annie, but rage subdued was twice as potent.

Releasing his shirt, Matt dug his fingers into Luther's broad, bony shoulders and shook him until his teeth rattled. "What the devil does it take to knock some sense into that thick skull of yours? Just what in hell were you trying to prove?"

Rose couldn't have moved away if her life depended on it.

"You all right, Rosie girl?" Crank spoke from the doorway behind her, and Rose gulped and nodded. Evidently reassured, they took the whimpering baby inside, Peg's rusty baritone muttering words meant to comfort.

Her gaze glued to the horrifying tableau before her,

she whispered, "Don't shake him so hard, Matt—oh, God, don't hit him!

It was like slipping into a familiar nightmare, only this time the sun was shining brightly. This time there was no rain, no deafening thunder, no jagged bolts of lightning tearing open the sky as there had been that other time.

Hearing the anger in Matt's voice, Rose cringed, trying not to hear the words, recognizing only too well the emotion that drove him.

"—trust you to stay away from that animal?"

"*—trust fund!*"

"—damned killer—!"

"*You damned cheating bitch!*"

"—know better than to risk your fool neck—?"

"*I'll teach you better than to lie to me, make a fool of me!*"

Her mind still trapped in another time, another place, she watched, horrified, as Matt shook the younger man one more time, released him and lifted his fist. "No! Please, don't!" Rose thought she screamed the words, and perhaps she did, because instead of striking him, Matt only shoved him so that he fell back onto the sand. Leaving him there, he turned and strode away, back rigid, hard hands fisted at his sides.

Utterly drained, Rose crawled farther back in the shelter of the porch and cowered against the wall, knees drawn up protectively, her head buried in her clasped arms. Slowly the bonds of fear eased their hold, but she was still trembling when Crank came and led her into the house. He made her sit at the table, poured her a mug of scalding tea and dosed it with brandy. "Helps with aching bones. Heard tell it's good for curing the shakes. Can't say I ever had 'em, myself, though, so I won't swear to it."

She forced a stiff smile. Hot liquid sloshed over her hand. She ignored it.

Crank pulled out a chair and sat across the scrubbed pine table. "Lute didn't mean no harm, you know. He was only trying to spark up to you, the way boys'll do when they fancy a girl."

"He doesn't fancy me," Rose denied too quickly. But she knew in her heart that the old cook was right. She had selfishly encouraged the admiration in Luther's eyes, basking in the rare feeling that someone found her attractive even though she was penniless, plain as a stump and both taller and older than he was.

"Luther's my friend, just as you're my friend, Crank. You and Peg."

"Aye, and don't forget the cap'n," the old man said solemnly.

Rose sighed and took a cautious sip of the potent tea. Was she that transparent? Did they all know how she felt about Matt? How odd, she thought, when even she didn't know how she felt. She only knew he frightened her as much as he fascinated her. She knew there were dark currents underlying the thin patina of civility.

Perhaps like the moth and the flame, she was drawn to dangerous, destructive men.

Matt poured a dipperful of water from the rain barrel over his head and shoulders. He'd sent Luther into

the village to fetch the mail, not because he expected
a letter, but because the boy needed a task and Matt
needed to put some distance between them until he
could work out the best way to handle it.

Damned if he would apologize. If Luther wanted
to make a fool of himself over a woman, that was
his privilege, but not when it endangered a good
horse. Not to mention two helpless females—although Rose hadn't seemed so helpless standing between Annie and the maddened stallion, flapping her
apron as if it were a weapon.

But Matt remembered another young man, remembered how his own negligence had led to Billy's
death. Luther had to be taught a lesson for his own
good. If Jericho had hurt either Rose or Annie, Matt
would have had to destroy him. God knows what that
would have done to Luther, whose heart was even
softer than his head.

Far easier to blame Rose for leading him on. She
was old enough to know better, even if Luther
wasn't.

Pouring another dipperful of water over his head,
Matt struggled to regain his perspective, but Billy's
violent death was too fresh in his memory. He remembered taking one look at the scrawny, red-faced
infant, the cord still dangling from her body, and
mentally consigning her to a grave beside her father.

Annie had fooled them all. Not only had she survived, she had thrived. And as much as he hated to
admit it, Annie wasn't the only one who appeared to
thrive here on this isolated stretch of barrier island.

For all her failings, Rose had come a long way from the pitiful female who had stumbled from the cart one cold, windy day in March wearing an ugly black gown, her face still green from retching her belly wrongside out. Bess said she'd been sick almost from the minute she set foot on the mailboat.

Matt shook his head in dismissal. He was too unsettled to return to the correspondence he'd left unfinished. Better to take Jericho down to the shore where they could both work off a few demons.

Inside the house, Rose managed to choke down half a cup of the potent tea before excusing herself to see to Annie, who, as it turned out, was sleeping peacefully. Feeling a powerful need to hold onto someone, Rose carefully gathered the small, warm body into the curve of her arm and settled into the cane rocker, staring blindly out the window at the shimmering glare of sun reflected from sand and water.

She croaked a few words of a half-remembered lullaby, then fell silent. Her arms were steady enough; her voice was not. She continued to rock, gradually regaining her composure as she went over in her mind what had happened.

Luther had been at fault for trying to ride a horse he'd been warned against. He'd even warned Rose never to go near Matt's stallion. "You don't never want to mess around no stallion," he'd said. "They're spooky. Jericho's worse than most because he was treated real bad before Matt took him in."

Matt had been right to take him to task, but it

should have ended there. Violence, no matter how justified, was never the solution.

Although, in all fairness, Rose had to admit that Matt had saved her from possible injury. He'd taken the time—at least someone had—to shove Annie's basket away from the edge of the porch, out of the reach of danger. He had remained calm so as not to excite the horse further, and as furious as he'd been with Luther—and rightly so, she had to admit—he hadn't actually struck him.

But try as she would to rationalize what had just occurred, she couldn't forget the image of Matt's towering rage and poor Luther's stark fear. She had come a long way, but evidently she still hadn't come far enough. Perhaps she never would.

Which left her right back where she had started. She could admit her deception and go on the way they had originally intended, staying here with Annie while Matt went back to sea....

Or she could pack her trunk and leave on that wretched boat.

One option was no more attractive than the other.

Chapter Seven

They had arrived in early spring. Summer was now at its peak. Rose was surprised that Bess had stayed as long as she had, but then, a writer, she supposed, could write anywhere. Still, the older woman was growing impatient. "Go ahead and tell him, Rose, I can't stay here forever. He'll make you a fine husband. He's a good boy."

Hardly a boy, thought Rose. "Why don't you tell him? After all, it was your idea, and besides, you're much better with words than I am." Her own talent lay in evading issues. Far easier to avoid making a choice than to have to live with another bad one.

"Of course I am, but as it happens, I'm off to visit with the magistrate, Dick Dixon. There's not a closet in any house on the island that don't have a few skeletons. He'll know where to look."

Evidently, the skeleton hunt proved rewarding, for Bess spent much of her time over the next few days in the village.

Rose, postponing the inevitable, spent hours on her

ridge mending, shelling beans, talking to Annie, or simply lying back on a spread and letting the warm, damp wind blow over her body.

What would he do when she told him? How would he react?

Impossible to know. He was such a puzzling man, quick to anger, but only when anger was justified; hiding a broad streak of tenderness under gruff manners that no longer frightened her. In spite of every grain of common sense she possessed, she was increasingly attracted to him.

Sitting up, she wrapped her arms around her knees and watched the two men in the distance. Once they'd taken care of the livestock this morning, they had dragged bales of hay to the shady side of the barn and settled down, Luther with a slate, Matt with a cup of Crank's powerful coffee.

Rose knew what they were up to. Crank had explained that with Billy gone, Luther would be chief mate as soon as Matt got his ship back, and Matt was using the interim to fill in the gaps in his education. "Boy's young, but Matt weren't too much older when he took command of the *Swan*."

This week they were working on mathematics. Amazingly, Matt never seemed to lose patience, not even when Luther stumbled badly over his times tables.

She watched from a distance, savoring the way sunlight glistened on that broad, bronzed back, the way he raked his fingers through the thick, dark hair and gestured with his hands to make a point. The same hands that were strong enough to control that wicked horse of his, yet gentle enough to stroke a baby's cheek and bring forth a smile.

"Lord, Annie, what have I done?" she murmured. "I'm pretty sure I want him for a husband, but I'm not at all sure he'll have me. I'm not even sure I know what I'd do with him if I got him."

Another sleepless night. Either she lay awake fretting or she fell asleep and dreamed. She knew very well that work wasn't the answer, but until she could screw up her courage to make a clean breast of what she'd done, it helped. So she went through all the bedrooms, even those not in use, gathered up every shred of yellowed linen and dumped it all into the washtub to scrub and rinse, wring and hang, then fold and put away.

Even using the twisting stick to wring the way Luther had shown her, the job took hours and left her with an aching back, a blistered nose, and rough, red hands, but at least staying busy kept her from worrying overmuch.

Luther offered to help her hang, but before he could peg the first sheet to the line, Matt stepped out onto the porch and ordered him to ride to the village with a letter for the magistrate.

"Them two's worse than a pair of banty roosters," said Peg, who had come out to the backyard with a bucket of scraps for the chickens.

Having no knowledge of roosters, Rose dismissed the comment, twisted another sheet using the stick, then flopped it over the line, spread it out and anchored it against the southwest wind.

She was going to have to get it over with. Better the agony of being rejected than the shame of knowing she was a coward.

With the laundry drying in the sun and Annie fed, changed and settled for her nap, Rose went in search of another task. Crank and Peg between them did the cleaning, refusing to allow her to touch a broom or wash a single dish. "Go pick some more o' them flowers you like so much," Crank suggested. "They set off a table right smart."

"I've picked every flower in sight and planted them around the house. They died," she said, as if accusing the old cook of sabotaging her efforts.

She'd be the first to admit she knew less than nothing about gardening, but she could learn. Goodness knows, Powers Point could use a bit of landscaping, especially if she decided to stake her claim. Which she might well be forced to do, whether Matt was willing or not, considering that she had no money and no other prospects.

Just like that, she made up her mind. No shilly-shallying. No more excuses, it was time to put an end to this charade. Still gritty and windblown from her morning's exertions, she marched down the hall before she could lose her nerve and rapped on his door.

Fingers crossed, she closed her eyes and said a silent prayer. *Please let him want me. Please let it come out right this time. If not for me, then for Annie. She needs me.*

The door opened before she could think her Amen, or even uncross her fingers. "Yes?" he barked impatiently.

He had a letter in his hand. His hair needed trimming. His shirt, a fine linen which she, herself, had laundered, was open halfway down his chest. Staring at the dark thatch on his chest, she swallowed hard and tried to remember why she was here.

"I'd like to borrow the cart, if you don't mind. While Annie's sleeping I need to ride to the village for seeds."

You stupid woman, you're doing it again!

"Seeds." He repeated the word as if he'd never heard it before. He was staring at her hands, and self-consciously she uncrossed her fingers and tucked her hands in the folds of her skirt.

"Flower seeds. But I could plant vegetables, too," she said anxiously, digging her grave even deeper.

"I see. You think you can handle her?"

"Handle who? Whom?"

"Angel."

"Oh. I drove my own gig. I hardly think a mule cart can be that much more difficult. It's not as though there were traffic to contend with." Feeling her competency challenged, she stiffened to her full five-feet-eight inches.

He pursed his lips, his intense gaze never wavering, and Rose fought the urge to turn tail and run. *Forget it,* she wanted to cry. *Just forget I was ever here.*

But of course, she didn't. She was, after all, a woman of her word...eventually. "Things do grow in sand. There are trees and shrubs and vines all over the ridge, and all kinds of wildflowers. Your house could certainly use a bit of landscaping." Knowing she had lost her nerve again, she resorted to belligerence.

He had stared at her until her mouth went dry. Just as she was about to slink away, he said, "Go ahead. If Bess don't need the cart, I've no objection, as long as Annie's not neglected."

"Annie will never be neglected as long as I'm here," she declared. "And Bess is in her room reading someone's diary that she borrowed from Mr. Dixon."

"Figures," he said. "Do as you see fit, madam."

If she did as she saw fit, she would crown him with the nearest hard object. Either that or reach up and touch that bristly jaw of his, to find out for herself if it was as hard and unyielding as it appeared.

Luther, just back from the village himself, hitched up the mule and instructed Rose on how to manage her if she acted up. "She don't always mind. Sometimes she takes to daydreaming."

"I'm hardly a novice. I had my first pony cart when I was twelve, my own gig when I turned eighteen."

But because she knew Luther's fragile self-esteem had been badly injured by the Jericho disaster, she listened, trying not to show her impatience. "Thank you, Luther, you've been a great help," she said gravely. Time to begin underlining the difference in their ages. She was twenty-four, after all, and Luther was barely twenty-two years old.

She and Angel made the four-mile trip with no mishap, if a severe trial of patience didn't count.

There was no such thing as a brisk trot in deep, powdery sand. It was trudge, trudge, trudge, battling flies and mosquitoes all the way. Despite her hat, she'd be burned to a crisp and eaten alive by the time she reached the village, nor was there such a thing as a shop once she arrived.

Not so much as a fresh market. She was told by a grizzled fisherman mending a delicate net he'd hung between oak trees that the next village south had a store, stocked weekly by a freight boat from across the sound.

"How far?" she inquired.

"Half a day's ride."

"Across the sound?" she marveled, remembering it as being more like half a century.

"To the store. Me and my woman'll be riding down in a few days if you need something. Luther or Bess can collect it next time they come."

Rose took a deep breath, absently scratched a fresh bite, and explained her mission. "Flower seeds, whatever grows best here. Perhaps come carrots and lettuce, too."

The tobacco-chewing fisherman smiled. At least the creases networking his face deepened. "Well now, I don't know about plantin' this time of year, but I reckon my woman could spare some collard slips."

Over the next half hour she met three women and several more fishermen, most of whom greeted her shyly and asked after Miss Bess. "I've not seen her around lately," one woman said.

"I believe she's doing research," Rose replied,

with no idea whether reading another's diary was considered research or snooping.

An hour later she headed home, hoarding a precious bundle of seeds, cuttings and slips, plus two letters and the news, for whatever it was worth, that the magistrate's son was coming home for the summer, and all the girls were excited about it.

Roughly halfway home, Angel lapsed into one of the daydreams Luther had warned her about. At least that was the only reason Rose could think of why the stupid creature stopped dead in its tracks, miles from nowhere.

Rose clucked and snapped the leads. She waited, thinking perhaps the hot sun would move it along. Who in their right mind wanted to linger outside on a day like this, when heat was shimmering off the sand in dizzying waves?

"Angel, anytime you're ready to wake up and move, I can promise you a treat." Did they have any dried apples left?

"How does a nice drink of water sound? And shade? The east side of the barn will be shady by the time we get home."

The stupid creature wasn't even grazing, it was just standing there. If the voice of authority wouldn't do the trick, perhaps a bit of bribery...

Reluctantly, Rose climbed down from the hard bench seat. Over toward the sound the lush, tall grass looked promising. At least it was green. She stood for a moment in the rutted road, eyeing a thick clump of prickly pear cactus. She'd had more than one unhappy encounter with those wicked spines.

The sound of the surf just over the dunes might have had a calming effect if it weren't for the raucous laughter of the seagulls and the drone of the ever-present mosquitoes.

With an oath she'd learned from Bess, she slapped a vicious green-headed fly away from her damp throat and glared at the somnolent mule. "I'm warning you, you stupid animal, I'll never forgive you for this. Your captain's going to think it's my fault, but we both know who's to blame here, don't we?"

With bribery in mind, she lifted her skirts and picked her way carefully, avoiding patches of pesky sandspurs and the longer spines of the cactus, toward the marshy edge of the sound, where the grass, however coarse and wiry, was at least green.

Later she could never recall what had alerted her. Whether it was the sound of a soft hiss, or the prickling at the back of her neck. Another few feet and she would have stepped on it.

Stricken with terror, Rose stared down at the thick, mottled brown snake, its beak-like mouth opened wide to reveal a cottony interior.

Ohmigod, ohmigod, ohmigod…

Once her heart resumed beating, she began edging away. If she could just reach the cart and climb up on the seat….

"Angel," she called softly without turning her head, "get ready to move." Her skirt snagged once or twice but she kept on moving backward, never once taking her eyes off the snake. It, thank God, didn't move. Curled in a loose S hook, it remained there, its wicked mouth open wide as it hissed a warning.

It was another sound that finally made her look over her shoulder. She gaped in disbelief. "Angel, you get back here!" With one last glance at the snake, she turned and began to run.

Angel, obviously thinking it some sort of game, began to trot.

"Come back here, you flop-eared jackass!" The more Rose yelled and the faster she ran, the faster that dratted mule trotted, with the cart bouncing over the ruts, shedding Rose's precious cuttings and slips along the way.

It took no time at all to exhaust her meager vocabulary. It took longer to collect the cuttings, limp now, and sure to die before she could get them into the ground again.

Flies swarmed. Heat sizzled. Rose swore, unbuttoned her shirtwaist all the way down to her camisole and snatched off her bonnet, using it to swat at the flies and mosquitoes buzzing around her sweaty face.

How far had they come from the village?

More important, how far did she have to walk?

Behind her, the dense maritime forest that sheltered the handful of cottages shimmered grayly in the ever-present salt haze. Ahead, the few buildings that constituted Powers Point were barely visible.

She'd been walking for nearly an hour as near as she could estimate when she saw something moving in the distance. By then she had removed her petticoat to make a bundle for the seeds and cuttings she collected along the way, fearing the heat of her hands wouldn't improve their chance of survival any more than lying in the road under a blazing sun would.

The idea of going back to beg for more had no appeal at all.

Her steps slowed as she squinted against the blinding sun. Was that—? Could Angel have changed her mind? Lost her mind, more like it. Lost her way and turned back. Dumb beast. Wicked, crazy animal. "You'll never get another apple from my hands, I can promise you that," Rose muttered.

At least she wasn't lost. On an island so narrow one could stand in the middle and toss a stone in either direction and strike water she had only to walk long enough in either direction to reach a destination. Perhaps not the one she'd had in mind, but any old port in a storm.

"As the good book says," she added, smiling as an alternative to cursing or crying. If Crank were to be believed, every cliché known to man came from the Bible.

Whatever it was she'd thought she'd seen in the distance was closer now. It wasn't Angel dragging the cart, it was...

Matt?

"Oh, no, please." She shook her head in denial as Matt, riding one of the mares, loomed up out of the shimmering heat.

She stood there, shoulders slumped in defeat, and waited for the inevitable. He could yell at her all he wanted, but if he shook her—if he laid a single hand on her, she would fight back. She would hit him with her bundle of collard slips.

"Decided to walk home, did you?"

Warily, she said, "Actually, it wasn't entirely my decision."

"Figured as much."

It was as close as he came to calling her stupid, idiotic, and all the other things she'd called herself. Without another word he climbed down, took the ruffled bundle from her hand and tied it onto the saddle. Then he boosted her up onto the mare's back, an awkward process at best, and swung up behind her. Rose couldn't have spoken if her life depended on it. She considered the possibility of dying of embarrassment, but didn't quite know how to go about it.

Matt collected the reins. His arms pressed against her sides and she caught her breath and held it, but not quickly enough. He smelled of horse, of clean, male sweat, of lye soap and sundried linen. Even dying of embarrassment, Rose found something enormously reassuring in the familiar aroma.

She smelled, she sadly suspected, of sweat and fear. And shame.

His heart thudded slow and steady against her back. She straightened her spine away, but it was awkward, hardly a position she could maintain for very long, seated sideways as she was, on the mare's sloping shoulders. With one arm, he pulled her back against him. Still not a word. The laws of gravity prevailed and she slumped against him, closing her eyes in defeat.

Safe, she thought.

Safe?

Safe was the very last thing she felt as the heat of

his body burned through the thin layers of her gown. He was hard as a rock...all over.

Luther was greasing the cartwheels when they rode into the yard. He glanced up, grinned, blushed and went back to his work.

No one spoke. Rose thought, this is absurd. She took a deep breath and said brightly, "How did you know I was in trouble?"

Matt dismounted, reached up and swung her down to the ground. "Cart came back. You didn't."

Well, of course. Nothing mysterious about that. Determined to make as dignified an escape as possible under the circumstances, she settled her hat on her head, took a single step, still holding on to her smile, and felt her knees buckle.

Swearing under his breath, Matt caught her before she could crumple to the ground. Forced to cling to him until she could regain her balance, she felt something hard pressing against her belly. "Oh my, this is as bad as getting off that wretched boat."

His belt buckle? Is that what it was? Or...

"Oh, my mercy," she whispered.

She heard the sharp intake of his breath—or perhaps it was her own. Stepping back, she turned away, but he caught her arm.

"Please," she said.

"Hold still," he said gruffly. To her amazement, he knelt at her feet. Numbly, she stared down at the top of his head. No hat. Thick, unruly hair, black, but shot with mahogany lights under the late afternoon sun. Her fingers trembled with the urge to touch him.

And then he lifted her skirt.

She slapped it down again, shocked to the marrow of her bones. Robert had—in broad daylight—she'd hated it!

But right here in the yard, in front of everyone?

The man was mad. "Stop that!"

"Dammit, stand still, or you'll have these pesky things climbing your drawers." Carefully, he removed a cactus pad from her skirt, dropped it into a pail and reached for another.

Rose shut her eyes as heat washed over her face. When his hand brushed against her lower limb she felt as if she'd touched a hot stove.

By the time he was done there was a layer of cactus pads and sandspurs in the bottom of the bucket. "Luther," he roared, "come set fire to these damned things."

He turned to Rose with a wicked smile. "Else the yard'll be full of 'em. Is that what you wanted? Weeds growing all over Powers Point?"

Ignoring his teasing, she said with as much dignity as she could muster, "Thank you very much."

"You're very welcome." When it came to mockery, the man was a past master. Now she knew why women wore stays and layers of underskirts, even in the hottest weather. She might not feel quite so vulnerable if she weren't half naked, soaked to the skin with perspiration, her face burned to a crisp because she'd removed her bonnet to keep sweat from trickling from her scalp into her eyes. Her skirt was probably clinging to her damp limbs, but she didn't dare look to see.

"Hot some, ain't it?" Luther observed, sauntering over to lead the mare away.

"Hold on," Matt said, and, reaching up, he untied Rose's petticoat with its bedraggled bundle of cuttings. "You forgot these."

Why don't I just lie down right here and die? A few years from now, no one will even remember my name, much less my shame.

Face flaming anew with embarrassment, she snatched it from him, hiked up her skirt and trudged toward the house. It could happen to anyone, she told herself. A runaway mule, a shared ride. Being caught against a man's body as he helped her down from the horse, feeling his arousal....

Or his belt buckle, she still wasn't sure which it had been, for by that time she'd been in such a state of agitation. And that was before he'd lifted her skirt.

"Tell Crank I'll be in for supper directly after I see to Jericho," he called after her.

Without stopping, she nodded and mounted the steps. She couldn't have spoken if her life depended on it.

That evening, determined to put the entire unfortunate affair out of her mind, Rose borrowed Crank's mail-order catalog. She would have liked to send for a pair of the high-topped canvas shoes and a lightweight straw hat, but even the two dollars and twenty-five cents for the shoes and the dollar for the hat were beyond her meager resources.

She turned to the infants' and children's section. Annie had little enough as it was, and most of what she had was too small, hand-me-downs from some of the village women.

Rose would have dressed her in silk saques and caps with the finest French embroidery if she could have afforded it, for she loved her dearly. While the hollow place in her own heart could never be filled, Annie had helped ease the pain. She could go for days now without thinking about how it had felt to wake up hurting over every inch of her body, and to be told that the baby she had carried for months had died without ever having had a chance to live.

She was terribly afraid she would lose Annie, too. If there was one thing she'd learned about her paper husband, it was that he demanded honor and integrity in all his dealings. No one in their right mind would dare lie to him, not even Bess.

Well...perhaps Bess could get away with elaborating on the truth, but the moment Rose confessed her own sins, it would be over. Her marriage, her tentative dreams. Matt would send her away. And the worst of it was that as much as it would hurt to leave Annie, that wasn't the loss she dreaded most.

How was it possible, she mused over the catalog, for one simple mistake to multiply until her whole life was affected? If she hadn't married in haste and then lost her courage, Matt would be her acknowledged husband now. He would have gone to sea again, leaving her here with Annie. There was a time in the beginning when she could have been content with that.

Instead she'd lost her nerve, done something incredibly foolish, and now she was forced to live with the consequences.

The next morning, having screwed up her courage once more, she rapped on Bess's bedroom door. "Am I interrupting? I need to have a word with you." And this time she refused to be put off with another excuse. "Now, not later."

"Had your breakfast yet?"

"I'm not hungry."

"Fried mullet. Forgot to salt the biscuits, but—"

"Bess, *please?* You'll be glad to know that I've decided to tell Matt the truth. Naturally, I'll take full responsibility and claim the whole thing was my idea, but if he sends me away, I'd like to go back with you. The thought of making that trip alone is— Well, I don't look forward to it."

Bess waved her toward a chair. Even this early in the morning, her typing machine was uncovered, a stack of paper on the table anchored by a glass paperweight against the breeze that blew through the open window.

"Dick Dixon sailed up to visit while you were out gallivanting yesterday," Bess announced before Rose could continue. "Says his son's coming to visit."

"I heard about it. I meant to tell you."

"Met him last summer. Handsome young fellow, got a good job, too. You could do worse, Rose."

Rose blinked in confusion. "I beg your pardon?"

"You heard me."

"Oh, for heaven's sake, Bess, this isn't one of your

adventure tales.'' Rose took a deep breath and said, ''Listen to me, I'm going to tell Matt the truth and that's all there is to it.

''Young widow like you, nice-looking fellow like that—I'd set my sights on him if I was you.''

Either I've spent too much time outside without a bonnet, or the poor woman has finally succeeded in pickling her brain with brandy. ''I have a husband,'' Rose said slowly, carefully, quietly. ''We both *know* I have a husband, even if *he* doesn't know it.'' She pressed her hands to her throbbing temples. ''At least, he knows he has a wife, but he doesn't know who she is. I mean—''

''Just letting you know there's options in case things don't work out. Not that there's any reason why they shouldn't, mind you, but it's not too late to back out. Still, Matt's a fair man. He'll give you a fair hearing. It's up to you to make him understand.''

''Understand what? That I'm a weak-minded coward?'' Rose's shoulders slumped. How could she make anyone else understand when she didn't understand, herself?

Matt was not in his office. She didn't dare knock on his bedroom door. Ashamed of the sense of reprieve, she bathed Annie, dressed her and gave her half a bottle of milk. ''Googoo,'' the baby chortled, waving her fists.

''All right, sweetums, we'll go have our googoo.''

As soon as she entered the kitchen, Crank began

filling a plate. "Oh, please—only coffee for me, thanks."

He plopped it down on the table before her. "Waste not, want not, as the good book says."

Unwilling to hurt his feelings, she managed to choke down a few bites. "I'm really not hungry," she said apologetically.

"Left off the salt again, didn't I? Man my age's got too much remembering behind him to keep up with every grain of salt."

Whatever that might mean, Rose concluded, and forced down another bite of the cold, greasy fish while Annie waved her sticky fists. "Would you mind keeping an eye on her for me?" she asked, carefully placing her knife and fork across her plate.

"I'll teach her another one of my songs."

Another bawdy ballad, Rose thought. Thank goodness Annie was too young to understand the words. She would miss them all terribly, she knew. It would be like losing yet another family. First her parents, then her baby—Robert hardly counted—and then her grandmother.

And now all this.

Standing outside Matt's office door for the third time in twenty-four hours, Rose smoothed her hair and brushed a wrinkle from her skirt. The knock she'd intended to sound bold and unafraid was barely loud enough to be heard.

Clearing her throat, she called through the paneled wood, "Matthew? I'd like a word with you, if you're not too busy—please?"

The door swung open before she could lose her

nerve and bolt. He was wearing another of the shirts she had laundered, this one so fine she could easily see the patterned dark hair as it swirled over the gleaming muscles of his chest.

She swallowed hard, wishing her heart hadn't taken up residence in her throat.

Without a word he stepped back, gesturing for her to enter. She tried and failed to gauge his mood. Easier to read the dark side of the moon.

"Sit down." He indicated one of the spoke-backed chairs. "I've been meaning to speak to you."

A wave of terror swept over her, leaving her limp with dread. *He knows,* she thought. *Bess has already told him.*

For several long moments, neither of them spoke. Like adversaries in a pitched battle, each used silence to measure the opposing force, waiting to see who would break first.

"Have a seat." Matt indicated a chair. Thus Rose won by default. Her mind raced, but her tongue simply refused to work.

He lifted his eyebrows.

She cleared her throat.

Do it. Do it now! The worst he can do is put you on that awful mailboat and send you away.

To her dismay, it wasn't even the seasickness she dreaded most.

Warm air drifted through the open window, carrying a hint of salt, more than a hint of horse. Closer at hand she detected the distinctive scent of shaving soap, books and something enticingly masculine.

Closing her eyes, she barged ahead before she lost her nerve. "I can explain everything…" she blurted.

Matt spoke at the same time, his words covering her own. "This won't take but a minute…" He studied her intensely, making her keenly aware of her hastily pinned-up hair, her ill-fitting dimity, and sunburned face. At least, she told herself, desperately trying to hang on to a single scrap of self-esteem, she could no longer be called sallow.

She stared at the shelves lined with books, at the brass instrument on the desk, at the stacks of correspondence there, some of it not even opened. Anywhere but at the man, himself.

"Is Bess paying you a salary?"

Her head snapped around. "A what?"

"You heard me."

Confusion tangled with relief. What had Bess told him?

"Well?" he prompted.

"No, of course not." Wrong answer. She caught her mistake and tried to correct it. "That is, I'm not actually working as a secretary while we're here, and—"

"Bess doesn't need a paid companion," Matt finished for her.

How on earth could she answer that without giving away the whole wretched plot? She had to do this thing logically, to explain step-by-step how it had happened, how she'd come to deceive him, else he would never understand.

"Well, now, you see—" she began hesitantly.

"I'll pay you the going rate for an able-bodied

seaman. With back pay,'' he added when her jaw fell slack.

''An able-bodied seaman? Oh, no—I'm sorry, but—''

''I always honor my debts. I expect no less from others.''

''But you're not in my debt.'' Was he? She would've thought it was the other way around.

''You've been taking care of Annie.''

''Oh, but I love—''

''Like I said, I honor my debts.''

Bess, the wicked woman, must have told him. Now they were both toying with her like two cats with a single mouse. That must be the reason she had stayed on so much longer than she had planned.

Rose felt betrayed. Bess, she knew, liked nothing better than stirring up a hornet's nest, if only so that she could take notes and add another paragraph to whatever tale she was weaving. She was devious enough for most anything, as Rose had learned to her sorrow, but Matt…somehow, she had expected better from him.

''There's not a bank closer than Manteo, and nothing to spend it on in the village, but you'll have it when you leave.''

And that was another thing. When she left. As inevitably she would, because even without their help she had mired herself over her head in this murkiest of messes.

Clenching her fingers to keep them from trembling, she said, ''Yes, well…I'm not at all sure about this seaman business, but you'll do as you see fit, I suppose.''

Was it her imagination, or was it amusement that sparkled in the depths of his eyes? ''Yes, ma'am, I usually do,'' he said, and Rose knew she hadn't imagined his crooked smile, even though it lasted only a few seconds.

Somehow, she managed to escape. Eventually, she even remembered to breathe.

Finally, she even remembered that she hadn't resolved a single thing.

Chapter Eight

Matt caught up with Bess just as she was putting on her hat and gloves to drive to the village. "Where the devil is she?" he demanded.

"Where the devil is who?" Bess asked without blinking an eye.

The woman was too guileless by far. "Don't play the wordsmith, I can always tell when you're up to something. You made a mistake, and now you're afraid to admit it, is that it?"

"Did I tell you Dick Dixon is fixing to retire? He was asking me just the other day what your plans were."

"Dammit, Bess, stop trying to change the subject, where the devil is my wife?"

"Well, you're not getting any younger, you know. Magistrate's an important man in a—"

"Bess," he said warningly.

"Oh, pshaw. Sit down, boy, I can't think with you towering over me like a blasted lighthouse."

Boy. God, she still knew how to get under his skin.

"Bess, I'm giving you a chance to clear your conscience. You misjudged the Magruder woman, didn't you? Admit it. Instead of the paragon of all virtues you described in your letters, she turned out to be just like all the rest. Promise not worth the paper it was written on. Wouldn't recognize the truth if it reared up and smacked her on the stern."

"The truth?" Bess assumed a look of utter innocence, which was always a tip-off. She was stalling. When it came to diversionary tactics, his aunt had written the book.

Matt had already given up on the Magruder woman and set his own course. He'd started by hiring Rose to take care of Annie. On his way north he planned to track down that lawyer friend of Bess's and make him tear up the marriage contract. Damned thing had been a mistake from the beginning. He blamed Bess for cooking up the scheme; blamed himself for falling for it. But Bagby had been the one to legalize it. Just to be on the safe side, Matt intended to pay the man whatever it cost to *il*legalize it.

First, though, he had a pound of flesh to extract.

"Tell me, Bess, was there ever an Augusta Magruder in the first place, or did you cook up this whole proxy marriage scheme to keep from having to come down here and help me with Annie?"

"Well now, I'm here, plain as day. I could have been cruising down the Albemarle and Chesapeake Canal on an excursion boat with a photographer and an ornithologist, and instead here I am, doing my best to make myself useful."

It was so patently false that Matt could only shake

his head in admiration. "Make yourself useful? How? By bribing my crew to supply you with brandy? By keeping them awake half the night pecking away on that confounded machine of yours? By—"

"Now, Matthew, you're my only living relative, my brother's own boy. Think of it this way—as long as I can earn a few pennies with my scribblings, I'll not be depending on you for support in my declining years."

"Declining, my sacred ass," he said, knowing full well his aunt wouldn't be offended. She could curse circles around him if it suited her purpose. At the moment, it suited her better to play the martyr, sacrificing her own comfort for the sake of someone less fortunate.

"It won't wash, Bess. I don't know why you're here, but it sure as hell isn't for my benefit. Have you talked your publisher into letting you write another series about the deer-eating wildcats and the goat-strangling pythons of the Outer Banks? That piece you wrote last summer was the biggest load of manure I ever tried to wade through."

"You're the one who told me there were wild boars in those woods."

"And you can't tell a hog from a cougar? Hell, Bess, they're not even in the same family."

"Wild boars can be every bit as dangerous as any wildcat. I saw an actual tusk from one of those creatures, and let me tell you, I've seen less impressive ivory on a full-grown elephant."

"Besides, they both have four legs, right? What

about the python? The picture in the paper showed a giant snake wrapped around the waist of a half-naked woman, dragging her off into a swamp. Is that the scene you described to the artist?''

"Well now, artists, being creative and all, occasionally take certain liberties—it's called artistic licence. Take it occasionally, myself.'' Matt rolled his eyes. "But I myself have seen dangerous poisonous snakes right here at Powers Point. For that matter, Rose—''

Matt sliced the air with an impatient hand. "Forget snakes, forget Rose. I want to know if you've seen my wife. Do I actually have a wife, or is she in the same category as all those jungle animals of yours?''

"Well now, you certainly do have a legal wife. I watched her sign the papers myself.''

"Or signed 'em for her,'' he muttered. "How much did you pay her?''

"How much?''

"I sent you a check to cover her traveling expenses, with enough left over to pay off any debts she owed. You said the woman was widowed and down on her luck, and that you'd had to lend her money to live on.''

"Well now, that's exactly what she is—was, and I'm sure—''

Bess watched the boy's powerful shoulders flex, stared at the pulse that throbbed on one side of his brow. She admired control in a man. Always had. Sure indication of strength, and he had that, all right. Strong of body, strong of will. A worthy adversary.

"Admit it, Bess. The woman cut and ran, so any contract between us is invalid."

"Now, don't be so hasty. We'll just ask Horace about—"

"That's another thing. That lawyer friend of yours has dropped off the face of the earth, too. Did the pair of them run off together? My wife and your lawyer friend?"

Bess plucked at a loose thread on her driving glove. There was always risk involved in the telling of a good tale. The thing was to skirt as close to the truth as possible and keep open all options. She'd been so certain Matt and Rose would suit each other, and with a wife in residence, Bess's rare visits would be all the more comfortable. Those two old men did their best, but lately their best had fallen a bit short of adequate.

"Well, now, I believe Horace did mention a trip he'd been meaning to take." The coward had as good as told her he didn't intend to hang around waiting for her chickens to come home to roost.

"So he's in on it, too. Just tell me why, Bess? For a few hundred dollars? It's hardly worth the trouble." He had mailed a check when Bess had described the woman's circumstances.

"Now, Matthew—"

"Did you plan the whole thing so you could write it and claim it as the truth? How the beached sea captain took a wife and couldn't find her? Maybe you got the idea from that damned fool poem."

"Couldn't *keep* her, not couldn't *find* her. That

was Peter, Peter in the nursery rhyme. Now, Matthew—''

''How the devil could I keep the blasted woman when I can't even find her in the first place? What happened, Bess? Did she sign the papers and take off with the money? Is that it? Then why not just admit it? Hell, we all make mistakes in judgment, I've made a few myself. If she pulled the wool over your eyes, we'll just chalk it up to experience and go on from there.''

''Speaking of that, Matthew, I just had an excellent idea.''

''No, thanks. I've had all the ideas I need from you and that lawyer. A word of advice, though: you might want to start looking for a new secretary. Next time you might even find one who can use that damned typing machine.''

''But Rose—''

''Forget Rose. She'll be working for me.''

''But, Matt, Rose is—''

''No point in arguing, she's already agreed to it.''

Bess opened her mouth and closed it again. She was sailing too close to the wind to risk giving herself away with a careless word.

Why the bloody hell had she gotten herself into this mess in the first place? She had an adequate income—of course, she could always use more. But she could have split the money with Rose, washed her hands of the whole business, and told Matt the truth—that his bride had had second thoughts. He probably wouldn't even have cut up rough about the money. The boy was tough as salt horse, but he was no skinflint. She'd known him to give a year's pay out of his own pocket to the widow of a common seaman who'd been killed in a tavern brawl. Told the poor woman it was her husband's due wages, when the truth was, the fellow had drunk and gambled away every cent he'd ever earned, leaving his poor wife to take in washing.

"Well now, as to that," she began without the least notion of where she was headed. One advantage of being a writer was that a body could make up whatever story served the purpose. "Mrs. Magruder, as I believe I mentioned, had this relative—an elderly aunt, I believe she said—and as it happened, on the very day of the wedding she received a—"

"Stow it, Bess. You tried and failed, and that's the end of it."

"What I was going to say is that—" *That what?*

Bess would have given anything to be back home, quietly sipping brandy and swapping tales with Horace. Instead, she was going to have to wiggle herself out of this mess without his help.

She should have left weeks ago instead of hanging on to see how it would all work out. What if she told the boy straight out that his bride had gotten cold feet, and she'd brought her down here to look him over before committing herself any further?

He'd wring her neck, that's what. No man with a lick of pride would allow himself to be put on the block and examined like a prize bull.

Think, Bessy, think! You've shoved a skiff up many a creek, only to have it peter out on you. You can

work your way backward, or you can drag your boat
through the marsh until you hit deep water again.

Arms crossed, Matt was obviously waiting on her
to say something. So she did, without the least notion
of where she was going with it. "I was about to say
that my friend Rose—"

"Friend? I thought you said she was your secretary."

"Secretary-companion. A sort of steward, you
might say. Does a bit of this and a bit of that." So
far, so good. Now what?

"Whatever you call her, I still want to know everything you know about her, seeing as I've already
hired her to take care of Annie when I leave."

'Ware the shoals ahead.

How much had Rose told him? If Bess said too
much and their stories got crossed, it might endanger
Rose's credibility. Although better that than endan-
gering her own, still she wouldn't risk harming the
girl if she could help it. Might be better to say as
little as possible.

She shifted her eyes and pulled another thread
from her glove. "Well, now, as to that…"

Matt disguised the intensity of his regard by dropping his eyelids to half-mast. He crossed his arms
over his chest. "Do you know, every time you start
a sentence with 'Well, now…' I know you're about
to pile on another layer of bull."

"It's purely a mannerism, boy. We all have them,
even you. You narrow your eyes and cross your arms
and I know you're not going to believe a word I
say."

"That's because you lie."

"I don't lie. What I do is try to present the facts in the most interesting manner. It's what I get paid to do."

"I don't want to be entertained, dammit, I want to be informed. Right now, I want all the information you have about the Littlefield woman. You claim she's a widow. Is that true, or is it another one of your fancy flourishes?"

"Matthew, I swear on my father's grave that—"

"We both know your father was buried at sea. I was there, remember?"

"I swear on the Atlantic Ocean," she said without missing a beat, "that Rose was married to a man who drowned shortly before she came to live with her grandmother, who happened to be a close friend of mine, which is how I came to know her—Rose, that is—in the first place. When her grandmother died, the poor girl was left with no home and no skills to support herself, which is why I took her on."

Bessy, my girl, you're treading on thin ice. If you can plot yourself out of this fix, you'll be ready to write your first novel.

"Now why does all that sound familiar? Have you taken up writing those fancy female stories?"

"What fancy female stories?"

Well, why not? If Matt was determined to hire his own wife, why not encourage a romantic interest between them before he found her out? By the time he learned the truth, Bess would be long gone. It would take Noah and a forty-day rain to get Rose back aboard a boat again. Meanwhile, any man worth his salt would already have given the girl a rollicking tumble or two. After that, they could set their own course and forget all about any discrepancies that might have cropped up.

Bess tugged off her ragged glove and fumbled in her dresser drawer for a fresh pair. ''If that's all, I need to be on my way to the village. I told you Dick Dixon's invited me to dinner, didn't I? His son's coming home for the summer, and I want to talk to him about Rose.''

''What does Rose have to do with Dixon's son?''

Her inventive mind at work again, Bess gave it her wide-eyed best. ''Well, now, Rose might be a widow, but she's still a young woman. I understand the boy's planning to go into politics. A nice wife would be an asset, and Rose could certainly use a husband.'' Nothing quite like setting the cat among the pigeons, if only to watch them scatter and see where they came to earth again.

Yes indeed, a novel might be just the ticket. Newspaper columns were well enough, but why stop there when she could be the next Brontë?

As Bess had taken the cart, Matt sent Luther off on one of the mares as soon as he sighted the mail-boat headed into the channel. Sooner or later, that damned shyster would have to admit what he'd done or risk being hauled before the bar by the scruff of his mangy neck. Matt had written weekly, wanting to know the whereabouts of his missing bride.

Bagby had written once, telling him nothing at all. Some hour and a half later, Luther came larruping back into the yard, leaped from the mare, dropped the reins and ran yelling toward the house, waving a letter. "We got us a letter from the *Swan*," he shouted.

Actually, it was from the broker Matt had commissioned to buy her back. Hardly daring to get his hopes up, Matt ripped open the envelope and scanned the contents.

"We going to Boston?" Luther asked eagerly, peering around his shoulder to read the letter.

Feeling as if a two-ton anchor had been lifted from his back, Matt nodded. He went so far as to grin. "Yeah, we're going to Boston. Take care of the mare while I go tell the others."

"Me, too?" Luther couldn't quite mask his anxiety. Evidently he hadn't forgotten the dressing down Matt had given him when he'd attempted to ride Jericho.

"Yeah, you too, son. Somebody's got to help me sign on a crew. I guess you're the best I've got."

The best he had *left*. The words went unspoken, but both men sobered, glancing out past the paddock to the lone sandy grave.

In the kitchen, Matt skimmed the letter aloud to Crank and Peg. "—negotiations in final stages, your presence required immediately for closing agreement."

"You done pulled it off, Cap'n" was Peg's comment.

"Hot diggety-by-damn," Crank swore admiringly. "We'll handle things here, don't you worry 'bout a thing. Peg can look after the horses, I can look after

Annie—we got enough fish salted down to last until—''

But Matt was already three jumps ahead. ''I'll send Luther back to hire a boy from the village to take care of the horses. He can come every day and bring whatever supplies you need from the village. Peg, you'll oversee the outside work. Bess and Rose can look after Annie—''

Rose. He would need to secure an ironclad agreement before he left, because he didn't trust Bess to hang around until he could get back. It would take at least a month, possibly longer, to complete the inspections, sign the final papers, hire on a new crew, arrange for cargo and deal with harbor officials.

He should have paid closer attention to those reports, then he'd know where to make the best deals on consignments.

His mind teeming with details, he went in search of Rose.

She was in the backyard. With Annie under a makeshift awning, Rose was kneeling beside a row of dead plants, carefully pouring water around each one. She glanced up. ''They're collard slips. I think they're supposed to stand upright, don't you?''

As far as he knew, they were supposed to lie dark and greasy in the pot with a slab of side meat. ''Forget the collards, I've got to go to Boston, but before I leave I want your word of honor that you'll stay until I get back.''

She forgot the collards. ''Boston?''

''It might take a couple of weeks, maybe even longer. We agreed that Crank and Peg can't handle

Annie on their own, and Bess is about as reliable as a—'' He swallowed the bawdy comparison. ''Anyhow, I need someone I can trust. Will you do it for me, Rose?''

She sat back, brushed the sand off her hands and gazed up at him helplessly. ''Matt, we really need to get something straight before I agree to anything.''

''Can it wait? I've got about three days' work to do in a few hours. There'll be a freight boat bound up the sound on the high tide. From Elizabeth City we can catch a train for Boston.''

''We?''

''I'll be taking Luther.''

''Oh.'' Rose wondered at his swift look of—of what? Satisfaction? ''And you want me to stay here and look after Annie. Even if Bess leaves?''

''I want you to stay on even if my wife shows up. She'll need help getting her bearings. We had an agreement, if you'll remember.''

He was clearly eager to be off and about his business. Rose had seen children on Christmas Eve look less excited. ''Of course I'll stay, but, Matt—''

It was plain to see his mind was already miles away. Standing there, legs braced apart, hands on his hips, with his head tilted back and his eyes narrowed against the glare of the sun, he was a magnificent man by anyone's standards. She could easily picture him standing on whatever part of a ship the captain stood on, with that same look of inner excitement sparkling in his eyes.

''Never mind,'' she said quietly. ''It's waited this long, I suppose another few weeks won't change anything." Let him go. Let him get his ship back so he could put to sea and forget Annie and Powers Point and…the wife he'd left behind. What difference could it make now? She'd made her choice, now she would have to accept the consequences.

She watched him head out to the barn, his long legs striding across the bright, hot sand. Glancing down at the pathetic slips she had planted so hopefully, she wondered why she even bothered. One thing, and one thing alone, mattered to Matthew Powers: his blasted ship.

They all, every last one of them, sang the man's praises. Luther worshipped him. Crank never ceased talking about the galley the captain had fitted out with the very best of everything. Peg bragged that after he'd gone and got himself all busted up, the captain had rounded up the best sawbones money could buy to patch him up, then hired another chips to work under Peg's supervision until Peg was on his feet again.

"Saint Matthew. Blasted man," she muttered. "Blasted, bloody, arrogant sailor." She jabbed the trowel into the sand.

This was what she'd wanted, wasn't it? To have her own home and a baby to care for without the risky ties of marriage? She had it all now, just as Bess had promised.

So why did it feel as if the sun had just gone behind a cloud?

Chapter Nine

Matt made the time to give Jericho one last work-out. As if the stallion were a member of his crew, he felt responsible for his welfare. It had been a mistake to buy him, he'd known it at the time, but the owner had been about to consign him to the glue factory.

"Devil horse. Dang near killed a feller working for me. Tell by the set of his eyes, he ain't normal."

Matt didn't know much about horses, having been raised at sea, but he'd read every western story he could lay hands on. If there was a Wild West show anywhere near whenever he was in port, he usually managed to attend at least one performance, some-times more. As a youngster he'd dreamed about growing up to be a cowboy.

How many boys, he wondered as he waded the stallion into the surf, had grown up on a ranch and dreamed about life at sea?

"We've got the best of both worlds, haven't we, boy? Easy there, watch your step now," he said softly.

He'd sent Luther back to the village to find someone to deal with the stock. Most of the boys on the island broke and trained at least one horse from the wild herd that roamed the Banks, partly for sport, partly necessity. Jericho shouldn't be too much of a challenge for a boy with that kind of experience.

Soon after he'd returned to the Point, Matt had sailed up to Currituck Banks towing a cattle barge, intending to buy a cow and a couple of mares. He'd come back with five mares, and Jericho. Almost as if he'd been sleepwalking, the rangy blood bay had followed the mares aboard, meek as a house cat. Not until they were out in open waters did he seem to wake up. He'd taken one look around, started bucking, and before they could get a line on him he'd busted up damned near everything in sight, including Matt.

"A regular heller, weren't you, fellow? Didn't trust anything on two legs." Matt continued to talk to the horse as he swam him out through the incoming tide to the bar, then turned and headed back to shore. "Yeah, I know how you feel." He'd fallen into the habit of voicing his thoughts when he was on board Jericho. Sometimes it helped ease frustrations; occasionally it even offered him a fresh perspective.

Once on shore again, with the light breeze playing over his wet body, he walked the stallion back over the dunes. "I'm going to have to trust the woman, Jeri," he said after several minutes had passed. "Got no choice. Funny thing, though—it's not as hard as I'd expected. Either I've learned a lesson or..." Back at the house, he headed for the stock trough, slid off the stallion's back and commenced to rinsing the salt off both their hides with bucketsful of rainwater. "...or I've not learned a damn thing," he continued. "Time'll tell which, I reckon."

With a three-hour lag between flood tide on the ocean and flood tide on the sound, he had just about enough time to pack a bag, instruct whoever Luther brought back on how to handle Jericho, and go over the duty roster with Crank and Peg before heading to the village.

No point in leaving orders with Bess, he concluded. If he read the signs correctly, she'd have her bags packed before he was even out of sight. The mystery was that she'd stayed as long as she had.

Which left Rose. Funny how he'd come to trust her for no real reason other than the way she looked him directly in the eye. Or the way she'd pitched in with the tasks Billy and Luther used to share with no complaint, much less any mention of compensation.

He wondered now if she'd intended all along to feather her own nest. It wouldn't be the first time a wily widow had set out to trap herself another husband. The trouble was, he already had a wife. It was no secret. Not much of a wife, to be sure, but enough to keep another woman from getting any ideas about staking a claim.

Whatever her intention had been, as long as she did what he'd hired her to do, he'd be satisfied. If she happened to stay outside too long and got all pink and damp so that her shirt stuck to her bosom, it was no skin off his nose. He wouldn't be around to see it.

If she laughed aloud at Peg's stories or sang her songs to Annie, he wouldn't be around to hear. What difference did it make if she bit her lower lip when she was embarrassed? He wouldn't be here to see it. To think the kind of thoughts that could land a man in trouble before he knew what had hit him. He had his ship back now. A couple of hours more and he'd be headed north. Once he had a deck under his feet again, no woman on earth could lure him off-course.

Still dripping, Matt strode into the house, mentally checking off things to be done before he could leave. Change into dry clothes, have a word with the men, leave funds with Crank to cover expenses for at least three months, throw a few things into a duffel, caution whoever Luther found to look after the stock to go easy with Jericho, and arrange to have their mounts collected from the boat landing and returned to the Point.

Crank had already packed his bag. "Thought you might be needin' your best blacks, Cap'n, seein's how you're gonna be mixin' with all them city folks up in Boston. I put in two shirts and a necktie and polished up your good boots. You leave them old ones here."

Both men glanced down at the big, salt-stained boots he'd meant to leave outside. "I appreciate it, Crank. I'd've forgot half my gear." Which wasn't true, and they both knew it, but the old cook had taken on the duties of steward once they'd settled ashore. "I've left expense money in the box in my office. If you need more, you can always reach me through the broker's office. Chances are, I'll be in Boston for a few weeks, maybe even a couple of months, before we tie up all the loose ends and get under way.''

Peg hobbled in, carrying a load of firewood, which he dumped in the basket behind the range. ''Gonna have a wet crossing. Looks like rain's fixin' to set in for a spell.''

''Rig a line in the attic for the wash if you need to.''

''Already done it.''

''Rose around?''

''Come in while you were out. Seeing to Annie, I reckon.''

''Tell her I said—'' He broke off and raked his fingers through his hair. ''Never mind, I'll tell her myself.''

He saw the look that passed between the two old men, but before he could deny whatever it was they were thinking, Luther called through the open window and he took the opportunity to escape.

They were still mounted, Luther on his favorite among the mares, the other man on a rangy gelding. ''You know John, don't you?'' Luther indicated a dark, wiry fellow Matt remembered seeing around the village. ''He can handle Jericho. He'll see to the stock and put out the net when Crank needs fish.''

Matt and the stranger sized one another up. Matt reached a decision based partly on instinct, partly on experience. Evidently the stranger did the same. Eyes met, minds were made up, and the deal was done. Satisfied, both men nodded.

"Obliged," Matt said.

"Seen your horse over on the mainland. Glad he's in good hands. I'd have taken him myself, but you beat me to it."

"If you have to approach from abaft the starboard beam, stand back and speak to let him know you're there. His right eye's not too good."

"I'll do it."

Leaving Luther to show the other man around, Matt went back inside. He stopped by Bess's room, heard her pecking away on her machine, and moved on. He'd say good-bye to Annie first, then check with Rose in case she had any last questions.

Rose was in Annie's room. Halting in the open doorway, Matt watched as the two of them played tumble on a quilt on the floor. They were both laughing. He'd never heard a baby laugh before Annie. The sound made him feel as if he'd taken too tight a hitch in his necktie.

"Rose?"

She rolled over, clearly startled, her skirts awry, her face flushed. "Oh—I didn't hear you come in." Still holding one of Annie's tiny feet in her hand, she sat up and brushed back her tousled hair. With the last red glow of sunset falling across her shoulders through the open window, she reminded him of a stained-glass panel he'd once seen in a church in Biloxi.

Looking flustered, she smoothed her skirt down over her legs. "The reason we're on the floor, in case you're wondering, is that Annie's quick as anything. We used to play on my bed, but I was afraid she'd roll off the side. I thought this would be safer.'' With a vague gesture, she indicated the rumpled quilt.

He nodded once, sharply. ''I came to say I'm leaving.'' Even to his own ears, the announcement sounded abrupt.

''So soon?'' That couldn't be disappointment he saw on her face...could it?

''Tide'll be high on the sound side within the hour. Before I go I just wanted to say—'' While she waited, her head tilted in that way she had, he struggled to remember what it was he'd wanted to say. ''I just wanted to say good-bye.''

The second attempt was no better than the first. He sounded angry. Anger didn't begin to describe his feelings. Threatened came close. Tempted, even closer. Seeing her this way, damp and flushed and rumpled—remembering the prim, starchy creature she'd been when she'd first landed on his doorstep— it was like looking at a painted picture of a ship, compared to seeing a real ship on the high seas, throbbing with life from keel to masthead, stem to stern.

Clearing his throat, he tried once more. ''I meant to say—that is—dammit, good-bye!'' Cursing his own ineptitude, he turned and fled. He got halfway down the hall before guilt overtook him. Wheeling about, he retraced his steps.

She was standing in the doorway, a puzzled look on her face. As he came closer, puzzlement gave way to wariness. He was half afraid she'd bolt before he could apologize for yelling at her.

Three more steps brought him close enough to see the green sparks in her golden eyes. "Rose, I'm sorry," he blurted. "I didn't mean to sound—that is, I just wanted—I needed—"

Oh, the devil with it. Like a guttering lamp, his mind flickered out, and he caught her in a hard embrace, buried his face in her hair and filled his lungs with her warm lilac scent.

Taken off-guard, Rose stiffened, but the strangest thing happened. Instead of pulling away, she found herself melting in his arms, the same way she'd done when he'd lifted her down from the mare after Angel had left her stranded miles from home.

She'd been furious at the time, embarrassed by her own reaction. Primed by the scent of him, the feel of him holding her against his heated, unyielding body on the long ride home, the rocking motion of the horse causing their bodies to move together, she'd been in no condition to think, much less to act properly.

Then, once the ride had finally ended, he'd lifted her down slowly, sliding her down the length of his body. For one searing moment he had held her against him then, just as he was holding her now.

And now, just as it had then, her heart went wild. With the top of her head brushing against his jaw, she drew in a deep, tremulous breath, filling her lungs with his clean masculine scent. A heavy urgency began to throb inside her. From the earliest days of her marriage, she knew what it meant, but this time it was far more powerful than anything she had ever experienced.

On the floor across the room, Annie made sleepy, contented noises as she sucked on her toes. Outside, the cries of gulls could be heard over the quiet rush of the surf. Somewhere a horse whickered, a man laughed. Held tightly in Matt's arms, Rose thought that if only she could capture this moment and hold it in her heart, she would never ask for anything more.

The last of her doubts faded away. For once in her life she had made the right choice. She lifted her face to tell him so, but the words went unspoken. She felt it again. The belt buckle thing. Oh, heavens, what now?

"Matt?" she whispered, her eyes widening.

"I'm going to kiss you." It was more threat than promise.

"All right." Relieved, she closed her eyes, puckered her lips and waited.

"I've got no right—you can say no, if you want to, Rose. I've got a wife…somewhere."

"All right." Eyes still closed, she nodded her understanding. Confessions could wait, this was far more important.

The whole world could wait, she thought a moment later when she felt his warm, firm lips come down on hers. He twisted his head, tugging her lips apart, and then she felt something hot and intimate slip between them. Shivers raced down her spine. Her legs went numb. Every particle of feeling she possessed was concentrated in the space between her mouth and her...

Well.

She tingled. Her small breasts grew heavy. When the tip of his tongue began to move in a rhythm that echoed the frantic throbbing between her thighs, she thought she might die. Torn between desire and a guilty conscience, she had no choice. She had to tell him—*now*.

"Matt," she gasped, "we're married."

She might as well have thrown a bucket of cold water in his face. He stepped back, his face expressionless. "I understood you were a widow."

"No, I mean—I am a widow, but you and I are—"

"I'm married. You're right about that, but I mean to take care of it as soon as I've got my ship back. In the meantime, all I require of you is that you look after Annie."

"Of course I'll look after Annie," she exclaimed, "but—"

"You have my apology, madam. We'll discuss it later."

"I don't want your blasted apology, I want—"

She wanted *him*.

Wanted him in a way she had never wanted another man, but he was leaving, and with no time to properly plead her case, it was pointless to try and explain what she had done and why she'd done it. Pointless and perhaps even dangerous.

Time and tide wait for no man. Crank would probably attribute that, too, to the Bible. Making the only choice she could possibly make under the circumstances, she lifted her chin and graciously accepted his apology, adding her best wishes for a safe journey.

"I'll be on my way, then," he said gruffly. If he'd been wearing a hat, Rose thought irritably, he would have tipped it.

And if she'd been holding a brick she might've thrown it.

Staring after him as he strode off down the hall, just as if he hadn't set her on fire and left her burning, she made a promise to herself. One day he would have to return, and when he did, she would be ready for him. They would settle this thing between them before she ever allowed him over the threshold. Then, if he wanted a life at sea, he could have it with her blessing.

But he would have to take her and Annie with him. If Bess could do it, then so could she. She was his wife, after all. His legal wife, even if he didn't yet know it.

Confidence swelling, she lifted Annie up off the quilt, settled into the rocking chair and began to rock. "He's going to love us, Annie, you just wait and see," she declared firmly.

Annie reached for a tendril that had escaped her braid, tugging with surprising force. She warbled a sleepy comment.

"That's all very well, but you're going to have to help me. If he wants you, he'll have to keep me. You're easy—anyone would love you, dumpling, but we're going to have to work on improving me if we want him to give me a chance. He thinks he can just sail off and leave us here, but we'll show him, won't we?''

She leaned her head back on the curved cane, her eyes half closed, and thought of what she was going to have to do to prove herself. Her stomach tightened uncomfortably as determination set in. She had made her decision. Now all she had to do was live up to it.

The next morning she took Annie out on the front porch to watch the new man work with the horses. Quiet and soft-spoken, he soon had Matt's stallion following him around the pen, nudging his shirt pocket for a treat.

''See there, love? Nothing's impossible. If that wicked beast can be tamed this quickly by a stranger, you and I can certainly tame our captain.''

She watched as a small sail skiff came alongside the wharf. She didn't recognize the gentleman at the tiller. Curious, she watched as he dropped the sails and made his way toward the house. Stout, dressed in a rumpled gray suit and a straw hat, he was sweating profusely.

Rose met him at the door, holding Annie in her arms. ''I'm afraid the captain's not here.''

He removed his hat. ''You must be Mrs. Littlefield. Bess told me all about you.''

''She did?'' *Oh, heavens, I hope not.* ''Yes, I am. Would you care to come in? I believe Bess is in her office.''

''Well now, I wouldn't mind a spot of shade for a spell before I go back, and that's the truth. Warm, isn't it?''

Rose agreed that it was warm indeed. The gentleman had yet to identify himself, but fortunately, Bess chose that moment to come and investigate.

"I thought I heard voices. Dick, how nice of you to come calling. Shall we go inside? I'll have Crank fetch us something cool to drink."

"I take it the boy got off on yesterday's freight?"

The boy? If they were referring to Matt, he was definitely no boy, as Rose could attest, had she cared to.

"Letter came yesterday," Bess explained. "Matt couldn't wait to leave. I know you wanted to see him about that matter we discussed, but he was champing at the bit the minute he heard the *Swan* was practically his again."

"My loss," the magistrate said philosophically. "He's been a big help to me, with his contacts all up and down the Eastern Seaboard, and that's a fact. I'm sorry things didn't work out. He'd have been a good 'un."

Turning to Rose, he extended his hand. "Dick Dixon, Mrs. Littlefield. Local magistrate. Catch-all title, catch-all position here on the Banks. Interesting, though. My, the tales I could tell you...." His hand was far softer than Rose's. His clasp, however, was surprisingly firm. "I believe my wife gave you some cuttings from her garden the other day."

Not a one of which had survived, Rose thought, but she smiled and said, "Please thank her for me, Mr. Dixon."

She wondered what it was Matt had helped him with, and what hadn't worked out. When Annie began squirming, she turned to leave, murmuring a polite excuse.

Bess waved her back. "Stay here, girl, you might learn something."

As it actually was somewhat cooler, with what slight breeze there was funneled through the windows, she sank into a chair and began bouncing Annie gently on her knees. Crank came in with tumblers of water, cool from the wet canvas bucket he kept on the back porch.

"Well now, as I was saying," Dick Dixon said after emptying his glass, "I thought of Powers as soon as I learned my boy wouldn't be following in my footsteps. Pity I didn't know sooner."

"Matt as magistrate? I doubt he'd have done it, anyway. Too much saltwater in his blood. Surprised he stayed put as long as he did."

"Still, if he changes his mind, you let me know. I approached him a year or so ago about becoming a pilot. With all the trade in and out of these inlets, it's hard to find enough qualified pilots. All he'd have to do is learn the waters, and they all have to do that. Shoals change, channels shift overnight. Takes a right smart man, keeps him on his toes, I can tell you."

In the cool, shadowy room, Rose allowed her mind to drift. Annie, her thumb securely between her swollen gums, leaned back against her bosom, generating a surprising amount of heat for one small body. Within minutes, she'd fallen asleep.

Within another few minutes, Rose, tired from another largely sleepless night, did the same.

"Don't snore in mixed company, Rose, it's not polite."

"Wha—"

Her mouth snapped shut and she sat up, amazed

to see that dusk had fallen and their guest was nowhere in sight. "Did I—is he—?"

"You did and he is. Son of his'll be here in a few days. Dick's promised to bring him out for supper. With Matt and Luther gone, you'll appreciate some company your own age."

Bess lifted the sleeping baby from Rose's lap. She held her awkwardly until Rose could take her again, then said, "If I was married to a seaman, blest if I'd leave him untended. Too many fancy women around. Seen 'em with my own eyes, the way they pile into the jolly boats all painted up and smelling to high heaven, and go out to meet every ship that comes into port. No sir, I'd move myself right into his quarters and there I'd stay to repel all female boarders, else he'll forget he even has a wife. Man's memory's no longer than his pecker."

Rose's lips twitched, but she was no longer surprised by anything the woman said, knowing it was meant to get a rise from her audience.

With a sly grin, Bess delivered her parting shot. "Growing up the way I did, there weren't much I didn't hear or see. You'd do well to keep a taut line on him, Rose, else you'll lose him, sure's the world."

She could hardly lose what she'd never possessed. All the same, Rose made up her mind to start on the course of action she'd decided on the very next day, as soon as Annie went down for her nap.

But lord knows, she wasn't looking forward to it.

Chapter Ten

The boat—a sail skiff, according to Peg, who looked after it while Luther was away—was much smaller than the mailboat, and far more graceful.

Nevertheless, it was still a boat.

Rose stood on the wharf, fighting the urge to turn away and forget the whole crazy notion. What had ever given her the idea that it would make a difference? Matt had planned from the first to leave her at home. It was the sole reason he'd married her, so that she could stay here and take care of his baby.

She looked at the boat, at the water, which was mirror-calm, then back at the boat. There was a flat, rectangular case of some sort rising up from the floor near the middle. She had no idea what that was all about. The front bench had a hole in it. Luther had told her it was for stepping—*stepping?*—the mast. She'd only seen him use oars.

Rose had no intention of using either mast or oars. She was determined only to climb down into the thing and see how long she could stand there without throwing up. With enough practice, sooner or later she should be able to go for hours without getting sick, which would be time enough to start learning about all the paraphernalia. Luther had mentioned that the first few times he'd sailed as a boy he'd been deathly ill. Then suddenly one day, he wasn't. Just like that, he'd been cured.

Well, if a cure could be had, then Rose intended to have it. When she finally laid out her case before Matt, she wanted to be able to tell him that she would stay ashore if he insisted, but she would rather follow him the way all the women in the Powers family had followed their seafaring men.

Now that she had herself another husband, she intended to be a better wife. And if she was a better wife, then Matt, whether at home or at sea, would be a better husband.

At least he hadn't married her for her money, as Robert had done, although she'd been far too naive to realize it at the time. Grieving for her parents, it had never occurred to her to wonder why a handsome, charming gentleman would suddenly fall blindly in love with a gawky, gullible girl with little polish and no looks at all.

Matt, on the other hand, had married her sight unseen. Given a choice, she would rather be married for her usefulness than for her supposed inheritance.

But then Matt had kissed her. More than a few times she'd caught him looking at her in a certain way. He had encouraged her to fall in love with him, which wasn't fair unless he meant to love her back.

And the one thing she knew about Matthew Powers was that he was a fair man.

It took her several minutes to lower herself into the bottom of the skiff. Arms flailing, it took less than thirty seconds to scramble out. Dismayed, she wondered if she shouldn't simply settle for having a roof over her head and a baby to fill the hours and the aching emptiness in her heart.

From the new train station on Norfolk's Main Street, Matt left Luther to guard their luggage while he went back outside to hail a hackney. "Hold on a minute, will you, Cap'n?" the young seaman called after him. "There's something I been wanting to ask you."

Luther had been chewing over something or other ever since they'd crossed the Virginia line. Probably concerning his rank, and who would take Billy's place. Matt had put him off because at the time he'd been too busy going over every letter, every report from Quimby since he'd first commissioned the man to buy back the *Black Swan*.

Now, with just over two hours before they had to make their Boston connection, he had in mind tracking down the source of his troubles and securing himself a few answers. After all the letters he'd written, he knew the address by heart. "Later," he called over his shoulder.

Some hour and twenty-five minutes later, he walked out into the drizzling rain again, his face a study in angry disbelief. By the time he reached the station, where his train was ready to board, disbelief had given way to a çold determination.

"As I recall," Horace Bagby had told him when he'd tracked the man to his office, "your wife was to have left Norfolk shortly after the wedding. A day or so, at the most. I believe your aunt planned to accompany her, but more than that I really can't say, as I never saw your, er—your bride, after she left my office. I thought surely by now she would have arrived."

Matt was beginning to have a bad feeling about this business. Beginning, hell, he'd been feeling this way ever since he'd signed the damned marriage contract. "According to Bess," he said impatiently, "my wife was suddenly called away to visit a sick relative. A week or so after that, Bess turned up with a companion, a Mrs. Rose Littlefield. Claimed they'd come down to help out until my wife could get there."

Bagby had shuddered visibly. "Oh, my, I was afraid of that," he whispered.

"Afraid?" All his doubts coalesced into a leaden weight in the pit of his belly.

"Mind you, I was never a party to…well, to anything other than the actual marriage. You do know, I assume, that your wife's full name is Augusta Rose Littlefield Magruder."

"*Rose Littlefield?* According to her documentation, I married one Augusta R. L. Magruder."

"Goes by her middle name. Named for her grandmother, Augusta Littlefield, who happened to be Bess's good friend and a client of mine until she passed away. Married a man named Magruder—

Rose, that is, not Augusta. Man drowned, I believe, which is when Rose came to live with her grandmother. That's when I first made her acquaintance.''

Now that it was too late, Horace Bagby was suddenly a fount of information. Stunned, Matt could think of nothing to say that would adequately express his feeling of betrayal.

The lawyer rushed to fill the silence. ''Do you know, now that I look back, it's plain as day what happened. I believe Bess did mention that your bride was having a few, er—second thoughts. I warned her at the time against trying any shenanigans. Told her whatever she did, I wanted no part in it.''

''Is that why you ignored my letters?''

The older man tried and failed to look indignant. ''I believe I answered the first one in a timely fashion.''

''Timely, my—! It took three weeks!''

''It's been my experience, Captain, that it's never wise to rush into anything of a legal nature.''

Matt prayed for patience. It was either that or wring the man's neck. ''You answered, all right. A bunch of 'whereases' and other legal bilge and not one damned fact.''

''If memory serves, you asked after your wife. And as I believe I told you at the time, while her name might have come up in conversation, I hadn't actually seen her since the day of the ceremony. Shortly after that as I recall, I left town on a bit of private business.''

''Private business, my sacred ass.'' Matt didn't bother to hide his disgust.

Bagby's jowls took on a pasty sheen. "Captain Powers, I've known your aunt for years. I am privileged to count her among my closest friends, but you have to understand, as I'm sure you do, seeing as how Bess is your relative, that sometimes—that is, on rare occasions, your—"

"The woman lies like a carpet. She'd sooner lie than tell the truth."

"Well now, none of this was my idea, in fact I believe I recall issuing a stern warning—"

"Just cut to the chase, Bagby, I have a train to catch. Bess hatched up a scheme and then lied to us both about what she was up to, is that the gist of it?"

"*Lying* is a relative term. *Prevaricating* might be a better way to put it." He coughed discreetly. "As you probably know, your aunt has a creative turn of mind. On occasion, that trait, as well as her, uh—natural enthusiasm—can lead her beyond the boundaries of common sense."

"In other words, when my wife decided to sneak into my house using a false name and worm her way into my good graces long enough to see if it would be worth her while to stay, Bess willingly went along with her. Probably even suggested it in the first place, is that what you're trying to tell me?"

"In a manner of speaking. Although I don't believe—"

"Annul it."

"Beg pardon?"

"Annul the marriage. Just do whatever it takes to cut me loose. I'll be damned if I'll have a cheating wife. Never wanted a wife in the first place, but I let Bess talk me into it.''

Matt had stood then, barely managing to control his anger until he could escape the small cluttered office. Once on the sidewalk, he lifted his face to the cool drizzle, took several deep breaths, then began striding off in the direction of the station. Two blocks down the street, he hailed a hackney. By the time he hopped off at the train station, paid the driver and went in search of Luther, he had settled on a course.

She was going to pay. It was too late for Bess; she'd been this way all her life, but one way or another, he intended to teach his conniving wife a lesson she would never forget.

Sanford Dixon, the magistrate's son, came to supper with his father the evening before Bess left Powers Point. He was young and presentable, and because she missed Matt even more than she'd expected to, Rose spared him more of her attention than she might otherwise have done.

"I'll be graduating from Chapel Hill next year." Between the clam chowder and the bread pudding he'd told her practically his entire life story. "I mean to go into politics. Did Daddy tell you?"

"I believe he might have mentioned it," Rose murmured.

"You see, I've made a study of ways to improve our public schools, and once that's done, I mean to do something about public transportation. Do you have any notion of how hard it is to get from one small town to another?"

Thinking of her own most recent experiences, Rose nodded. It was all the encouragement Sandy needed to lay out his plans for a network of macadamized roads, and fleets of regularly scheduled hackneys and celerity wagons connecting every town of more than a few hundred souls between Charleston and Norfolk.

By the time the two men left, Rose was yawning, Crank had washed and dried and put away the last plate, Peg had brought in the morning's firewood, and both men had retired to their rooms.

"Well now, from the way that young man took to you, I'd say we have a promising situation on our hands, wouldn't you?" Bess was big on "promising situations."

Rose closed the front door and momentarily leaned her forehead against the cool wooden panel. "Before you say another word, don't. Just don't."

"Don't what?" the older woman inquired, all innocence.

Turning, Rose shook her head. "Sandy's a nice young man. Luther is a nice young man, and so is John, for that matter. But you seem to forget, I have a husband."

"Matt's my own blood kin and I love him like a son, but the boy don't know the first thing about women, much less his own wife. Before it's too late, you have to spark his interest, else you'll not see hide nor hair of him until you're both too old to remember why you married one another in the first place."

"We married because I needed a job and he needed a nanny," Rose said flatly. Exasperated, she flung out her hands. "Besides, he's not even here. If your idea was to make him jealous, how can I do that when he's in Boston? Even if he were here, he wouldn't care."

"That's all you know."

"I know I never should have gotten myself into this fix. I know cheating never works. I know—"

"Ballocks. If you hadn't come down here flying false colors, you wouldn't have come here at all. Instead you'd be in a hot attic earning slave wages working for some woman who treats you like dirt, while her husband sneaks into your bed every night to have his way with you."

"Oh, for heaven's sake, would you stop turning everything that happens into one of your blasted novels? This is my life we're talking about! I'm trying to make choices I can live with, while you—"

"What d'you think novels are all about? Did you ever bother to read one, or is all you read those shelf-fillers your grandfather left by the ton when he died? Gussy never cracked a one of them, I can tell you that. I'd bet my bloomers that stick she married never did, either, but they looked mighty fine in that library of his. Waste, if you ask me. All those written words and not a one of 'em ever got read."

"Goodnight, Bess."

"Wait a minute, I'm not finished."

"That stick was my grandfather."

"You don't even remember the man, he died before you were born. He was a stick. Now listen, I'll be leaving on the mailboat tomorrow, but before I go—"

"I'm staying. False colors or not, I gave my word. And in case you're still interested, I can sit in that blasted boat for nearly five minutes now without feeling even faintly queasy."

She left without seeing Bess's smile, nor did she hear the softly spoken comment. "Well now, isn't this interesting? Now that the pot's boiling, we'll just see what floats to the top."

It was late when the train pulled in. Too late to go down to the harbor. As tired as he was, Matt should have fallen asleep the minute his head touched the pillow. Instead, he went over in his mind the steps necessary before he could reclaim his ship.

Luther was snoring in the next bed. The boy had been practically sleepwalking for the past few hours. Matt had planned on booking two rooms, but after going over his figures again on the way north, he'd felt a sudden need to watch his funds. As things stood he was going to have to scrape the bottom of the barrel to come up with the purchase price alone. Putting the Powers Point property back in order had taken more than he could spare.

Luther snored on. Matt envied the boy his ability to snatch sleep when and where he could. Staring into the darkness through red-rimmed eyes, he went over his mental lists.

Repairs; sure to be a few of those. Stem-to-stern inspection. Hire a crew. Take time to get the right men.

Cargo. He'd have to jockey for position when it

came to bidding on cargo, he'd been out of touch for so long.

Rose. Damned deceiving woman. Kneeling in the sand trying to force a dead weed to live, lifting her sun-flushed face to smile at him....

Across the room, Luther muttered something in his sleep. Matt rolled over onto his belly, punched his pillow and commanded his brain to shut down. Dammit, he needed to be fresh come morning.

What seemed only moments later, he opened his eyes, blinked twice to get his bearings, then groaned and sat up. His head was pounding like a hundred kettledrums, but in spite of that, he began to grin.

Four years. Four long years, and she was finally his again.

Or would be once he signed the papers and handed over a bank draft for practically every cent he possessed.

"Get up, you lazy scoundrel, you want to sleep your worthless life away?" He swung out of bed, knuckled his eyes, then grabbed his trousers and headed for the washstand. "I'm due at Quimby's at seven. We've just got time for a bite of breakfast, then you head on down to the hiring hall and start sizing up the lot. I'll meet you there once I'm done with Quimby."

Less than an hour later, feeling remarkably refreshed considering a lack of sleep and a hastily consumed breakfast, Matt strode off toward the harborside offices of one Asa Quimby & Associates, his mind fairly seething in anticipation.

Luther trotted along behind, picking his teeth.

"Hold up a minute, Cap'n, I never got to ask you about—"

"The answer is yes. You're my new chief mate, if that's what's on your mind. Think you can cut it?"

"Yessir, I sure do—that is, I'll try like the devil to take Billy's place, but that weren't what I was fixing to ask."

"No?" Matt didn't slack his pace.

"It's about Rose, Cap'n."

That brought about a slight hitch in his gait. "Rose?"

"Yessir, you see, I was thinking—that is, if you've got no objection, I'd like to pay court to her next time I see her, but I don't have much to offer. So what I was thinking was that if she married me, then she could stay on at the Point, and when your wife comes, she could sort of be company for her—maybe help out with Annie and all?"

Hellfire. Slowly, Matt turned to stare at the good-looking young seaman. "You *what?*"

Two drunks, apparently just headed home after a night of debauchery, stumbled against Matt. Instinctively Matt clapped a hand over his wallet, caught the hand snaking inside his coat and gave it a crippling twist. The pair of pickpockets turned tail and ran, and Matt turned back to Luther.

"You want to marry *Rose?*"

"If she'll have me. I'm not in any hurry, but it strikes me that a man needs a wife and a baby or two, else when he's gone, he's just plain gone. You take Billy—"

"We'll talk about this later," Matt snapped. "I've had about all the distractions I need."

He strode off toward the waterfront office that housed the brokerage, a ship's chandler, an insurance firm and a flock of maritime lawyers.

He would need them all before he was done.

Chapter Eleven

She broke his heart. There was no other word to describe the pain he felt as he stood on the dock and stared across the harbor at the *Black Swan*. She was like a grand lady fallen on hard times. A proud young beauty who had been forced to take to the streets. Coarsened, ashamed, the pride that had once been so much a part of her now a thing of the past.

Matt swore at great length. By the time he had run out of words, there were tears in his eyes.

"We'll take care of you, lady," he whispered.

If he had to sell Powers Point—and it well might come to that—he would see her clean and gleaming once again, her damaged superstructure properly repaired, with a brand-new set of sails sparkling above her deck instead of the filthy, badly patched rags she wore now.

What he saw from here was bad enough. It was what he didn't see that had him worried sick. God knows what condition her bottom was in. Riddled with worm, more than likely. Quimby had warned him there'd been some damage to her keel and rudder when she'd gone through that bad blow off Barbados, but Matt had taken for granted that the damage would have been quickly repaired. No man who owned a valuable ship would allow structural damage to go unrepaired, certainly not on something so crucial.

Unless she was insured well beyond her value....

"Oh, Jesus. Oh, Jesus, Cap'n, that ain't her, is it?"

Luther had come up behind him. The two men stood silently, staring across the water at the ship they both loved, the only home other than Powers Point that Luther had known since he'd gone to sea a dozen years ago as a ten-year-old lad.

"We'll not be bidding on cargo anytime soon."

"No sir, I reckon not. Can she make it as far as Norfolk? If we could get her there with a skeleton crew, we could send Peg up to oversee the work."

Matt nodded. He'd been thinking along more or less the same lines. She drew too much water for the sounds inside the Banks, but Norfolk wasn't all that far away. A damn sight better than Boston.

"John could stay out at the Point to help out while me and Peg stay aboard the *Swan*," Luther continued.

The boy had a solid head on his shoulders, for all his occasional foolishness, Matt reminded himself. "We'll see. I guess the first thing to do is pump her bilges and see if she's fit to sail."

By the end of the day, Matt had commissioned Luther to hire the best men available capable of making a preliminary inspection and patching the *Swan* up enough so she could make the journey south.

Once she was back in Norfolk harbor they could undertake a thorough overhaul.

Matt went back to the bank and arranged to borrow enough to cover the cost of temporary repairs; the rest could wait until he got her closer to home.

Home? For as long as he could remember, the ship herself had been his home.

Not until two days later when the *Swan* had been pumped dry and he had personally inspected every inch of her hull and superstructure did Matt allow himself to think beyond the moment. With debt already beginning to accumulate, he had tracked down the company that had held her insurance policy only to learn that coverage had lapsed nearly three years ago, which doubtless explained why she'd been allowed to fall into such a state of disrepair. No one in his right mind would insure her in her present condition.

As he had already scraped the bottom of the barrel to come up with the purchase price, plus Quimby's commission and emergency repairs, Matt made another appointment with the banker. As much as he hated it, he was going to have to mortgage the Point.

Considering its location, the bank officer was reluctant. "If it were in one of your major cities—Charlotte, perhaps, or Charleston—"

"Charleston's in South Carolina," Matt had said, disgusted with the provincialism of the Yankee banker.

"But there's nothing there," the man had gone on to say, to which Matt had replied that there was a ten-room house, a herd of horses, a slew of outbuild-ings and dockage. Not to mention several towns to the north and south.

Which might have been something of an exagger-ation, but if the man didn't know any more than to shift Charleston a couple hundred miles to the north, he didn't deserve any better.

It took him four hours to convince the banker to lend him three thousand dollars against his ship and an estate that extended from the Pamlico Sound to the Atlantic Ocean, and four miles from north to south.

It sounded a hell of a lot more impressive than it was.

Meanwhile he commissioned Luther to hire on four good men, preferably men with some carpentry skills in case further repairs had to be made on the trip south. He had never sailed her with fewer than nine, but Luther could stand double watches. As for himself, Matt knew he wouldn't sleep until they were secure in a familiar port.

Fortunately, it was late in the season for the nor'easters that could lay offshore and batter the coast for days at a time; early for hurricanes. With any luck at all they could be in Norfolk in three days—four at most. Having wired ahead to arrange for moorage, they set out on a Tuesday, with two men taking turn and turnabout at the pumps.

Calm seas, scarcely enough wind to ruffle the sur-face, meant slow going, which was safer than the alternative as long as they could stay ahead of the leaks. With her crudely repaired rudder she had a tendency to yaw. Matt manned the helm, first shedding his boots so as to be aware of her slightest vibration.

Hour after hour, he eased her along, talking softly, encouraging her, reminding her of the good days they'd shared in the past, and the many that lay ahead.

They passed two northbound steamers; three more passed them, headed south. Off the mouth of the Delaware they passed the new steel warship that had just been built at Newport News. It was a sad reminder that the days of sail were rapidly coming to an end.

For two hours out of every twenty-four Matt allowed Luther to spell him at the helm. The boy was everywhere, measuring the levels in the bilge to see that the pumps kept up, checking the rigging for signs of weakness they might have missed, overseeing the crew. Twenty-two was young to make chief mate, but he was a good, experienced man. Matt knew his strengths and weaknesses. Given another ten years, he would make a fine captain.

Thank God one of the new men kept a pot of coffee boiling on the stove. At regular intervals he handed Matt a thick mug of the stuff along with two stale, shore-bought biscuits stuffed with sausage and cheese.

By the time they passed Cape May the wind had picked up, but the sun was damnably hot. His beard was itching and he could swear his hair had grown three inches longer. Luther, making his rounds, dipped a gourdful of water from the juniper barrel on deck and poured it over his head and shoulders.

"Want me to bring you your razor?"

"I'm not shaving until we drop anchor," a red-eyed Matt growled, but his tone was cautiously optimistic. Sailors had always been a superstitious lot. Matt was far too intelligent to believe in such nonsense, but when the chips were down, why take chances?

The boy grinned and dipped up another gourdful of water to add to the coffeepot on his way past the galley. "We'll make it just fine, Cap'n. She might not be much to look at now, but she's still got what it takes."

Now why the devil, Matt wondered, did that make him think of Rose? Because Rose had tumbled out of the cart a few months ago looking like a bundle of old rags washed up on the shore? Because she'd come around to where she was almost pretty?

Hell, she was beautiful.

She was also a cheating, conniving woman who had set out to deceive him before she'd even met him, he reminded himself. He still hadn't made up his mind what to do about that. At least he was no longer married to her, not if Bagby had followed his instructions.

His mind ranged ahead, exploring several possibilities. Once the *Swan* was safely berthed, he would send for Peg to oversee the work. It would leave them shorthanded at the Point, but he'd be damned if he'd send Luther back there.

He would go himself. By that time he would have thought of a way to deal with his ex-wife.

Trouble was, he needed her.

Correction: *Annie* needed her. Matt had never needed any woman, except in the most fundamental sense.

Yeah, say it often enough, Powers, and you might even believe it.

Swearing, Matt removed his leather-brimmed cap, wiped a hard forearm over his burning eyes, and jammed the cap back on his head. He was too old to go without sleep more than thirty-six hours. It messed up a man's mind, caused it to play tricks on him.

"All you need to remember is that the woman lied to you," he told the wind.

"It's the flying tails she likes," John said quietly. He said everything quietly. He was a quiet man, an even-tempered man, which appealed to Rose enormously. Even when Jericho had thrown him up against the paddock fence and kicked down yet another gate, John had simply picked himself up, brushed off the sand and walked slowly after the bucking stallion, still talking in that quiet way of his.

Annie smacked her hands together and chortled. She loved watching the horses, and John was right— when the wind blew their manes and tails, she loved it most of all.

And the wind had blown steadily for three days without once letting up, not even at what Peg and Crank called the calm o' day, the hours just before daybreak. There'd been no rain, yet clouds constantly threatened. Rose, tired of being housebound, had come outside, braving the stinging sand, to watch John work the horses.

At least there were no biting insects. Blown all the way out to Diamond Shoals, according to Crank, who had a bit more spring in his step now that he was taking the patent medicine he'd ordered out from the mainland.

Rose suspected it was the high alcohol content, but if it worked, then who was she to complain? Besides, a case of Porter's Cure-All cost far less than a case of brandy.

Not a day passed that she didn't climb the ladder that led to the widow's walk on the roof to watch for Matt's ship, even though she knew very well the *Black Swan* would most likely put into Norfolk Harbor if she even came that far south. She'd listened to the men talk, picking up bits of information to store away until she could fit them all together. A sea captain's wife should at least know enough to be an intelligent listener.

The two old seamen had described Matt's ship right down to the gold-leaf curlicues surrounding her nameplate. To hear them tell it, she was the fastest thing under canvas, the most beautiful ship that ever sailed, with the finest crew's quarters and a captain's cabin fit for a Persian prince.

All of which she fully intended to see for herself someday.

"John," she called now, "do you think you could teach me to ride?"

The dark-eyed young man from the village turned to study her. She could never tell what he was thinking. He didn't say much at all. "Why?"

Nonplussed, Rose considered telling him the

truth—that she wanted to impress her husband when
and if he ever came home. Goodness knows she'd
had little to brag about when he'd left. Practically
everything she had planted had died. Obviously, she
was no gardener, but if she could learn to be more
self-sufficient, he might overlook her shortcomings.
"Just teach me, that's all. I can drive the cart, but I
don't trust that mule."

That drew a smile that disappeared almost before
it could be appreciated. He was a handsome young
man, Rose had to admit. She wondered if he had a
wife. And if he did, did the woman resent his spend-
ing so much time at the Point?

"No woman's saddle," he told her.

"Then teach me to ride without one, the way you
men do."

"Ma'am, I don't think the captain would like it."

"The captain's not here."

"He'll know."

"How?"

"I reckon I'll tell him."

Exasperated, Rose shook her head. "Never mind,
I'll teach myself." She had taught herself not to be
seasick. At least, not to be sick sitting on a bench in
the skiff on a calm day when the skiff was tied up
at the wharf. It was a beginning.

The very next day while Annie napped, with Crank
sitting outside her door shelling beans, Rose had her
first riding lesson. She had borrowed a pair of Luther's trousers, tied them around her waist with a yellow dimity sash, and now she stood on an upturned

barrel, working up her nerve to throw her limb over the horse's back again. Her first attempt had been a spectacular failure.

"You'll be sore," John warned her.

"I'm already sore. I might as well have something to show for it."

Face set in lines of disapproval, he held the mare steady. Seeing that she was going to do it with or without him, he had reluctantly agreed to help. "If you're going to mount, then climb aboard. No, not that side. Always come up on a horse's port side, else they'll spook."

It was the most words he'd said at one time. Impressed, Rose took a deep breath, hung onto a handful of black mane, and threw herself onto the horse's back.

"There now, Katie," she said nervously when the mare pranced a bit. "We're going to be very gentle with one another, aren't we?"

Good Lord, she'd done it. She was finally sitting on top of a horse. She'd been driving since her dog-cart days, when her nanny had walked her around the block in a wicker basket behind a patchwork pony, but until the day Matt had rescued her and brought her back to the Point, she had never actually sat on a horse before. Her mother had refused to consider letting her have a saddle horse. Riding, she'd said, was an unsuitable pastime for unmarried girls.

"Later, when you're married, you can ask your husband if he'll allow it. By then, it won't make a difference."

She had finally reasoned out, after several whispered conversations with other girls her age, that it had something to do with being a maiden. Evidently, riding horseback robbed a girl of her virginity.

Hogwash, she thought now, wishing she hadn't been such a coward. She'd been afraid to do anything that might cast her into any more disfavor than her unfashionable height and lack of looks already did. She'd once heard her mother confide to her father that the poor child would never find a husband.

"Then she'll be a comfort to us in our old age" had been his reply.

Neither of them had lived to find out, and Rose, after all, had found herself a husband. Or rather, he'd found her.

And now she had yet another husband, one who probably wouldn't want her once he realized who she was, so what difference could it possibly make if she raced a dozen horses bareback on the beach and spent all day sitting in that blasted boat not being sick?

"Just hand me the reins, if you please. I can do it," she snapped.

"Yes, ma'am," John said, his black eyes sparkling with what looked suspiciously like amusement.

Crank heated a small sack of rice on top of the range, tactfully leaving the room so she could apply it where she hurt the most. He laced her tea with some of his patent medicine, which didn't improve the taste.

Then he called through the door. "Dixon said last time he was here he might have some good news for the captain by the time he come home."

"That's nice," Rose said absently. Groaning, she wondered if she had inherited more from her dotty old grandmother than flyaway hair and a pair of pale amber eyes.

"Never again," she vowed to Annie, whose crib had been placed beside her bed. "Pinch me if I ever go near another horse."

Pinching was Annie's newest achievement. Ears, for the most part, but lips were a second target. Especially moving lips. Motion seemed to fascinate her.

"All right, call me foolish. It seemed a good idea at the time. Other women ride, I used to see them all dressed up in fancy habits, circling the statues in Monroe Park."

Annie batted her tiny hands at the wooden gee-gaws Peg had carved to hang suspended over her bed. When she'd outgrown her cradle he had built her a small bed with sides so that she wouldn't tumble out.

"I wonder where he is tonight." She sighed. How many times had she voiced that thought? A dozen?

More like a hundred.

Grimacing, she rolled over and rubbed her behind to see if the ache had disappeared. It hadn't. "No one told me I'd flop like a sack of oats when the blasted horse took off. How was I to know I shouldn't allow my feet to touch her sides? John didn't tell me."

He might have tried to, but Rose had insisted on doing it all her own way.

Which was the wrong way, as attested to by her various bruises.

"Comp'ny coming," Peg sang out.

Rose groaned. "At this time of night?" It was still light, even though supper had been hours ago. Still, she'd better be up and dressed in case her presence was required. With Bess gone, she had assumed the role of hostess. The magistrate's wife had ridden out to visit one day last week.

"Well, I'll be-swigger," she heard Crank say. Both men had tried earnestly to clean up their vocabulary after she had reminded them that Annie was getting old enough to pick up a few words. She'd even said, "Mm, mm" the other day. It had sounded enough like "Mama" to bring tears to Rose's eyes.

Stiffly, she pulled on the dress she'd removed earlier when she'd put on Luther's trousers. Like just about everything lately, it felt damp. She dragged a brush through her hair and bundled it back, tying it with a ribbon. It would have to do, she told herself irritably as she walked stiffly through the house. Anyone who came to call at this hour of the evening deserved...

"Matthew?" she whispered. Oh, my mercy, he was home.

Chapter Twelve

He looked older. Silhouetted against the last streak of light in the western sky, he looked gaunt, as if he'd been ill. Rose stood and stared for a full minute before realizing she was barefooted, wearing a limp gown with no undergarments, not so much as a single petticoat. Her hair was not even braided.

"Matt, are you ill?" she whispered. From the way he was staring at her so intently, she thought he might be feverish. His eyes were burning like banked coals.

"I'm not ill. Where's Bess?"

Even his voice sounded different. "She left a few days after you did. Something about seeing her publisher about another project." Her response came without thinking as her mind raced ahead. *He's home. He's exhausted. Something's wrong. He needs me.*

Crank had gone outside to bring in his saddlebags. Peg was taking care of his borrowed horse. Heavenly days, he didn't even have the strength to do that, she thought. The Matt she knew would have taken care of his horse, even a borrowed one, before seeing to his own comfort.

Standing in the open doorway, Rose glanced past him. Correctly interpreting her look, Matt said, "He's not here."

"Is everything all right? Did you get your ship back? Is Luther all—"

"In answer to your questions, no, it's not, yes, I did, and yes, he is. Now, if you'll kindly step aside, madam, I'd like to come inside my own house."

Rose jumped back as if she'd been scorched. "I didn't mean—that is, of course you may. I was only—"

He'd called her madam. There'd been nothing even faintly respectful in his tone.

"Tell Crank when he's done outside, I'll have a bit of whatever he has left from supper and a kettle of hot water."

It was a command, not a request.

What did you expect him to do, embrace you? For all he knows, you're no more than another employee.

She turned away too quickly and staggered against the wall as tortured muscles protested. Before she could recover, his hand gripped her elbow. "Steady, there. Have you been hitting Bess's brandy?"

Close. She'd had a generous dose of Peg's painkiller. "If you must know, I was almost asleep."

"This early?" He steered her toward the kitchen, his grip no longer quite so punishing. Once inside, Rose pulled away to light the table lamp while Matt dragged out a chair and dropped onto it. His shoulders slumped, as if he'd been holding himself erect by sheer will alone.

Despite her own discomfort, it was all Rose could do not to gather him in her arms. Besieged by a storm of conflicting emotions, she turned toward the kindling box, bent too quickly, yelped and clapped a hand to her back.

Matt's chair clattered against the wall. He was beside her instantly. "What the devil is wrong with you, woman?"

"Nothing is wrong with me," she snapped back. *Nothing, that is, but a serious lack of common sense.*

You'd think she had never before felt pain. Heavens, this was nothing. A few bruises, a bit of chafing, a few aching muscles... "Sit down while I get the fire going. Crank left some fish stew in the cool house." She turned toward the back door, moving as gracefully as one could possibly move with a strained back, a bruised behind and badly chafed thighs.

"Sit down," Matt said gruffly. He dragged another chair away from the table and seated her none too gently. When she couldn't hide a slight grimace, he demanded to know what in God's name had been going on. "Dammit, Rose, you're in even worse shape than I am."

The slamming of the screen door announced the arrival of the two old men. Rose was torn between making her escape and staying to hear the news. Matt might be reluctant to tell her what had happened when he'd gone to buy back his ship, but he could never hold out against Peg and Crank.

"Ruint another good pair o' boots, I see." Crank

stared accusingly at Matt's sandy, salt-rimed foot-wear. "You set right there, boy, while I get you some supper. Peg, stoke up the fire. Rosie, what the devil are you doing out of bed? That dose I give you should've laid you out till dinnertime tomorrow."

His haggard face a study in confusion, Matt looked from one to the other. "Has something happened to Annie?" It was the only reason he could think of why Rose would have taken to her bed at this hour with one of Crank's homemade remedies.

"Annie's fine. She's growing so fast you won't recognize her." Rose shot Crank a warning look that only added to Matt's suspicions.

Something was wrong. As tired as he was, he knew he'd never sleep until he got to the bottom of it. "Anybody want to tell me what the devil is going on here?"

It was Peg, now that he'd stoked the fire and set the kettle on to boil, who filled him in. Rose could have swatted him if she hadn't been quite certain that any sudden movement would have done her in.

Lord, she ached. The cornstarch she'd used on her chafed thighs was damp and sticky. She wasn't sure, but she thought she might've scraped the skin on her back when she'd fallen against the fence.

"Our Rosie's been busy since you been gone," the carpenter said smugly. "Soon's she told us what she wanted to do, me and Crank offered to help out by standing watch over Annie's nap. John, he's been a big help, too. Dixon's boy's about as useful as tits on a boar hog, but he tries. Seldom a day goes by that he don't ride out to see how she's coming along."

Matt sighed. Leaning back in his chair, he heel-toed his boots off, leaving them where they lay. "Go on," he said darkly.

Taking him at his word, Peg cleared his throat and prepared to launch into a recital of everything Rose had done since the day Matt had left.

"I'm sure Matt would much rather hear about Annie's new skills," Rose suggested.

Ignoring her, Peg cleared his throat again and settled back to disclose every pathetic detail of her shabby attempts at self-improvement. "Well, now, I reckon it commenced when her garden died. First off, we had us this three-day blow out of the nor'east, and then—"

Her small store of patience exhausted, Rose interrupted. "To make a long story short—"

"As the good book says," Crank put in, and she glared him to silence.

"If you must know, I decided to learn how to sail and how to ride, since gardening clearly isn't among my skills. I've never been taught a single useful thing in my entire life, and it's about time I learned. And you might as well know that once I've mastered the art of sailing and staying on top of a horse, I'm going to learn how to cook. Crank's promised to teach me. I already know how to wash clothes." Her fierce look defied him to comment.

Over a three-day growth of beard, Matt's eyes took on a decided gleam. Damned if she wasn't something, all right. Just what, he hadn't yet figured out, but she'd bear watching until he made up his mind what to do about her.

"What's Annie been doing all this time?" he asked mildly.

"Playing. Napping. She's a happy baby. She doesn't demand my constant attention." It was more of a challenge than an explanation.

Matt lowered his gaze to the steaming mug of tar-like coffee Crank placed before him. "Then I take it you're preparing for your next position."

Some of her belligerence gave way to wariness. "My next position?"

"After you leave here. Once my wife arrives, I'll hardly be needing your services."

With a look of dismay, she started to speak, then bit her lower lip and fell silent. If he weren't so damned tired from getting by on three hours' sleep out of every twenty-four, Matt might have felt some satisfaction. He had her right where he wanted her, didn't he? Even if she suspected he'd stopped off in Norfolk to see Bagby, she couldn't be certain how much he'd learned. Evidently she intended to bluff it out.

Two, he mused, could play that game. "Go to bed, Rose, you look like hell."

What happened next wasn't mutiny, but it came close to it. Scowling, Peg issued a rebuke as Crank shook his head and said, "Now, son, that ain't no way to talk to a lady. Rosie, he don't mean to hurt your feelings, the boy's not himself, anybody can see that."

Matt shot the old man a withering look. However,

Crank was right. Better to wait and fire the opening volley when he wasn't too tired to take aim.

Crank plopped a tin plate of cold stewed fish and potatoes in front of him. Peg scowled at the simmering kettle. Rose, with a look that defied interpretation, stood, bade them all a gracious good-night and walked stiffly from the room, the effect only slightly spoiled by the fact that she had a tendency to waddle.

Long after he stretched out on his own bed that night, fully prepared to fall instantly asleep and not wake until hunger drove him in search of food, Matt remembered the look on her face just before she'd taken her leave. If he didn't know her for the conniving woman she was, he could have sworn her feelings were hurt.

Something was going on around here. His two old crewmen, men who owed him their allegiance whether on land or at sea, were in on it. Before he headed north again, Matt promised himself, he damned well intended to find out what it was.

Rose opened her eyes, yawned and stretched, and broke off with a gasp. Steeling herself, she tried again.

Oh, drat! Crank had warned her, telling her about the time he'd been carrying a fifty-pound sack of beans over his shoulder when he'd tripped over a cat and fallen down the companionway. "Picked myself up and put in a full day's work, I did," he said proudly. "Next morning, I couldn't get out of bed. For near onto a week I couldn't move without it hurt something awful. These things always gets worse before they get better.''

There was nothing seriously wrong with her, nothing a decent night's sleep shouldn't have cured. Gritting her teeth, she forced herself, one protesting muscle at a time, to get out of bed. Annie was already awake. She'd be soaked through and hungry by now, and eager to tell the world about it.

Matthew was home again.

The knowledge struck like a tidal surge, and as miserable as her body was, her spirits took flight.

He'd been gruff, but that was understandable. He'd been utterly exhausted, his cheeks gaunt and unshaven, his eyes dull and red-rimmed. Either the lines in his face had deepened, or he'd developed a few new ones. Evidently the repurchase of his ship hadn't gone quite as smoothly as he'd expected.

''But today, my dear Annie, is a brand new day. After a good night's rest in his own bed, your papa's bound to feel much better, especially when he sees your beautiful toothy smile, hmm?''

Rose had never been one to hold a grudge. Well, perhaps she had, but not over a few harsh words. Today the sun was shining brightly; there was enough of a breeze from the southwest to blow away the mosquitoes, and stiff or not, she was more than ready to forgive and forget.

She only hoped Matt would be as generous.

Walking gingerly, she collected a clean diaper, leaned over the crib and barely suppressed a groan. ''Don't even think about riding, darling. Papa can buy you a gig and a pretty little mare, and you can travel in style.''

She peeled off the wet diaper, dropped it in the pail, and wondered how the simple act of sitting on top of a horse could do so much damage.

Well, of course it hadn't been quite so simple. The first time, when John had held her foot and boosted her up, she'd slid clean over the animal's back and fallen against the fence, which accounted for her aching back. John had hurried to her side, obviously concerned, but he'd barely been able to suppress his laughter. If he hadn't assumed the lesson was over, she might have given up then and there.

The second time started out much better. She'd managed to climb up on the mare's back and sit there for almost a full minute before the stupid thing decided to go for a run. With no choice other than to jump and risk being trampled, she'd grabbed a handful of flying mane along with the bridle and hung on, bouncing like a rubber ball, which no doubt accounted for her bruised behind.

John had run after them shouting orders and laughing fit to split a seam. ''Hold on,'' he'd yelled.

''I'm trying!'' She'd been holding on every way she possibly could, with both hands and both legs, which explained her blistered palms and chafed thighs. It had seemed hours before she'd hit ground the second time, but it couldn't have been more than a few minutes.

''But I'm not giving up,'' she told Annie as she lifted her up and blew a kiss in the creases of her neck.

Annie chortled. She was delightfully responsive, so Rose kissed her again and said, "Next time, though, I'll dust down with cornstarch *before* the damage is done. No wonder men walk the way they do. If I had to wear those scratchy old trousers, I'd probably walk that way, too. Do you think we should tell your papa to powder his thighs before he pulls up his trousers?"

She bathed the pink, plump bottom and pinned on a fresh diaper. She might as well take advantage of the sunny weather and wash the diapers and Annie's bedding this morning. It was an excellent excuse to postpone another riding lesson.

As for her sailing lessons, Sandy usually came in the afternoon while Annie was taking her nap. She was learning how to handle the different ropes, which on a boat were called lines. As confusing as it was, so far sailing hadn't bruised anything.

"Come along, sweetie, let's go see if Crank has your breakfast ready. I'll bet your papa's never seen a young lady who can drink from a cup without spilling more than half her milk."

With nothing save her own growing experience to go on, Rose had decided that Annie was an exceptional child, advanced in all ways. Poor Billy must have been a wonder. He had certainly been a charmer, if Annie was as much like her late father as Crank and Peg said she was.

"Here we go, blue eyes, let's go show off for Papa."

Crank had breakfast waiting. Bacon and eggs for Rose, milk and burgoo for Annie. Now that she insisted on participating in the process, breakfast took twice as long.

No sign of Matt. Not even to herself would Rose admit she was disappointed.

"How're you feeling?" the cook asked as he poured himself a mug of coffee and sat down to watch the performance.

"Wonderfully well, thank you."

"Still sore, huh? Told ye so."

Rose shot him a fulminating look and steered Annie's fist-held spoon to her mouth. She was dying to ask if Matt was up yet, but she wasn't ready to face one of Crank's knowing smirks. In some ways he was even worse than Bess. As far as Bess was concerned, the world was a stage and she loved nothing more than moving the players around at will.

Crank and Peg, having made up their minds that their captain's proxy wedding had been one of Bess's tricks, were determined to find him another wife. As soon as Bess had left, Peg had said, "It's been months since he signed them papers. No woman's turned up to claim the title, which means something went afoul on the other end."

"Better a bird in hand than one in the bush," Crank had said, making no secret of which bird Matt held in the palm of his callused hand.

Once Rose had realized what they were about, she'd been tempted to tell them the truth, but she owed it to Matt to tell him first. Which she fully intended to do, just as soon as she could get him alone.

"If you're looking for the captain, he took that

horse of his out to the beach. Didn't even stop to eat breakfast first.''

Pretending a lack of interest, Rose wiped a smear of burgoo from her arm. ''I believe the sun will hold long enough to dry a line of wash, don't you?''

''He got her back, but she's in bad shape.''

''The diaper pail's overflowing, and—'' She broke off to stare at him. ''Who got *who* back?''

''The cap'n. He bought the *Swan* back, but she's been treated shameful. Peg's headed out this afternoon to see to her.''

So then, of course, she had to hear the entire story, about how Matt and Luther and a handful of deckhands had sailed the *Swan* from Boston to Norfolk, had had to stand off for nearly twenty-four hours before they were allowed mooring space, and how Luther had stayed behind until Peg could get there to oversee the repairs.

''No wonder Matt looked so...so—''

''Yes'm, he was plumb tore up. Heartsick, I guess you could call it. Loves that ship like she was a woman, he does.'' The old cook shook his head, then went on to say, ''But that don't mean he don't need a wife. No sir, a man needs a woman if he wants to raise himself up a crop of sons. Don't do no good to lay by a mess o' worldly goods without begetting a flock of sons to take over. The Good Book talks a whole lot about that.''

Before Rose could think of a response, Sandy Dixon called through the open back door. ''I heard Powers is back, didn't know if you wanted to sail today or not, but if you want to go out, I can come back when Annie's taking her nap.''

Without waiting for an invitation, he came inside and sat down at the table, careful to avoid the blobs of mush Annie had distributed generously on every exposed surface.

The official sailing lessons had begun little more than a week ago. Once she'd mastered the art of sitting quietly without expecting to lose her dinner at any moment, Sandy had offered to teach her how to handle the small sail skiff. ''Having something to focus your mind on will go a long way toward keeping it off your belly,'' he'd told her.

So far it had worked, at least as far as her belly was concerned. She was no sailor and probably never would be. Twice she had nearly knocked him overboard by losing her grip on the rope—the line—it was also called a sheet, which had only added to her confusion when he'd yelled at her to grab it. The stick thing that was attached to the mast to hold the bottom of the sail swung around and struck him in the back before she could catch it. It had been one of several minor disasters, but at least she hadn't disgraced herself by getting seasick.

''Sandy, today's not really a good time, but thank you for offering. I started my riding lessons yesterday.''

''And?'' he prompted. Sandy Dixon had an easy, disarming way about him. He would have made a wonderful brother. As it was, he was becoming a good friend.

"Shall we say, I'm every bit as good a horse-woman as I am a sailor?"

"That bad, huh?"

"With blisters and bruises to prove it."

They were laughing—even Crank indulged in a cackle or two—when Matt strode into the kitchen. He looked from one to the other, nodding at Dixon, glaring at Rose, then turned to Annie.

Rose watched his reaction. His eyes widened, then softened, and her heart nearly burst her bodice when he knelt down and captured one tiny, sticky hand.

"She's changed." It sounded almost like an accusation. "Her hair's longer."

It was also matted with cereal at the moment. Annie blinked solemnly and stared back at him. Even plastered with oatmeal she was irresistible. If anyone could soften his heart, Rose thought, it would be Annie. And she definitely wanted his heart as soft as possible when she told him who she was.

"It's even starting to curl," she said proudly. "She has a tiny little tooth right in front, and she's learning so fast—show him, sugar. Show your papa how you can drink from a cup." She carefully held the cup to Annie's mouth. Obediently, the baby slurped, then with the cup still in place, she grinned. Milk leaked out from both sides of her mouth to soak her sticky bib.

Rose beamed approvingly. Crank looked proud enough to crow.

Dixon looked utterly bored.

As for Matt, he looked almost—well, she didn't

know what it meant, but his eyes were suspiciously bright.

A moment later, his scowl firmly back in place, he told her he would see her in his office as soon as he got back from the village.

Rose was pinning the last few diapers to the line when Peg came to say good-bye. Her gaze flew past him to where Matt waited with the horses. If she'd been busy, he'd been even busier. Their paths hadn't crossed since breakfast.

Peg was wearing a rusty black suit and a leather-brimmed hat. He smelled suspiciously of vanilla extract. "You take good care of him, y'hear? He don't sleep much when he's worrying, and he's real tore up about the *Swan*. Don't let him go to fretting. If he gets real quiet and broody, you swish your skirttail at him. He'll likely fuss at you, but he don't mean nothing by it, it's just his way. He feels real deep, but he don't like to admit it. What he needs is a good woman to pull him up short when he sinks too low. Strikes me, you're just the woman to do it."

The old man was obviously referring to Matt. Confused, Rose stammered, "But I—he—"

Faded eyes sparkling with good humor, he said diffidently, "I weren't always this ugly. Had me a few good women in my day. I know what I'm talking about, Rosie. The wrong woman can cripple a man, but the right one's like a good sea anchor. Come a hard blow, she'll keep him off the rocks. Trouble is, the boy never learned how to tell a good'n from a bad'n."

"But—but what about—I mean, he has a wife."

Peg shot her a knowing grin and looked as if he would have said more, but Matt's patience finally snapped. "Dammit, let's shove off! Once the mail's called off, the boat'll be bound out, and you'd damned well better be aboard her!"

Chapter Thirteen

She had them all eating out of her hand, Matt thought angrily. Every last one of them. If he didn't know better, he might've been taken in as well. Thank God he'd learned the truth about her in time, that she was as deceitful as all the rest, Bess included. Else he might have been tempted to—

Forcing his mind away from a matter that could wait, back to one that couldn't, Matt told Peg, "I've arranged with the bank to honor your signature. Make yourself known to them before you write a check, though. We've got credit at Stevens's Lumber Yard and Shoemaker's Chandlery. Luther will be signing on a crew. Remind him they'll be working directly under him. Try to find older, more experienced men, but choose carefully. Pay bonuses if necessary, but get sound men, no drunkards, no bullies, no grumblers."

"Round up a bunch o' hymn-singers, 'n'other words."

Matt acknowledged the remark with a wry grin.

He'd never known a sailor who didn't drink; a bit of grumbling was only to be expected, but he wouldn't tolerate a bully. "The four he hired on in Boston will do for a start if they're still around."

Peg nodded. "I've got a few more good years left, if we can't find us another chips."

"I'm obliged to you," Matt said, but they both knew which way that particular wind blew. After more than forty years at sea, Peg had settled surprisingly well ashore. With Crank for companionship and enough work to keep him occupied, he was content with his lot. And while Peg would miss his old life—and Matt would sorely miss the man who had served first under his father, helping to raise and train the boy Matt had been then—neither man would have dreamed of voicing the sentiment.

"Them new iron ships don't need no carpenters," Peg muttered. "Reckon half the hands'll be scaling rust."

"No worse than holystoning, but you're right. Times are changing," Matt agreed.

The two mares, Peg's a handsome bay, Matt's a rawboned claybank, plodded through the powdery sand. Had the tide had been low they would've taken to the beach and made better speed, but with high tide lapping at the dunes, the rutted cart road was easier to navigate.

"Time was, I thought you'd be building yourself a shipping line," the older man commented.

"Time was, I thought so myself," Matt admitted. He had picked up his father's dream when the elder Powers had retired. "Start with one good ship, a good crew and a bit of luck, son. Put your profits where they'll grow, build a solid reputation for speed and dependability. After a few good years you'll have enough to invest in a second ship.''

And then a third. Matt had quickly expanded the dream. Small, fast schooners designed specifically for hauling freight from the West Indies to every port along the mid Atlantic. It was a modest enough dream in a day when great ships were sailing every sea in the world.

Oh, yes, he'd inherited his father's dream along with his name and his reputation for fast, dependable service. That reputation, he was proud to say, had never been sullied. Thank God he'd let it be known the day he'd sold the *Swan* that she was no longer associated with the Powers name.

Just when, he wondered now, had the dream begun to fade? Had it ever been truly his own? After four restless years spent ashore, he was beginning to wonder. He'd been born at sea, reared at sea, treated by his own father as one of the crew until he'd earned his salt and the rank of chief mate.

The invisible wall between a captain and his crew, so vital to maintain a proper chain of command, had included the captain's son. After his mother had deserted ship when he was eight years old, Matt had been consigned to crew's quarters, eaten at crew's mess, expecting no quarter from his father, receiving none. The crew had become his family. Crank and Peg, standing in for his father, had meted out punishment for boyish misdemeanors and stood between him and one or two unsavory characters until he'd grown old enough to look after himself in that respect.

Matt had been given his first command the same year his father had retired. Nearly every man who'd sailed for his father had signed aboard. They'd still been with him two years later when he'd bought the *Black Swan,* good men, one and all. By then he had learned firsthand the necessity of that invisible wall between captain and crew.

It was over the past four years spent ashore that the wall had tumbled, brick by invisible brick. The last fragment had crumbled when Billy was murdered. Since that day he hadn't even attempted to maintain a semblance of rank. Not that it would have done him much good, not with two old men who had known him since he'd been scampering about the decks on all fours, bare-ass naked.

Having foolishly thrown away everything two generations of Powers men had built up, Matt was only now coming to realize where the true value lay. It was not in the ship he commanded, but in the men who stood with him along the way.

Which meant, God help him, that the rules he'd lived by all his life might no longer apply.

The mailboat was ready to cast off when Peg tossed his duffel aboard and leaped onto the deck, his nimbleness belying his age and infirmity. "I'll get back to ye soon's I look her over," he called across the widening strip of water.

Matt nodded acknowledgment, his mind torn between Norfolk Harbor and Powers Point. Under normal circumstances he would have personally supervised every nail driven into her hull, every board foot of lumber, every inch of oakum used to caulk between the planking. It was his duty as captain and owner.

But circumstances, he told himself as he turned away and headed home again, were far from normal. Not only did he have a child whose welfare depended on him, he had a wife. A wife he didn't want. A wife he was in the process of shedding. A wife who was supposed to take Annie off his hands so that he could go back to his profession.

And now, dammit, he couldn't seem to steer a straight course no matter which way the wind blew.

He *knew* what he had to do.

He also knew it wouldn't be clear sailing, not when all he had to do was glance out his window when she was hanging out the wash, with the wind blowing her gown against her body, revealing the curve of her breasts, the inward sweep of her waist, even the handspan of roundness that was her belly and the slight mound at the juncture of her long limbs.

He'd be salivating. Hard as an ax handle.

Devil take it, he was swelling now, just thinking about her.

After talking to Bagby, he'd been convinced she had done it deliberately. But since then he'd had time to think, and he was no longer as certain. Could the best actress in the world sustain a role this long? The first week she'd been there she'd been timid as a ghost, afraid of her shadow. She had gradually come around, mostly because of Annie. He had to admit that whatever game she was playing, she had done him right on that score.

The first time she'd laughed aloud it had stopped him dead in the water. Who would have thought such a grim female, one who dressed in thick, ugly black gowns, could make a sound like water running over small pebbles in a stream?

Not long after that she'd started singing to Annie. He would find himself lingering outside her door to listen.

Could she have known? Had she done it deliberately?

She fell into the habit of sewing outside on the porch where the light was better. Was it so he could look up from whatever he happened to be doing and see her there? See the way she frowned and bit her lower lip. He'd told himself it was only because she needed reading glasses, but maybe it had all been an act.

He couldn't count the nights he had lain awake burning, throbbing, cursing his own weakness. Reminding himself that Rose was a respectable woman, a friend of his aunt's, and that he was a married man.

And then she'd started leaving off her corset. He'd noticed it right off—a new freedom in the way she moved, the way she breathed. Even the look on her face, part relief, part guilt, as if she expected to be hauled before the mast for indecent exposure.

He'd wanted to expose her, all right. Expose every hidden wonder, explore every delicate curve, every soft swelling, every secret treasure…

The claybank twitched her ears as he began to

swear. Peg's bay picked her way daintily along behind. "Damn your lying tongue, Mrs. Littlefield," he said aloud.

His wife, he reminded himself bitterly. To think that all the time he'd been lusting after the woman, he could have had her in his bed.

Had it amused her to torment him that way? She had to have known the shape he was in, it wasn't something a man could hide.

Besides, she'd been married before, unless that, too, was a lie. He hoped to hell she'd enjoyed herself, making a fool of him, because the last laugh would most definitely be his.

As he neared the Point, the various structures looming above the ever-present salt haze, he set about charting his course. If he faced her directly with what he knew, he'd have no choice but to send her packing.

But if he sent her away, he'd be right back where he'd been when this whole disastrous chain of events had started. Needing a woman to look after Annie; stuck here, high and dry, until he found one he could trust.

As much as he hated to admit it, he still needed her.

Worse, he still wanted her.

"Judas Priest," he muttered aloud, "How the devil did I fetch up on this particular reef? My ship's barely afloat, my land is mortgaged, I'm married to a shameless liar."

The one bright spot on the horizon was Annie. Matt didn't even attempt to define his feelings where

Billy's daughter was concerned. He only knew that from the very first day—well, perhaps it had been the second or the third—that tiny speck of humanity had laid claim to a portion of his heart that had never before been touched. Whatever it took to insure her welfare, he would do it, and if that meant dealing with Rose, so be it.

Turning toward the paddock, he weighed the two courses open to him. He could either confront the woman with the truth and watch her try to spin her way out of the tangle, or he could pretend he didn't know the truth and see just how far she would go.

No closer to an answer than ever, he unsaddled Peg's mare, rubbed her down and turned her into the paddock, then did the same for the claybank. Glancing at the sky, he judged the time to be just past four. An hour before Crank would have supper cooked.

His belly grumbled, reminding him that he hadn't taken time to eat dinner. Should he tackle her on an empty stomach?

The wind was out of the southeast, laden with moisture from having traveled thousands of miles over the warm waters of the South Atlantic. "A mean wind," his father's old bosun had called it. Jerome Guidry, dead these past ten years, had carried more charms than a gypsy peddler. He used to warn the crew against bickering when the wind was out of the southeast, claiming it invariably led to bloodshed.

Matt had never put much stock in superstitions; nevertheless, it wouldn't hurt to wait a day or two longer before he set his plan into motion. Hell, he didn't even have a plan. Seducing the woman and sending her on her way was no plan, it was an outright catastrophe.

Dripping with sweat, he sloshed a dipperful of water from the wooden trough over his head, savoring the momentary coolness generated by his wet shirt. He turned toward the house, but before he'd gone many steps, he heard the sound of laughter coming from the sound side.

Rose's laughter. He would recognize it anywhere. She'd been here almost two months before he'd heard her laugh at all, but now it was an all-too-familiar sound.

And for some reason, it made him mad as hell.

Having placed Annie's basket in the only spot of shade, under a twisted live oak tree, Rose stood in the dappled sunlight, trying discreetly to scratch her various itches while she watched her two visitors attempt to outdo one another. Amused and even a bit saddened, she thought of all the years when she would have given a king's ransom to have even one young man trying to impress her.

The only thing worse than being homely, awkward, without a smidgen of style, was being intelligent enough to know it. She'd been all of that, to her sorrow.

How very young they were, she thought now, watching the two good-looking men showing off like two little boys on the playground. And how very sweet. Sandy was two years younger than her own twenty-four years, but tried to appear older. John was probably about her own age, but with his serious mien and his weathered features, he looked older.

"Watch this, Rose," called Sandy. "I'm going to throw a bowline around that piling."

With nothing better to do, she had strolled with him down to the dock so that he could show her a few more knots. He hadn't offered to carry Annie's basket, which was getting almost too heavy for her to lug around. Then John had joined them, riding a horse he claimed to have cut from the wild herd that roamed the Banks. "I've had her less than a week and she's already saddle-broke," he said with that quiet pride that was so much a part of him.

Rose admired the shaggy mare, then turned and watched dutifully as Sandy flung a rope toward the post, flicked his wrists just so, and then stepped back to show off what looked like a perfectly ordinary knot.

She applauded.

From her basket, Annie chortled and waved at a butterfly.

John grunted. "You like rope tricks? How about this?" He swung a loop of rope over his head a time or two, then let fly. The loop drifted down over Sandy's startled face to settle about his waist.

It was the expression on Sandy's face that set her off. She was laughing so hard she didn't notice when Matt joined them, his approach silent in the soft sand.

"If you've nothing better to do, madam—"

Caught off-guard, Rose turned too quickly, caught her foot in a tendril of vine and flailed her arms wildly to recover. "Of all the sneaky, underhanded things to do!" she exclaimed.

It wasn't so much that he'd frightened her as that he'd caught her looking frazzled and windblown, dripping with perspiration, her hair escaping her braids to stick to her damp face. She had planned to be bathed and changed into her most becoming outfit by the time he returned. He had mentioned wanting to see her in his office, at which time she fully intended to set the record straight.

Still, it wasn't like her to speak out that way, she didn't know what had gotten into her. The heat, probably. That and her own guilty conscience.

Taking a deep breath, she composed her features and said, "Please excuse me. Annie and I will be in shortly. As soon as I have her settled with a bottle, I'll see you in your office, if I may."

Looking thoroughly out of sorts, Sandy yanked the lasso off his shoulders, glared at John and mumbled something about seeing her tomorrow at the usual time.

John, his expression as inscrutable as ever, calmly coiled his line and hooked it over his saddle horn. Ignoring Matt, he nodded to Rose. "Send word when you're ready for another lesson."

With a sigh, Rose thanked both young men. Why had she ever thought learning to sail and to ride would help her standing? She watched Matt pick up Annie's basket and march down the sandy slope toward the house, shoulders rigid, long, powerful limbs covering ground without the least regard for all the hazards she'd been warned against.

It was with a mixture of dread and anticipation that she picked her way through sandspurs, cactus, and a swarm of gnats that were obviously attracted to her damp, sunburned flesh.

This time, she vowed, she was going to tell him the truth if she had to tie him to his chair to make him listen. She would tell him everything, from beginning to end.

Well, perhaps not *everything*.

If after that he wanted to send her away she would go without a word of complaint. Go and spend the rest of her life grieving over another broken dream.

Not until the sun had set in a sulfury glare of color behind a bank of clouds did she appear at his door. Matt had purposely left it open to catch whatever slight breeze there was. Some thoughtful ancestor had deliberately planned the house to take advantage of the prevailing winds, setting it high enough off the ground to avoid the tides and catch the slightest breath of air.

Sometimes even that wasn't enough to break the stifling heat. Tonight, though, the wind was switching more to the east. With any luck, it would swing on around to the northeast and bring some relief.

"Come in," he said without glancing up from his desk. He'd bathed and changed into fresh linen, but he was soaked to the skin again.

Hellish weather. Worse than the doldrums.

"You wanted to see me?" She stepped inside, hands clasped so tightly he could see her white knuckles. "That is, I wanted to tell you something. You see—"

"Take a seat." Lilacs. Dammit, she had to go and smell of lilacs.

She collapsed onto one of the straight chairs, then stiffened her back. Matt had about made up his mind to tell her he'd had the marriage annulled, then sign her on to stay with Annie. But it might be more interesting to cut her some slack and see how far she would run with it.

He waited. She drew in a deep breath, closed her eyes briefly, then said all in one burst, "I'm the one you married. By proxy, I mean. I never deliberately set out to deceive you, but you see, I didn't really want to marry anyone—I'd been married before, and—well, but that's not important. What's important is that I love Annie, and I'd like to keep her. That is, if you'll still have me."

She was obviously waiting for a reaction. Matt steepled his hands before him, his eyes never leaving her face. He'd set grown men to trembling in their boots with just such a look.

If it bothered Rose, she didn't let on. Too wrapped up in her own story, more than likely. "Go on," he prompted.

"Yes, well—you see, I needed to find work, only nothing I could find suited, so when Bess said her nephew had a baby and needed help, I said yes, only she thought it wouldn't be proper for a woman to stay in a house full of strange men, and so—"

She caught her breath, prepared to plunge on. He had to admire the way she looked him straight in the eye, even knowing she'd been lying through her pretty teeth ever since she'd tumbled out of the wagon onto his doorstep.

"As soon as I did it, I tried to undo it, but Mr. Bagby said it was too late. He did say, though, that I could behest my way out of it any time I wanted to, as long as the marriage was never—that is, as long as we didn't— And of course, we didn't, so—"

Watching the flush of color rise above her collar, staining her face, Matt wondered if it extended down over her body. "We didn't?"

"Certainly not," she said quickly. "At any rate, we—that is, you—I mean, if you'd like—"

Oh, I'd like, all right. And I will, madam, before this farce is ended. I believe we owe each other that much.

Chapter Fourteen

Not tonight, Matt decided. Better to wait until he could look at her without feeling angry, betrayed. The last time he'd lost his head over a woman the results had been disastrous, and he was honest enough to admit that Rose affected him in ways that Gloria never had.

A cautious man, he thought it better to wait until he could see his way past every shoal, every snag, every conceivable hazard. As captain, his policy had been to mete out punishment quickly once guilt had been established rather than to allow the culprit to wallow for days in fear and uncertainty. He prided himself on being a just man, not a vindictive one.

Rose's guilt had been established beyond a shadow of a doubt; she had even confessed, if that rambling discourse could be considered a confession. What punishment could be more fitting than to take her at her word? To treat her as he would a wife?

That was neither revenge nor vindication, it was simple justice.

But not tonight. Not until he could think about what she'd done without wanting to wring her delicate little neck.

Restlessly, he turned to the window where his gaze was captured by the rising moon and the golden trail that spread across the surface of the water. Was there anything more beautiful in God's creation than moonlight on the water?

Soon he would be free to leave, to follow that golden highway over the horizon and beyond. But first…

First he would send those two young jackanapes on their way. For as long as he was here at the Point, he could take care of his own livestock, and if Rose wanted to learn how to sail, he would teach her himself. He'd do a damned sight better job of it than any jumped-up clerk in a collar and tie.

As long as she didn't think about it, she would be all right.

As long as she could sit here in the rocking chair, holding Annie's soft warmth in her arms, gazing out at the path of moonlight across the water, she could go for hours without thinking. For whole minutes…

Somewhere in the house, a clock began to chime. Now and then the old house protested as the heat of the day slowly faded. A familiar sound, Rose found it oddly comforting.

Well, you told him. He didn't send you away. What now?

She didn't know what, she simply didn't know.

She knew he needed her, and not just for Annie's sake.

She knew he wanted her, and that he was angry because he didn't want to want her. Given time and experience, even the most witless woman could learn to recognize certain indications.

Robert had wanted her money, but because she was a woman and she'd been available, he'd used her that way when it had suited his purpose. Matt wanted her services for Annie's sake, but he wanted her body, too.

And heaven knows, she wanted his. The trouble was, she wanted far more than his body, because that sort of thing had never really appealed to her. She wasn't good at it. She'd been told so enough times that she believed it.

She wanted those rare smiles he offered Annie, and sometimes Crank or Peg, but never her. She wanted his strength for when her courage began to flag, and the kindness that had prompted him to adopt a new-born infant when he hadn't the least notion of how he would look after her. She wanted that streak of tenderness he tried so hard to deny.

What she *didn't* want was his anger. Not until she was certain of her own strength, and she was working on it. Growing more self-assured with each day and every new accomplishment.

But oh, how she wanted him to love her, at least a little bit. Wanted him to think she was beautiful and brave and beguiling, all the things she was not.

Oh, you don't want much, do you, Augusta Rose? Only the moon.

* * *

It rained the next morning, a string of light showers that promised to clear, but never quite went away. Rose gave up and did the baby's wash, boiling it on the kitchen range and hanging it on the lines in the attic. She needed to hem more diapers. Three dozen wasn't nearly enough.

Annie was fretful. Rose thought she was cutting another tooth, and rubbed her gums with a finger dipped in honey. She'd have dipped it in brandy if she'd dared, but she didn't. With Matt watching her every move, she was walking on eggshells.

"I'm moving Annie's bed back into her own room," he'd told her before she'd even had her breakfast. "She needs to learn to be independent."

Taking the words as an accusation, Rose had gone on the defensive. "I fully intend to teach her to be independent, but don't you think she's a bit young to start learning?"

"No, I don't."

"Yes, well I—" She started to say she did, but caught herself before she could pick a fight. It wouldn't serve her purpose. "You're probably right. I asked Crank to move her to my room in case she woke in the night, but it was really because I like having her nearby."

"Don't tell me you're afraid of the dark?"

"I'm not afraid of anything," she said quickly. Then, remembering the promise she'd made to herself to be honest in all her dealings from now on out, she said, "Not of the dark, at any rate. I'm a little bit afraid of lightning, but I'm working on it. I'm a little bit afraid of snakes and spiders, but John promised to show me which ones are dangerous and which ones are our friends."

"Our friends?" Matt was beginning to enjoy himself. She was a disarming wench, and he couldn't afford to be disarmed. Couldn't afford to start liking her, not when he fully intended to seduce her, then denounce her.

"Snakes eat mice, and I do dislike mice. Frogs and lizards eat bugs, and I don't particularly like bugs either, but then, snakes eat frogs and lizards, so I'm not sure yet how that works out."

"Snakes also eat birds. Baby birds, right out of the nest," he told her solemnly.

Her eyes widened, but she recovered quickly. "I knew that, of course. There are some things I prefer not to think about." She said it with quiet dignity.

Matt had been enjoying their little game, which was a good reason to cut it short. He'd never been skilled at games, especially not games played with women.

"I'll just bet you don't," he muttered, and left without waiting for a response.

He could almost feel her eyes boring into his back. Those cat eyes of hers, more yellow than brown. Even her hair was more yellow than brown these days, with streaks that were almost white from staying out in the sun without her bonnet.

Eager to be away where he could think without being distracted, he slammed out the front door, took the five steps in a single leap and strode toward the barn. A few minutes later he was racing across the damp sand on Jericho's bare back, a light rain plastering his shirt to his back, his hair to his scalp.

"Dratted woman," he muttered.

The stallion, intent on reaching the surf, didn't so much as flicker an ear.

"You've got six of 'em to deal with, old fellow. Any advice would be greatly appreciated."

And thus the day dragged on. Rose managed to stay busy. Unfortunately, the things that engaged her hands did little to distract her mind.

In honor of Matt's return, Crank produced another of his favorite meals. This time it was baked flounder surrounded by potatoes and onions and topped with strips of crisp bacon.

Rose couldn't eat a bite. Oblivious to the splendid view out the back door, where a drift of pink clouds presaged the sunset, she mashed fish and potatoes together with her fork and helped Annie feed herself. Held the cup for her to drink her milk, and ignored it when Crank coaxed a smile while she was still drinking, then cackled when milk dribbled from both sides of her mouth onto her bib.

Matt had filled his own plate and taken it to his office. He hadn't shared a single meal with them since his return. Obviously he hadn't forgiven her for deceiving him. Either that or he'd decided he didn't want to be married to her and was trying to think of a tactful way to tell her.

Oh? And since when did Captain Powers bother with tact?

More likely he was trying to think of someone to come and take care of Annie. "Well, we'll just see about that, won't we, sugar?'' Scowling, she wiped a gray blob of fish and potatoes off Annie's chin and offered her another spoonful.

''She's growing like a weed, ain't she?'' The old man sat across the table, beaming proudly.

''Not like one of my weeds,'' Rose observed dryly.

Some time later, having dragged the rocking chair back into Annie's room, Rose rocked her to sleep and went on rocking until the sun had set and the first few stars appeared.

Surely he wouldn't come to her bed. She had worked herself into a state of nerves for nothing. She'd been on edge all day. Ever since he'd left her to go off on that horse of his, she'd been waiting for the ax to fall. If he hadn't taken his supper into his office and shut the door she might have followed him there, but in this house, where comfort depended on a free circulation of air, a closed door had to be taken seriously.

The rain had finally stopped. The air was perfectly still. Rose had bathed this morning, but after settling Annie for the night, she bathed again, using the last of her lilac soap.

She was his wife. If he came, he came.

If he wanted her, he wanted her.

If he didn't, then she would leave, and that would be the end of that.

He came. She had worn her lightest nightgown because it was a warm night, not because it also happened to be her prettiest. She had sprinkled lilac water on her hairbrush before her obligatory hundred strokes because it was cooling, not for any other reason.

And she was lying to herself because she didn't dare admit to the truth, that she had fallen in love for the first time in her life, and she was terrified that he could never love a woman with no looks, no money, and no more backbone than a snail.

A woman who had lived a lie for so long.

She had just crawled into her bed when he appeared in her doorway. He'd changed from his worn denim trousers and the frayed cotton shirt he wore when he was working with the horses to his best white linen shirt and a pair of black trousers that fit his loins like a glove. If he wanted to make a favorable impression, he'd have been better served to wear a smile.

"Did you want something?" Her voice sounded like a hinge that needed oiling.

"You claim to be my wife. I thought we might as well establish the relationship before I leave again."

He moved to stand beside her bed, yellow light from the single lamp delineating the sharp, angular bones of his face. Determined not to be intimidated, she managed to say, "You don't have to—that is, I don't expect you to—"

"Rose." His voice was quiet.

Hers was barely audible. "What?"

"Move over."

She scooted as far to the other side as she could without falling off the bed. Mesmerized, she watched in the flickering lamplight while he shed his shirt, then deliberately unbuttoned his trousers and slid them down over his narrow hips.

He was wearing nothing at all underneath. She tried and failed to tear her gaze away from the center of darkness at the apex of his powerful thighs. He was fully, proudly aroused. She felt her mouth go dry. After the first few months of her first marriage she had come to think of the male part as a weapon.

Oddly enough, she was not afraid of Matt. What frightened her most was her own reaction.

Matt allowed her to look her fill. He was what he was, a plain man with no pretense of fancy manners. If it wasn't enough, then she should have taken the first boat out and left him in peace instead of hanging around until he...

Until he got used to her.

Now, having finally dealt with his anger, he intended to take as much time as necessary to pleasure her. Just why he needed to watch her eyes darken with passion, he couldn't have said. Pride, perhaps. She'd held off long enough, keeping her options open. That still rankled. She had deceived him, and he meant to have his revenge, but the truth was, he wasn't entirely sure of his own skills when it came to bedding a respectable woman. The other kind— the only kind he'd ever bedded—usually took the lead. They were paid to squirm and groan, whether they felt any pleasure or not. The quicker they sent a satisfied customer on his way, the sooner they could take on another one.

He'd been almost fifteen when Peg had taken him to his first brothel. Flush with eight weeks' earnings, plus the money his mates had chipped in and donated to the cause, he'd spent the entire night and come away late the next afternoon with barely enough strength left to stagger back to the ship.

But he'd been grinning. He'd grinned for days, just thinking about it.

"Would you rather be on top or bottom?" He thought it only polite to ask, but the feel of her beside him, warm and smelling of lilacs, was making it hard for him to remember his anger.

"Um—whatever you want."

"I'm heavy. I wouldn't want you to be uncomfortable." The words were strained between his teeth. They were sitting up side by side, backs supported on the cool iron spokes of the bedstead as she hadn't rearranged her pillow.

His foot brushed against hers under the light spread, and a jolt of electricity shot through him. He sucked in his breath.

Why not just take her, dammit? Spread her and bed her and be done with it!

"We could wait," she suggested hesitantly. "There's no law that says we have to do it at all if you don't want to."

"We could argue all night, too, but we're not going to."

Turning suddenly, he took her by the shoulders and pulled her around so that she was facing him. His fingers bit into her flesh, but when her eyes widened with something that looked almost like fear, he eased his grip, clumsily smoothing her skin as if to take away the pain.

He'd never intended to hurt her, dammit, but he'd been half erect all day, just thinking about what he was going to do tonight. If he didn't get on with it now he would lose his nerve.

Or lose his priming.

So he kissed her. He'd done that much before, and enjoyed it a bit too much, but it was a beginning.

It was more than a beginning; it was enough to scatter his wits to the four winds. The scent of her skin clouded his senses, its flowery essence mingled now with something spicy, exotic.

Driven to taste her, he twisted his mouth on hers, parting her lips. Guided more by instinct than experience, he began to explore. He used his teeth gently, his tongue seductively echoing the throbbing of his groin.

Sometime during the kiss he lowered her onto the mattress and followed her down, still without breaking contact. Her gown was twisted beneath her body, and he fumbled to lift it, then gave up, broke off the kiss, and said, "This won't do."

He should have doused the lamp. Seeing her like this, her lips wet and swollen from his kisses, her darkened eyes staring up at him, he had to remind himself of his original plan: to take her and then to tell her he'd had the marriage annulled.

With unsteady hands, he sat her up, tugged the thin cotton gown from beneath her hips and dragged it over her head.

"Don't do that," he said when she crossed her arms over her chest and drew her knees up protectively. "I want to see you. You took your own sweet time looking me over," he reminded her.

If she heard him, she gave no indication. Gently, he clasped her wrists and brought her arms down to her sides. Her breasts were small, the nipples dark and erect, as if begging for attention.

Painfully aroused, he shifted onto his knees and eased himself between her updrawn thighs, all his fine plans of retribution forgotten. He touched her breast first with his lips, then with his tongue. His nostrils flared to the scent of her woman's sex, spicy, musky, unbelievably intoxicating, and he began to suckle her.

She whimpered. He lifted his mouth from her nipple to her lips and kissed her again, cradling her fragile breasts in the palms of his hands. Still on his knees, knowing he was on the verge of losing control, he deliberately moved away and took several deep breaths. In a voice that was hoarse, but totally without inflection, he said, "Please spread your legs, Rose. I'll be as quick as I can, and then I'll leave you alone."

He gave her time to prepare herself, warning himself not to jump on her like a rutting stallion. Even Jericho had enough manners to do a bit of sniffing and nuzzling before he got down to business.

Reaching out, he turned the lamp down until there was only a flicker of yellow light. He should have doused it completely. When he came about, she was lying there with both arms held stiffly at her sides. Her eyes were shut tightly—too tightly. He could see, or thought he could see, the shadow of a quiver on her flat stomach.

What the devil was he going to do if she started crying? No woman had ever cried when he'd made love to her.

When he'd bedded her, not made love. Love had never been involved, he had simply paid his money, taken his pleasure, and left until the next time he made port.

Not love, he reminded himself as he came down over her. "Don't be afraid, I won't hurt you," he whispered, and wondered why he bothered. Wondered where the thought had even come from. It wasn't as if she were a virgin.

Primed to go off at a single touch, he reminded himself once more that if she'd been a whore, he'd have been in and out, his money on the dresser, and gone by now.

The trouble was, this was Rose. The woman he had married. The woman who had brought a hundred dead weeds down from the ridge and tenderly planted them around his house. The woman who sang to Annie, and washed her diapers, and laughed at the same old jokes over and over from Peg and Crank.

Closing his mind to all that, he slipped his hand down between their bodies, opening her so that he could get on with what he'd come here to do.

She was damp. She was wet, and hot and swollen and slick, and he nearly lost it before he could get into position. With his heart pounding so hard he could hear it, his body trembling until he could scarcely support his own weight, he took his sex in one hand and moved the head of it slowly back and forth over her nest to prepare her for his invasion.

He heard her catch her breath. She gasped, shuddered, and when her hips thrust upward to meet him, the last remnant of sanity fled. He found her entrance, pushed himself inside her, drove into her again and again, oblivious to all but the earth-shattering sensations that ripped his world asunder....

Sometime during the night he awoke, his shoulder aching, his groin tight and needy. And then it all came back in one heady, intoxicating rush. Half in disbelief, he went over the incredible experience all over again in his mind. At his body's eager prompting, he considered waking her and taking her again.

He'd do better to wait until he could think more clearly. The fact that he was still here in her bed, with her head on his shoulder and her fist curled trustingly on his chest was more than enough to put him on guard. He'd planned to return to his own bed as soon as the deed was done.

He slipped away just before daybreak, got halfway to his own room before he remembered his clothes, then tiptoed back to collect them from the floor where he'd dropped them. Physically, he was spent, but he knew better than to try to sleep. Instead, he dressed and quietly let himself outside.

By the time he returned from the beach with Jericho just as a fiery sun was breaking through the morning mist, he was no closer than ever to coming to terms with what had happened.

This wasn't the way it was supposed to work out. His plan of retribution had been fair without being cruel. She had lied to him. He couldn't allow her to get away with that. His intention had been to mete out a fair punishment, then tell her that he'd had their marriage annulled, and offer her a generous allowance to stay and look after Annie.

But the fact was that they'd both lied. One had been a lie of commission, the other a lie of omission. Did one offset the other?

Chapter Fifteen

Matt rinsed away the salt from his early-morning swim, changed into dry clothes, then went in search of breakfast. He ate what was put before him, accepted seconds and cleaned off his plate once more. Swimming always made him hungry.

After that he wrote a long, detailed letter of instructions to Peg, knowing full well that the old man would likely ignore it, then went and asked Crank for a list of needed supplies. "I'll be riding south this morning. If you need anything from Cape Woods, I could ride on down there while I'm out."

The old cook gave him a knowing look. "Rosie said something about taking the young'un up to the ridge after breakfast. Told her it'd be too hot, but you know how she is."

He didn't know how she was.

Hell, he didn't even know how *he* was. He was half afraid to find out. All he knew was that he had taken a complicated situation and complicated it still further.

To make matters worse, before he could get away her two lovesick swains turned up, John riding that shaggy, half-trained mustang of his, and young Dixon in his father's gaff-headed sail skiff.

Taking the supply list Crank handed him, he scanned it to be sure he could read the old man's crabbed handwriting, tucked it in his pocket, and turned to go just as Rose appeared in the kitchen door. For once, she avoided meeting his eyes, staring instead at a place just beyond his left shoulder. Her face was as composed as any marble saint's, but there was nothing she could do about the deep color that stained her cheeks.

Feeling an unaccountable lift of spirits, Matt said, "Good morning, Rose."

"Good morning, Matthew," she replied evenly.

She went to edge past him. Some devil prompted him to block her passage, but he made it seem accidental. "Pardon me. Nice day, isn't it?"

"Yes, it is," she said with the slightest catch in her voice.

She moved to pass on the other side. He shifted his weight and grinned at her, trying to keep from laughing out loud. He wanted to lift her off her feet and swing her around. He wanted to kiss that pinched, disapproving mouth until it was all soft and swollen, the way it had been last night.

"May I please pass?" Her voice was cool, her cheeks ablaze.

He was half tempted to bow, just to watch her reaction, but he stepped back and gestured for her to pass. When she edged by in a wave of lilac-scented warmth, he said quietly, "It really is a fine day, Rose. I'll bring you something from the village."

She turned, a stricken look on her face. "You don't have to do that. Please, I-I'd rather you didn't."

Rose watched him all the way to the horse-pen. Had he really done all those things to her last night? Made her feel things she couldn't even find words to describe? Was that how it was when a woman loved a man?

Other than a few vague longings that had eventually withered and gone away, she had never felt anything faintly like it before, and she'd loved Robert at first. At least, she'd convinced herself she had, until he'd made even the pretense impossible.

Matt had said he would bring her something. Was he courting her? How was a woman supposed to know? She knew about as much about courting as she did about—about horseback riding.

John was already here for her lesson, and she hadn't even had her breakfast yet. Both he and Sandy were showing up earlier each day. She wasn't sure if they were trying to beat the heat, or each other. He was sitting on top of his horse, one leg cocked up before him as if he were seated on a kitchen chair. He did that sort of thing, especially when Sandy was around. Showing off, like the trick with the rope.

He was a nice man, though. Old for his age in some ways, surprisingly young in others, but nice. She watched as Matt stopped to speak to him. The two men exchanged a few words and then John wheeled away and rode off. She thought about calling him back. If she wanted to learn to ride, Matt had no business interfering.

The trouble was, she didn't. Not really. Some people had an affinity with horses, others didn't. She was one of the others. Later, after Matt went back to his ship, she might try again. Or she might simply limit herself to Angel and the cart.

Matt saddled one of the mares and swung himself up in a move that was surprisingly graceful for so large a man. He stopped to watch as the sail skiff glided alongside the wharf, made his way down to the waterfront and spoke a few words to Sandy, then wheeled away and headed south.

Sailing. Another of her failures. Still, she had tried, which was more than the old Rose would have had the courage to do. In a dire emergency she could probably climb up on top of a horse and make it go. She could sit in a boat and hoist a sail, even venture a little way out into the sound on a calm day, but she'd as soon stay on dry land.

So much for her dreams of competency. She could barely manage adequacy. The best she could hope for was that Matt would come home now and then, perhaps even give her another child, a brother or sister for Annie. She was good at babies, if little else.

Oddly enough, Sandy sailed off without even coming in the house. Not until Matt was nearly out of sight did she go back inside. She'd intended to tell Crank she wasn't hungry for breakfast when she realized, somewhat to her amazement, that she was starving. "I'll be back in about five minutes. I left Annie finishing her bottle. Could I possibly have two boiled eggs this morning? And some bacon? Is that biscuits I smell? Oh, good!''

It was late when Matt left the village, the most important part of his mission yet undone. Having been told that Dick Dixon wanted to see him, he'd been frustrated at not finding the man at home. As things had turned out, he had a few questions of his own, questions about his marital status. He'd written to Bagby, but judging from past experience, it could be weeks, or even months, before he heard anything.

Dixon was no lawyer, but as magistrate, his business was enforcing, and even interpreting the law in a limited fashion. If he didn't have the answers Matt sought, he might at least have a book that covered the subject. It was damned embarrassing. The last thing he needed was to give the gossips something else to gnaw on, but he needed to know where he stood. Belatedly, he had remembered Rose's reputation as a young widow living alone with two men and a baby. When Bess had been there, it had been different, but now Bess was gone and he was back, and everything had changed.

So he'd given Crank's supply list and his letter to Bagby to the captain of the freighter that brought supplies out once a week, then sought out the woman who was the nearest thing the village had to a dressmaker. A widow, Miss Sal, as she was called, supported herself by making sails, shrouds and occasionally sewing for those whose eyes and fingers were no longer up to the task.

He ordered a dress made for Rose. ''Something

yellow," he suggested. "Not egg-yolk yellow, but paler, more like those flowers that grow near the shore."

"Cost you fifty cents, you buy the cloth. I'll need me some measurements."

"I'll pay you three dollars, you order the cloth and I'll get you the measurements in a day or two. You've seen Mrs—" He cleared his throat. "You've seen her. She's about this high, sort of thin, but not too thin—built like a regular woman."

He was sweating like a horse. Miss Sal promised to send for the material, and Matt promised to bring her measurements, but he had one more request before he could escape.

If he'd been in Norfolk or Boston, or most any other port city in the world, he would have sought out a florist. Instead, he ended up borrowing a shovel and pail, handed over another dollar and dug up a rosebush from the dressmaker's front yard.

And tried to ignore her gap-toothed grin as he rode off with the thing, his ears burning like fire.

"I just happened to see it and thought I might as well bring it home and see if you could do anything with it," he told her when he got home. "I didn't steal it, if that's what you're thinking." He'd seen it blooming and wanted it for Rose. A rose for Rose. If he'd thought about having to tote the long-armed, thorny thing home on horseback, he might not have bothered.

Yeah...he would've.

Dropping the pail beside the porch, he clumped

off, muttering under his breath, "Take it or leave it, you'll probably kill the damned thing anyway."

With both Peg and Luther gone, there was enough to do to keep him busy until dark. He fed up, gave Jericho a run on the shore, nailed up a nest box in the henhouse and set out a net. The wind was due for a change. Which meant he'd be up to his armpits in guts and scales come morning, but at least they'd have fresh fish, which would be a relief from the salt mullet Crank favored.

In a rundown boarding house in the waterfront town of Beaufort, Tressy Riddle tapped her front teeth with the crumpled envelope and thought about what she'd just read. No wonder Cat hadn't answered any of her letters. She was dead, murdered by that no-account husband of hers.

Tressy, who was younger but a whole lot smarter, had warned her sister to wait. Told her if she'd just be patient a little while longer, something better would turn up. But Cat claimed she was tired of people looking down their snooty noses. "Just because we don't have no money. Just because Papa drank himself to death and Mama run off owing half the people in town, they think we're dirt."

So Cat had up and married some old man she met down at the docks. Tressy had warned her about hanging around there. "You're not never going to meet the right kind of man if you don't learn to talk right and dress right and go where they go."

"Where do they go?"

"To the 'piscopal church, dummy."

"I went there twice. It's no fun."

"No, well let me tell you something, what happens to girls that hang around the docks is no fun, either. Leastwise it is for a while, but once the ship leaves out, you're stuck with a brat in your belly and no man and no money. That's what happened to Louella."

"I'm smarter than her."

"You're dumber than dirt, is what you are."

Well, look who was right and look who was wrong, Tressy thought smugly as she replaced Mr. Dixon's letter in the envelope.

Abner Murdoch, the man Cat had married, had had a house, at least. Tressy, finding herself in need of a roof over her head until her luck changed, had considered paying the Murdochs a visit. She'd written to Cat and not heard back, so she'd written again. A man named Dixon had answered her letter, telling her what had happened.

"Your sister left a child, who is at present in the custody of one Captain Matthew Powers of Powers Point."

That had impressed her right off. People who had places named after them had money. The next line had confirmed it.

"Captain Powers is a man of some means, and well respected. You may be assured that even without a wife, he will care for your niece until other arrangements can be made."

"Mmm-hmm." Once again, Tressy tapped her front teeth with the corner of the envelope. A man of means, no less. With or without a wife.

Well, maybe she'd just spend her last few dollars on boat fare and see what else she could see. She wasn't interested in any baby, but Cat and her old man had had a house, and maybe a few other things, like furniture that could be sold. Sailors usually brought back all kinds of knickknacks from foreign places just to prove they'd been there.

Matt was late for supper; the others had started without him. He took time to wash up and change into a clean shirt, then remembered who it was who had to wash and iron his clothes, and wished he hadn't.

"You do too much," he said by way of greeting.

"I beg your pardon?"

They were both turning red in the face. Crank was grinning all the way back to his gills, and Annie sat in the tall chair with the tray Peg had fashioned for her, slapping her food, spattering it to kingdom come.

"Ironing. It's too hot to iron."

"Too hot to cook, too," Crank put in.

"You want to eat raw fish, you go ahead, but I want Annie's food good and done."

What with passing this and passing that, the tension eased, but by the time Crank stood to dish up the molasses pudding, Matt still couldn't look across the table without thinking about what he'd done last night.

And what he fully intended to do again tonight, as soon as the household was settled.

Later, Rose tried to pretend it was no great thing, having him come to her bed again. They were married, after all. Husband and wife, although he didn't feel like a husband. At least, not like the only other husband she'd known.

"Think it'll live?" he asked, adjusting the window now that the wind had swung around.

"I shoveled some of the barn scrapings into the hole. Luther said before he left if I used ma—material from the oldest pile, it would be all right."

Matt knew about as much about manure as he did about roses, but he nodded sagely. "Should be. I think you're supposed to water it now and then."

She swallowed visibly. "I will."

"Well. It's been a long day." He stretched and pretended to yawn, which made him feel even more like a fool than he already did. How the devil did a man approach a decent woman? Diving into the bed on top of her didn't seem like the proper tactic. How had he done it last night?

Damned if he could remember. All he knew now was that it was like nothing he had ever experienced before. If he weren't careful he might find himself agreeing to take one of those shore jobs Dixon had mentioned, just so he could have her in his bed every night.

"Matt?"

He wheeled away from the open window. "What? Are you too sleepy? If you'd rather not, I don't mind. That is—"

"Why don't you come to bed?"

He awoke in the night and lay there, staring up at the dark ceiling, feeling the northeast wind blowing across his naked skin, feeling his arm tingling where the weight of her head cut off circulation, the small fist curled on his chest, the slender thigh she had drawn up over his crotch.

He shifted his hips so that his pecker was no longer trapped. It sprang free, tall, throbbing, in search of the same mind-numbing pleasure it had already experienced twice tonight.

She was probably too tender. He'd used her hard.

"Mmm..." She mumbled something in her sleep, and he stroked her hair back from her face. Was she too warm? Too cool? Was her neck half broke from propping her head on his shoulder?

"Rose," he whispered. "Roll over, you'll get a crick in your neck."

After a moment she answered him. "No, I won't. Is your shoulder sore?"

It was. A head must weigh near as much as a watermelon, but he'd be damned before he admitted it.

She turned over on her side and poked her bare bottom against his hip, and that was even worse. Once last night, twice tonight—things were getting out of hand. He really owed it to her to tell her what he'd done before things went any further, but how could he tell her when he wasn't sure himself? If Bagby had dragged his heels, she might still be his wife. And if she was, then she would stay his wife. But if he had to marry her all over again, he'd do it, and the sooner the better.

He rolled onto his side and curled around her backside, looping an arm over her body, but he couldn't find a comfortable position, not with his rod standing out like a flagpole.

She sighed, and then she turned over again, and this time she was facing him, and his flagpole knew just where to go.

He lifted her, swung her up so that her thighs hugged his sides, maneuvered her into position and settled her astride him. Neither of them spoke a word, but he groaned. And she gasped as he eased himself into her hot, slick depths.

"Oh, my," she said when he thrust upward against her. And, "Oh, my," again when she caught the rhythm and thrust back. It was touch and go for a while, hit and miss, but near the end, he grabbed her shoulders and held her still while he drove into her, quick, quicker, quickest.

And then he shuddered—might even have cried out. When she collapsed on top of him, he held her close and felt like laughing, crying—or maybe dying.

From the next room, Annie whimpered.

"Did I wake her?" He could barely think clearly, much less speak.

"She'll go back to sleep if we're quiet."

Placing his mouth against her ear, he breathed, "I'll be quiet if you will."

She giggled, and he placed his hand over her mouth. When he felt her teeth score his callused thumb, he tucked his forefinger between her lips and moved it slowly in and out, with no real notion of why he did it, he only knew he wanted her in all the ways there were. Given enough time, he would have her in all those ways. Perhaps together they might even discover a few new ones.

But first he was going to have to tell her what he'd done.

No more was heard from Annie. He whispered, "Are you cold?"

"Hardly," she whispered back. "Did you ever back up to a fireplace?"

"Don't think so."

"You're like a hardwood fire."

"Honey, I'm hard and I'm hot, but I don't think there's anything wooden about me."

"Hush," she whispered, her body trembling with suppressed laughter, which didn't do much to help his control.

"Are you sore?" he ventured, half hopefully.

"A little bit. Sort of, um—stinging."

"I could—" he began, hardly knowing what he'd been about to say, but she caught his arm and held him back when he went to get out of bed.

"No, please—don't leave. It's just that—well, it's been a long time since—"

"Since you were widowed."

He could feel her nod her head, and he wanted to know more. Wanted to know everything about her. If he'd been sure of his rights—not that he had a right to her past—he would have pressed, but as it happened, he didn't have to.

"I don't know what Bess told you about—well, about my first marriage. I'm not even sure how much she knows, but I lost a baby."

His arms tightened instinctively. "Lost it?"

"She was born prematurely, the night my husband died."

He started to speak, thought better of it, and finally said, "I'm sorry." It was inadequate, but what was a man supposed to say? He was just beginning to understand how devastating the loss of a child could be. If anything happened to Annie...

"Yes, well...Annie helped heal my heart."

The simple statement made his eyes sting. His arms tightened, but this time there was nothing at all sexual about it. He held her until the wind fell off just before daybreak, and the rain started. It came down in a heavy drone, silencing the questions, the half-formed thoughts that churned in his mind.

They both slept until Annie let the world know she was wet and hungry and not at all happy about either condition.

By the time Rose had Annie ready for breakfast, Matt was nowhere in sight. She wasn't quite sure how she felt about their new relationship, much less how he felt about it. Or if he felt anything at all.

The nicest thing of all was that they'd laughed together. Lain in bed in each other's arms and laughed.

Well, perhaps not the nicest thing, she thought in a rush of warmth.

"Comp'ny coming," Crank sang out just as Rose, still in her wrapper, buttoned on Annie's gown.

It was early for company. Even the mailboat didn't usually arrive until mid-afternoon. Perhaps John...or Sandy, she thought.

It was neither.

Chapter Sixteen

Rose saw no reason to hurry. Through her bedroom window she could see Mr. Dixon's black gig with the canvas sunshade and wide wooden wheels for driving through sand. It was a strange-looking vehicle, but practical for the terrain.

Opening the clothespress, she pawed through her meager selection of gowns. The blue, or the yellow again? They were both getting a bit sun-faded. The pink silk was out of the question. It had been another of her infamous bad choices.

As it happened, Rose shared a birthday with the daughter of her parents' best friends. The two girls, although never friends, had been forced to share their birthday celebrations. On the last such occasion, Serena had worn a new wasp-waisted pink taffeta with a flounced skirt and a daring neckline. Not surprisingly, she'd been the belle of the ball, with everyone exclaiming over how pretty she'd looked in pink.

Rose had prevailed on her mother to have a gown made in the same shade, of a similar style. Unfortunately, the low neckline had accentuated her own lack of bosom, the strawberry-ice color, her sallowness. She'd worn it only once, miserably aware all evening of how unflattering it was in both cut and color. Before she could dispose of the wretched thing, her parents had been killed. Someone—the maid, no doubt—had packed it away when she'd gone into mourning.

She decided on the blue voile. What difference did it make? It was only Mr. Dixon to see Matt.

Matt. Oh, my. Grinning, she quickly pulled on a pair of white cotton stockings and reached for her shoes. "Don't fret, sugarpuss, you'll have your googoo as soon as Mama puts on her shoes."

"Googoo!" Annie called her cereal googoo, which Rose thought described it perfectly. While Rose laced up her white kid high-lows, Annie went through her repertoire, which expanded daily. "That's right, precious, say Ma ma."

At first Rose had felt guilty about encouraging her, but Annie was going to have to call her something. And since Matt had obviously forgiven her and decided to keep her, then Mama was the logical choice.

She was halfway down the hall on her way to breakfast when she heard the sound of a shrill voice that made her think of a fork scraping against a tin plate. It wasn't Mr. Dixon, she'd heard his voice before. It definitely wasn't Matt.

Mrs. Dixon? If she'd ever heard the woman, she couldn't recall, and anyway it was awfully early to be paying a social call.

"—fetch her in a minute." That was Matt.

Fetch who? Me?

Well, if she must, she must. "Come along, sugar, we'll pop in and pay our respects and then slip away for breakfast. You're my excuse not to linger."

She paused outside the door long enough to smooth the braid she'd anchored at the back of her head, straighten Annie's tiny collar and fix a smile on her face. "Good morning, Mr. Dixon, Mrs...."

The smile faded. This was definitely not Mrs. Dixon. The woman couldn't be a day over twenty. Although the eyes...

There was something old, almost calculating, in the violet-blue eyes that confronted her. Rose turned to Matt for guidance, finding none. His face had that familiar shuttered expression. Drawing on the training of a lifetime, she stepped into the room and, holding Annie against her shoulder, extended a hand.

Matt said in a curiously flat tone, "Rose, I believe you've met Mr. Dixon. Miss Riddle, Mrs. Littlefield."

Mrs. Littlefield?

She felt the first quiver of unease. Wasn't it time to end the charade?

The next thought that flew through her mind was that Matt had sent for someone to take care of Annie before he'd discovered Rose's identity, and the someone had finally showed up.

"Miss Riddle," she murmured politely. Matt would send her away, surely. They didn't need her. Besides, she had the look of a troublemaker, Rose could tell that much right away.

Her smile was forced as she said, "And this is our

Annie. Say bye-bye, darling. Annie's late for her breakfast, so if you'll excuse us?"

"Oh, so this is Cat's precious little Annie!"

Before Rose could react, the woman rushed forward and tried to pry the startled child from her arms. Annie grabbed handfuls of blue voile and started to whimper. Rose backed away. Undeterred, the woman tried again. "Here, give her to me. Oh, you sweet thing, you."

By then Annie was shrieking in Rose's ear. Matt said, "Dammit, begging your pardon, ma'am, but I told you to wait."

"Now, Miss Riddle, be patient, the baby don't know you yet," said Dick Dixon. There were wide wet circles under the arms of his rumpled gray suit.

Rose, shielding the howling baby with both arms, glared at the other woman, then at the two men. "Will someone please tell me just what's going on here? Who *is* this woman, Matt?"

"This is Annie's aunt from Beaufort. She only recently heard about what happened to her sister and she's come for Annie." Matt repeated what he'd been told by the magistrate, but he was obviously as shocked as Rose was. "I've explained that Billy— beggin' your pardon again, miss, but Billy was Annie's father, not Murdoch, and Billy gave her to me before he died."

"Well, that's just too bad, because Cat was my sister, and whatever she left is mine, ai—isn't that right, Mr. Dixon?"

Dixon looked as if his stomach hurt. "Now, that would be a fact, in the ordinary turn of events, but like I tried to explain last night, Miss Riddle, this is not an ordinary situation.''

''I don't care if it's ordinary or not, Cat wrote me all about her house, and it's mine now.'' She turned as if to appeal to Matt. ''I was fixin' to stay there when I got in, but it was late and Mr. Dixon said I couldn't because there was people living there, so I had to sleep with him and his wife.''

Not literally, Rose sincerely hoped. Matt looked as if he didn't know quite what to make of her.

''Can you beat that? Strangers livin' in my house, and me not even knowing about it?''

''As I explained, Miss Riddle, Abner's folks—'' Dixon began. He was sweating profusely.

''I don't care whose folks they are, Cat was that old man's widow, so what was hers is mine now, so you can just tell 'em for me to get out. You're a magistrate, they have to do what you say. You tell 'em I'm fixing to sell my house, and I want 'em out today!''

''You see, miss, the thing is—''

''And tell 'em I said not to steal anything, neither, 'cause Cat says old Abcess gave her everything.''

''Abcess?'' Rose and Matt echoed the word together.

''That's what Cat called him. Anyhow, he's dead, so all his stuff was hers, and now it's mine, 'cause I'm her next of kin.'' She shot Dixon a triumphant look. ''I do know my rights.''

''Well now, as I tried to explain last night, Miss Riddle, there's not all that much, er—stuff. And in the absence of a will, I'm afraid what little there is belongs to Abner's next of kin.''

Miss Riddle opened her mouth, then closed it again. Her eyes, a truly lovely shade of blue, went from Matt to the magistrate and back again while Rose watched, fascinated and increasingly convinced that this woman didn't want Annie any more than Annie wanted her. Rose made up her mind on the spot that she could have whatever worldly goods her sister had left behind, but under no circumstances could she have Annie.

"Didn't you tell her?" Matt asked Dixon.

"Tell me what? That Annie gets it all? I'm her aunt, what you might call her guardian, so I guess it's up to me if I want to sell the house and put the money away for Annie's future.''

A helpless look on his pudgy face, Dixon turned to Matt. "I tried to explain, but evidently I didn't do too good a job of it. Like I said, when the letter came addressed to Murdoch's woman a few months after the fact, so to speak, it was handed over to me. I took it upon myself to inform Mrs. Murdoch's next of kin of the unfortunate incident, and explain how you'd taken the baby and how Mrs. Littlefield had stayed on after Bess left to look after her, and that she— that is, Miss Riddle—shouldn't worry on that account.''

"And I can see you've taken real good care of her, too, Captain Powers. Can I call you Matthew? You can call me Tressy. It's really Theresa, but everybody calls me Tressy. Anyhow, now that I'm here, we won't need Miss Littlething anymore. I can take over. You just show me what to do, I'm a real fast learner.''

Matt's scowl deepened. Standing off to one side of the room, Rose thought irrelevantly that if only Bess were here, she'd be scribbling madly in her notebook, plotting her next fanciful tale.

Oddly enough, Rose wasn't worried about losing Annie. The Riddle woman wanted a crying, teething baby about as much as she wanted a bad case of poison ivy. She most definitely wanted something, though, and might even try to use Annie to get it.

Over my dead body, Rose vowed silently. Having made more than her share of disastrous choices these past few years, she was finally learning to respect her instincts. At the moment, those instincts whispered that Tressy Riddle would bear close watching.

Miss Littlething, indeed.

''Didn't Dixon tell you how your sister died?'' Matt asked bluntly.

Dixon said hurriedly, ''I believe I indicated that the deceased had expired shortly after giving birth to a daughter.'' He sent Matt a helpless look.

''You want the unvarnished truth? Your sister took herself a lover while her husband was away. Murdoch came home to find his wife lying in bed with a new baby, and knew damned well it wasn't his. He shot his wife, brought the baby here to the Point, where he shot his wife's lover and then turned the gun on himself.''

For a full minute no one spoke. The stark horror of such a tragedy lay like a pall over all four adults.

Only Annie seemed unaffected. Squirming in Rose's arms, she switched to her I-want-breakfast howls.

"In a little while, sugar," Rose whispered, bouncing her in her arms. "Miss Riddle, I'm so very sorry," she said, and meant every word of it. No amount of sympathy, however, could change her mind about Annie.

Tressy Riddle blotted her beautiful, but quite dry eyes, with a slightly grimy handkerchief. "Oh, my poor dear sister. Cat never was real strong. I always used to tell her, I said, Cat, you got to behave yourself, else you'll get in trouble, that you will. The world's a wicked place for us poor orphans, and now there's Annie." She let out a wail that startled them all and even silenced Annie for the moment.

Rose edged closer to the door. "If you'll excuse us," she murmured, jiggling the baby in her arms.

"Not yet, Rose," said Matt, looking as if he'd rather be anywhere else in the world.

Actually, he looked almost vulnerable, Rose thought, her protective instincts expanding to include him along with Annie.

"I'd best be getting on back," the magistrate said with every appearance of relief. "Wife's waiting breakfast. I'll set your trunk out on the porch, Miss Riddle. Matt can bring it inside."

Her trunk?

"Her trunk?" Matt echoed Rose's thoughts.

"I can't hardly move into Cat's house until Mr. Dixon gets those people out, so I reckon you'll just have to put up with me." Tressy gave Matt a tremulous smile that didn't quite match the calculating look in her eyes.

"You still don't understand, do you?" Grimly, Matt explained once more. "Miss Riddle, your sister died first. Neither she nor her husband left a will, so you don't stand to inherit anything. The property belonged to Murdoch and he survived his wife, that's all there is to it. I'm sorry you had a long trip for nothing."

The magistrate nodded emphatically. "Couldn't have said it better myself."

"B-but he killed her. A murderer can't inherit his wife's stuff, can he? That ain't fair."

She might be a greedy little baggage, but Rose couldn't help but feel sorry for her. If she was truly alone in the world, then she needed all the help she could get. "Matt, if you'll bring Miss Riddle's trunk inside, I'll go get Bess's room ready. She'll be comfortable in there for a few days until she's ready to go back to—where was it, Beaufort? I've heard that's a lovely little town." She managed a smile. Not a particularly enthusiastic one, but it was the best she could do at the moment.

Tressy Riddle sniffed and blinked away invisible tears. "Thank you, I'm sure, Miss Littlething."

Miss Littlething said, "Just let me get Annie started on her breakfast first. Perhaps you'd like to join us? I warn you, it's rather a messy business. Annie's learning to feed herself."

"Captain Matt, do you think you could show me around? I mean, as long as I'm going to be living here, I need to know where everything's at." Ignoring Rose, she placed her hand on Matt's arm and gazed trustingly up at his face.

Seeing that pudgy little hand, the fingernails gnawed to the quick, Rose felt a reluctant surge of sympathy. *Oh, Lord, don't let me make another foolish mistake.* At least Annie was in no real danger. She was fairly certain of that.

Matt was another matter. The poor girl thought he was single. They really should reveal their marriage. It might be embarrassing right at first, for not only had Rose deceived her husband, she had deceived the entire village. But embarrassment was rarely fatal. If it were, she'd have been dead long before now.

Matt disengaged his arm and, on the pretext of collecting the Riddle woman's trunk, followed Dixon out to his gig. "I need to talk to you on another matter if you've got a few minutes."

"You've changed your mind about taking over my position when I retire?"

"I appreciate the offer, but I don't have the background. This is about something else. You see, I need to know—that is—" How the devil did he find out what he needed to know without admitting that the woman they all knew as Mrs. Littlefield was, in fact, Mrs. Powers. Once the truth came out, Rose would be branded an adventuress at the very least, and he'd be called a fool.

He cleared his throat and tugged at his collar. "Now, this is not personal, you understand, but say a man married a woman and then they both changed their minds. How long would it take to dissolve the union? Would it be done as soon as the request was made, or would it take more time?''

"Well now, that would depend, wouldn't it?''

"Depend?''

"On whether this hypothetical couple changed their mind before or after the, er...the honeymoon. You're talking divorce in one case, annulment in the other.''

Matt could feel his face starting to burn. Grimly, he plowed ahead. He had to know, and Bagby was taking too damn long to answer his mail. "Say the request was made before the, uh—the honeymoon.''

"Hmm.'' Dixon stroked his chins, then ran a finger under his limp collar. "Now this is lawyering, and I don't have any real experience in this sort of thing, you understand, but my guess would be...depending on how quickly the paperwork could be done, a matter of days. Perhaps less. Maybe longer.''

Well, hell. He'd have done better to hop the next boat to Norfolk and get his answer straight from the horse's mouth. He muttered his thanks, shouldered a Saratoga that looked as if it had barely survived a war, and headed for the house again.

For the sake of Rose's reputation, he would have to keep to his own bed until he knew for sure they were still married. His groin tightened in protest, but until they could get rid of the Riddle woman, he couldn't afford to take chances. His legal claim to Annie would never stand up in court if there was so much as a hint of scandal.

He'd give it three days. If he hadn't heard from

Bagby by then, he'd get Dixon to tie the knot, and this time it wouldn't be any slipknot.

Somehow they got through the rest of the day. Miss Riddle monopolized Matt, which left Rose and Annie to their own devices. Rose watched from the ridge as he showed her over every inch of the estate, right down to the henhouse.

Oddly enough, she wasn't jealous. She knew he was only trying to keep the woman away from Annie until he could find an excuse to get rid of her. They would each do whatever it took to protect Annie, and if that meant bribing the woman to go away, then that's what they would do.

Not that Rose had anything to use as a bribe. The pink gown, perhaps… "But not you, sugar. And not our Matt, either."

Annie gnawed on her fist and began to fret. Reluctantly, Rose stood, dusted the sand from her skirt and headed back down the ridge.

He loves me. The words echoed in her heart again and again as she went through the rest of the day, a silly grin on her face as often as not. He hadn't actually spoken the words, but she knew him well enough by now to realize he would never wear his heart on his sleeve.

Supper turned out to be a circus. Sandy Dixon came by and was invited to stay. Crank, despite having what he called "comp'ny," served the meal in the kitchen, as usual. And as usual, Annie splashed her milk and dropped fistfuls of food on the floor.

Tressy edged away from the high chair until she

was practically sitting in Sandy's lap. Sandy stared at her yellow ringlets as if he'd never seen hair that color before. It really was rather striking, Rose had to admit.

Once or twice she tried to catch Matt's eye, but he avoided looking at her, even though she sat across the table from him. He had little to say, and as Rose was busy seeing that as much of Annie's supper ended up inside her as outside, it was left to Sandy to entertain their houseguest.

Which he did with a discourse on the condition of the roads in rural North Carolina, while Crank misquoted the occasional applicable Bible verse.

All in all, Rose decided, it could have gone far worse.

Once the household was finally settled for the night, Rose, feeling a glow of anticipation, bathed and dressed in a simple ivory batiste gown. Sprinkling a few drops of lilac water on her hairbrush, she did her hundred strokes slowly, sensuously, remembering each touch, each langorous look, every thrilling moment of the night before.

After turning the lamp down low, she climbed into bed to await her husband. Unsettled at having a stranger in the house, Annie had taken longer than usual to fall asleep. Rose wasn't happy about it, either, but it wouldn't last long. As soon as Matt made her understand that there was nothing for her here, the poor girl would move on to greener pastures.

Matt would probably end up paying her passage and even giving her a little something to tide her over. Rose decided that if there was a tactful way she could give her the pink silk dress, she would do it. As unfortunate as the style and color had been on Rose, the thing had cost dearly. With Tressy's coloring, it would look lovely.

She might even offer her a few suggestions for finding work. Goodness knows, her own experience hadn't been notably successful, but she'd thought about it a lot since then. At the very least she could advise against a few of the more common pitfalls.

Rose yawned. What on earth could be keeping him? Crank had washed the last dish and gone to his own room hours ago. The poor man had been muttering all day about Jezebels and foxes in henhouses.

It had been a long day. Endless. As soon as breakfast had ended, Matt had been pressed into giving his guest that guided tour. Dutifully, he had shown her everything with the exception of the bedrooms and his office. Judging from what she'd seen from a safe distance, Rose didn't think either of them had particularly enjoyed the excursion.

She yawned again and tugged at the neckline of her nightgown. Mercy, it was hot tonight. Tressy had come to supper wearing a tight blue taffeta gown that Rose could have told her was a mistake. While the color might enhance her eyes and the style certainly did things for her figure—she bulged both above and below the tightly corseted waist—taffeta, with or without stays, was utterly miserable in this climate.

Poor child. The very last thing Rose would have expected was to find herself in sympathy with the woman who had come to take Annie from her. And,

quite possibly, Matt. Still, she couldn't help but remember her own similar circumstances.

Not long ago she herself had been without family
and utterly without prospects. Then Bess had come
along—Bess and Mr. Bagby—and Rose had let herself be talked into something she would never have
dreamed of doing if she hadn't been desperate.

Obviously, Tressy had taken a leap of faith in coming here. Rose hoped things turned out well for her.
Hoped her sister had left something, after all. Perhaps
she could find work in the village, or even a husband....

But not *my* husband, Rose thought firmly, wishing
Matt would come. Wishing with all her heart they
had declared themselves man and wife from the beginning.

And not my baby, either, she added as she drifted
off to sleep.

Matt couldn't sleep, picturing Rose alone in her
bed, waiting for him to go to her. He had fully intended to do the honorable thing and explain that they
might or might not be legally married. Before he'd
had a chance to explain anything, the Riddle woman
had shown up. All day long she'd stuck to him like
a barnacle. He'd never got the chance to see Rose
alone.

Honor would just have to wait, he decided, because he damned well couldn't. She was in his blood
worse than a fever, setting him on fire, rattling his
mind until he could no longer think clearly. Three
days, he'd allowed himself. If he didn't hear from

Bagby by then, he would marry her all over again, as if the first marriage had never taken place.

Thus resolved, he moved silently down the hall and let himself into her room. He'd heard there were ways to keep from getting pregnant. Not that he would have minded, but it wouldn't be fair to Rose. Remembering too well how the village had shunned the poor Murdoch woman, he vowed never to allow a shadow to be cast on Rose's reputation.

"Rose," he whispered. A streak of moonlight fell across the foot of her bed, revealing one slender white foot. He took it in his hands, then slid his hand up over her calf.

She didn't move. Her foot was cool, her calf warm, and he was damned near burning up. "Rose," he whispered again.

He waited. Waited, watched and listened until he heard the soft, puffy little sound she made with her lips when she was sleeping. Then, aching with disappointment and still painfully aroused, he pulled the sheet over her feet and silently returned to his bed.

He could read. He had books he'd never even cracked, but if he lit a lamp, the Riddle woman might take it as an invitation. After today, he didn't dare give her any opening.

So instead, he turned his mind to the *Black Swan* and occupied himself with wondering how Peg was getting on with the repairs. After that, he thought of possible ways to rid himself of Tressy Riddle, and from there he went on to wondering how he was going to explain his irregular marriage to Crank and

Luther, not to mention the rest of the world, without looking like a fool.

Just as the eastern sky began to show light, he got up and went outside to douse himself with a bucket of water from the rain barrel. Then, without regard for anyone who might still be sleeping, he plopped a chunk of oak onto the chopping block and raised the ax over his head.

Plop, whack, crack. Plop, whack, crack. Splits of kindling piled up on either side. When the pile reached high enough, he buried his ax in the chopping block and began to stack it, as Luther wasn't here to do it.

From inside the house he heard a whining voice that was far too familiar after but a single day. Damned, pesky female. He'd caught on quickly enough to what she was after, and it wasn't Annie. Something about the way she gazed up at him and swatted her eyelashes, the way she hung on to his arm and his every word, reminded him a little too much of Gloria.

The woman had come here looking for an easy mark and thought she'd found one. He was half tempted to send her back to Dixon with orders to stay the hell away from Powers Point, but if he did, she might turn nasty and try to take Annie away from him just for spite. And while he didn't know much about the law, he had a feeling her claim might be stronger than his own.

She couldn't have Annie. Annie was his, and besides, it would break Rose's heart, and he'd cut off both his hands before he would hurt Rose.

He should have explained to her. Between them they could have presented a united front.

Explained what? Explained how you planned to seduce her without telling her you knew who she was, just so you could watch her struggle to redeem herself?

Whatever his initial plan had been, he hadn't counted on two things: that Rose herself would confess, and that he would want her as much as he did. For all he knew, he might even love her. Not that he knew what love was supposed to feel like, but if it was anything like this fever that was burning him up, this ache inside him at the thought of losing her, then it had to be love. Either that or he was desperately, incurably ill.

Rose woke with a headache. Grimly determined to ignore it, she quickly fed and dressed Annie, collected basket, blanket and book and headed for the ridge, the one place she was sure of being left alone. She had some serious thinking to do before she was ready to confront Matt and his houseguest.

The air was completely still. Mosquitoes whined, frogs croaked sporadically, and from the very top of a wind-stunted yaupon, a mockingbird sang melodically, never once repeating a single verse.

Annie warbled back, waving her pudgy fists and kicking her tiny bare feet. There was a speck of dried googoo in her hair, but it could wait until later. For now, Rose only wanted to be alone with the troubling thoughts she'd woken up with, which weren't quite as charitable as the ones she had taken to bed last night.

All evening she'd kept waiting for Matt to announce that they were married. Crank already knew, at least she was pretty sure he had guessed the truth, but Matt hadn't said a word.

At first she'd been puzzled. There was no real reason that she could see to keep their marriage a secret. She had fully expected him to explain when he'd come to her bed, but he hadn't even done that. She'd wakened up alone this morning—hurt, puzzled and a bit angry.

If he had changed his mind and decided he didn't want her for a wife, that was one thing, but even considering her poor judgment where men and their motivations were concerned, she refused to believe he would throw in his lot with Tressy Riddle in order to better his claim to Annie.

Chapter Seventeen

Too hot to sleep. Too hot to eat. Too hot even to move. Having a stranger constantly underfoot, asking nosy questions about things that were none of her concern, only made matters worse. Rose did her best to be patient, but with so much on her mind, it wasn't easy. How long was the woman going to stay? What was she waiting for? For Rose to go away so she could have free access to Annie?

Hardly. She wouldn't even change a diaper.

Sandy visited daily. As Rose had given up on sailing lessons, he spent most of his time with Tressy, encouraged by her flattering attentiveness to elaborate on his varied interests and plans for the future.

Rose had heard it all before, so she excused herself and went about her business. Heat or not, things had to be done, and she'd rather do the wash than watch Tressy flirt and Sandy show off.

As miserable as the sticky weather was, it was not the heat that bothered her most. Something was wrong between her and Matt.

They had been on the verge of announcing their marriage…hadn't they? So then, why was he avoiding her? Was it something she had said? Something she'd done? Could he have changed his mind?

All the uncertainties of her youth came rushing back to haunt her. *For goodness' sake, Rose, why can't you stop growing? You certainly didn't get your looks from my side of the family, I've always been dainty.*

That was the year she had shed her baby fat and shot up like a beanpole. From then on she'd been too tall, too sallow and too gauche, despite all her mother's attempts to turn her into a fashion doll. When she was old enough to begin making her own choices, she had invariably chosen the wrong girls to emulate, the wrong boys to develop a crush on, the wrong colors and styles, despite her mother's advice.

While she had clung to the fading hope that one day the ugly duckling would turn into a beautiful swan, common sense told her that biologically it was unlikely, if not impossible.

And then suddenly, her whole life had changed. In her own defense, she'd been young, inexperienced, and still stunned by the loss of her family when Robert had wangled an introduction and offered his condolences.

She still couldn't recall those first few weeks after the accident clearly. She did remember that her parents' friends had been kind, and that the middle-aged bachelor she'd been encouraged to call Uncle Harold, even though he was no relation, had invited her to stay with him so that he could help her in her hour of need.

Fortunately, Robert had talked her out of that, telling her it might be perfectly innocent, but it wouldn't look right. He had offered advice without a hint of implied criticism, held her when she needed to cry without making her feel weak or homely or vulnerable, even though she'd been all of those things.

It hadn't helped that her father's lawyer had been out of the country, and that her father's record-keeping had been even worse than her grandmother's. Perhaps it was a Littlefield failing.

In all the confusion that followed, Robert had been there, offering comfort, advice, and then marriage. She had never once questioned his attentiveness until it was too late.

Matt, she reminded herself now, was nothing at all like Robert, yet she was beginning to wonder if she could have misunderstood his intentions, too. She'd been so certain he had forgiven her for deceiving him. He had accepted her as his wife. He'd come to her bed. He'd shown every evidence of enjoying it, too, and goodness knows, she certainly had. It had been wonderful beyond belief. Even now she had only to look at him to recall in vivid detail the intimacy they'd shared. The aching, throbbing, desperate drive for completion that had far exceeded the meager bounds of her limited imagination.

She could understand why he wouldn't come to her bed with a stranger in the house, but why was he avoiding her?

Because he was. There was no longer any doubt

of that. He would take one look at her, mumble something about work to be done, and disappear. Every single animal in the horse pens, even Angel, had been polished to a high gloss.

They had enough firewood to last a hundred years. There had once been seven dead oak trees bordering the sound, killed, according to Luther, by the encroaching tide. Yesterday Matt had chopped down and cut up the last one.

Rose tried to convince herself that it was only the wretched heat that was making him act so strangely. It affected them all. Tressy sulked. Annie fussed, but then she was probably cutting another tooth. Crank grumbled. Normally the kindest of men, he had taken Tressy in dislike from the first, the feeling being entirely mutual.

Thank goodness for Sandy. As he didn't seem to object to Tressy's mindless chatter, Rose left them to entertain each other. The woman irritated her beyond bearing, but she couldn't help but feel sorry for her. As someone who had lost her own immediate family in a tragic accident, Rose knew how she must feel. She herself had Matt and Annie now. Poor Tressy was alone in the world.

Annie clicked her newest tooth on her cup and grinned, dribbling milk from both sides of her mouth. With absent-minded patience, Rose blotted her chin. They had come early to breakfast because it was too hot to sleep much beyond sunrise.

"I woke up wringing wet," declared Tressy, who had wandered into the kitchen in her dressing gown, her hair a disheveled mess that managed to be wildly becoming.

"I know, it always seems worse just after sunrise. Never a breath of air." Rose, fully dressed and groomed, watched the other woman attack a plate filled with fried croaker, fried potatoes, pickles and crusty biscuits. Rose herself had eaten so much seafood lately, she was heartily sick of it. Crank had stewed a chicken yesterday, but in this heat, no one had been particularly hungry.

"That bed's got bugs in it."

"I beg your pardon?"

"I got bites all over me."

The two women and Annie were alone at the moment, Crank having stepped outside to refill the kettle.

"It's probably mosquitoes. We've had rain lately, and now there's no wind to blow them away."

"You think I never seen a mosquito before? These is all over me, under my corset and ever'wheres."

Rose had suffered her share of bites, but only where her skin had been exposed to the pesky devils. "You didn't...well, no, of course you wouldn't do that."

"I didn't do what?"

"Well, I saw you and Sandy walking down by the sound side yesterday evening. Did you—"

"—did I what, Miss Priss? Take off my clothes the minute we was out of sight behind the bushes?"

Rose gaped at her. "I didn't mean—"

"For your information, Miss La-de-dah, we just talked. We sat down in that patch of grass behind the net shed and I told Sandy all about how I was going to better myself by reading books and going to church and all, and he told me how he was going to fix the roads and the schools. It wouldn't surprise me none if he didn't end up as governor one of these days. He might not look like much, but he's real smart.''

"I think he's a nice-looking young man, and you're right, he is smart. He's also kind.'' Despite her own concerns, she felt sorry for the poor girl, who was scratching first her waist and then a place behind her knee. "I suspect it's chiggers. The grass is full of them. I'll make you a poultice after breakfast, but first, if you'll excuse me, I'd better see to getting Annie cleaned up.''

Just as she swung Annie up from her chair, Crank came back inside. He set the kettle on the range to heat, looked at her untouched plate, lowered his brows and shook his head. "Off yer feed again, are ye?''

"It's the heat, I suspect.''

It wasn't the heat that troubled her, it was her heart.

Miss La-de-dah?

Matt was fit to be tied. He no longer believed the Riddle woman would actually try to take Annie from him, but she wasn't above using her as a pawn. She was after something. He was beginning to believe she might have lined him up in her sights. Him and young Dixon and any other unattached male. There was nothing to be gained from her sister's estate,

Dixon had explained all that. And if she didn't want Annie, then why the devil was she still hanging around the Point? He'd offered her no encouragement.

So far, he'd avoided a direct confrontation by keeping his distance, but he'd run out of chores to do and wood to chop. He could have caught a boat across the sound and then headed up to Norfolk to see how the work on his ship was going, but he didn't dare leave her here with Rose and Annie, with only Crank to protect them. Not until he knew what she was after.

Dipping his discarded shirt into the bucket of water he'd been about to pour into the horse trough, he mopped his face, then slung the wet shirt around his neck, reveling in the momentary coolness.

He'd be the first to admit he was no good at dealing with women. He'd proved that much when he'd tried his hand at revenge and ended up falling in love with his victim. Men he could deal with, having lived in a man's world all his life. If Tressy Riddle had been a member of his crew he'd have kicked her off his ship before he ever left port. He'd sized her up right away as a snoop and a troublemaker.

Crank said he'd caught her going through the locker in his bedroom. Claimed she'd been looking for a handkerchief. Matt had been tempted to drive her to the village and load her aboard the first outward-bound boat right then, but the woman had him over a barrel. Any way you looked at it, her claim to Annie was stronger than his.

There had to be a way, dammit. If he and Rose

were married... The trouble was, he didn't know if
they were or not, and not knowing, he didn't know
which tack to take. He'd been on the verge of declaring himself—of declaring something, anyway—
when Dixon had dumped the Riddle woman in his
lap. Now, every time he tried to get Rose alone,
Tressy was there with her confounded meddling and
her endless questions.

"How big is your ship?"

"Big enough."

*"My, I bet it cost a heap, didn't it? I never met a
man that owned a whole ship before. I've knowed—
known lots of sailors, though."*

No wonder Crank was threatening mutiny and
Rose was looking so peaked, if they had to put up
with that prattle all day long. He would like to blame
it on the summer doldrums, but this wasn't the first
hot spell they'd had since Rose had been here. The
heat had never seemed to bother her before. She
wasn't eating enough, according to Crank, who put
it down to the fact that the Good Book warned
against eating seafood and drinking milk in the sum-
mertime.

Matt couldn't help but wonder if there might be
another reason. How long did it take for a woman to
catch? How long before she began to show symp-
toms? Was a week long enough?

God, he wished he knew more about women. All
men, especially those without mothers or sisters,
should be forced to take a course in the subject of
women, understanding how they were put together,

how they functioned, what made them different from men.

From the woman who had deserted him as a child he'd learned that women smelled good, cried a lot, and weren't interested in anything a little boy had to say. Growing into manhood, he'd been too proud to ask questions, afraid of revealing weakness, but he'd learned a few more things from the whores he'd done business with over the years. He had learned still more from a woman who had played him for the fool he was.

His aunt Bess didn't count. She defied all understanding. But now there was Rose, and he was more at sea than he'd been in all his seafaring life.

Rose dragged herself in to breakfast the next morning, but regretted it almost immediately. Leaving Annie with Crank and Tressy, she hurried from the kitchen, her face almost as green as it had been the day she'd arrived at Powers Point.

Matt, on his way inside from seeing to the livestock, heard rapid footsteps on the bare wood floors followed by the slamming of a door. He peered into the kitchen. Tressy's scowl turned instantly into a smile. Annie was patting globs of burgoo on her head.

"Rose?" He looked to Crank for an explanation.

"Sick, I reckon. Looked like she was headed for the rail."

Oh, hell, he'd fouled his own nest. Got her with child before he could settle the marriage question. Even with his meager knowledge of society's rules,

Matt knew what that meant. The proof was right there before him.

Annie.

"I never been sick a day in my life," Tressy declared proudly. "Stop that," she snapped at Annie, who had leaned over to share a handful of cereal with her aunt.

Matt turned to follow Rose, but Crank called him back. "Leave her be, Cap'n. Women don't like a man to see 'em on their knees, heavin' into a chamber pot." When Matt hesitated, the old man went on to say, "I had me five sisters, all older'n me. Why'd you think I went to sea when I was no bigger'n a gnat's behind?"

While he was still trying to make up his mind whether to go after her, Rose returned, her face pale as new canvas, but quite composed. "Good morning, Matt," she greeted him.

He studied her intently, searching for some sign she was breeding. Against all decency, his groin tensed at the thought that they might have made a baby.

"I need to talk to you," he said softly. They were standing in the kitchen doorway, close enough to touch, but carefully not touching. Matt wanted to hold her, not necessarily to make love to her, just to hold her and promise her that everything would be all right, but he didn't dare, not until he knew he could keep that promise.

"Crank says you're fixin' to go back to Norfolk to see to your ship, Matt." Tressy broke the tension, a coy note in her thin, nasal voice. "I never been to

Virginia. I heard it's a real pretty place, though. I wouldn't mind seein' it.''

Rose slipped past him to take her seat beside the high chair and Matt managed not to swear aloud. "I won't be going anytime soon," he said.

Crank served him a cup of steaming black coffee, strong enough to dissolve nails. Then the old man touched Rose on the shoulder, and Matt watched Rose incline her head toward his gnarled hand and felt a stab of jealousy.

What in hell was happening to him? He'd all but banished Luther, sent John on his way, and now he was worrying about a man old enough to be his own grandfather?

"Anybody home?" Sandy Dixon called out. There was a pause as he stomped the sand off his shoes, then let himself in with the ease of familiarity. "Brought you a letter, Cap'n Powers."

With a nod that was barely polite, Matt took it, glanced at the return address, then hastily excused himself. A moment later they heard his office door slam shut.

Sandy looked from one to the other. "Must be important. You ladies mind if I join you? How about you, Annie, you want to share your breakfast cereal with me? Mama had the headache this morning. The heat, I reckon. She didn't feel like cooking breakfast."

Crank had no sooner set a plate of fish, potatoes and the few remaining biscuits, cold by now, before the magistrate's son when Matt returned. He paused at the door to say, "I'll be back in a couple of hours. Rose, be here, will you?"

As if she had any choice.

"Wait for me to get dressed and I'll go—" Tressy stood eagerly, then sank back into her chair. "It wouldn't have took me but a minute," she grumbled as he left the house and headed out to the horse pen.

Sandy picked up his fork. "Boat got in just before dark yesterday. I probably should've brought the mail out last night, since nobody came in to collect it, but there was just one letter. Some lawyer in Norfolk, probably something to do with his ship."

"We'll need to throw out the chicken stew," Rose told Crank.

"We got ice boxes in Beaufort, with ice delivered fresh ever' day."

"Electric ice boxes, that's the coming thing," Sandy announced, and would have elaborated on the topic had Rose not cut him short.

"That will hardly do us much good until they can bring electricity out here on the freight boat." She lifted Annie from her chair and excused herself. "It's tinned milk and burgoo for you, young lady, until this awful weather breaks."

Rose removed the wet diaper and sticky nightshirt, bathed and powdered the plump, squirming body, then selected the plainest of the fancy gowns the men had ordered from the mail-order catalog. Annie had outgrown most of them, thank goodness, but Rose still felt like crying, picturing four rough seamen, Matt, Crank, Peg and Luther, poring over the layette section of the catalog, ordering the fanciest, most expensive things available without the least notion of what was suitable.

"Your papa will be home any time now. He'll want to see your new tooth, so let's practice our best smile."

Dear Lord, she loved this child. Rose was quite certain Tressy didn't really want her, even though she was a blood relative and the courts would probably side with her if it came down to a fight.

It was this awful uncertainty, she decided, as much as the weather and the spoiled chicken that was making her feel so wretched. Waiting for the other shoe to drop.

What was bothering Matt?

Why was Tressy still here?

Rose lingered as long as she could, throwing back the covers to air the bed, gathering Annie's laundry, taking a few of her own gowns out onto the back porch to sun. With the awful humidity, everything was prone to mildew.

Just as she turned to go back inside, she saw Sandy ride off. She really should have stayed to entertain him, but she no longer thought of him as company, not when he came every day.

Returning to her bedroom, Rose found Tressy standing in front of her dresser. Ignoring Annie, who was sitting up in her crib chewing on a knotted rope toy Peg had made for her, the woman had uncapped a bottle of lilac toilet water and was sniffing the contents.

"Were you looking for me?" Rose asked politely.

Tressy whirled around, dropped the cap, but mercifully hung on to the bottle. "You didn't tell me you two was married," she accused.

Rose's mouth opened, then closed. Cautiously, she said, "I...was married before I came here." Which was both true and ambiguous. By the time she'd picked up the cap from the floor, replaced it on the bottle and set it on the dresser, her mind was racing, trying to pinpoint the danger she sensed.

"What happened? Why'd he get it annulled? I bet I know—he got tired of your la-de-dah ways, didn't he? A man wants more than fancy manners in his bed, I can tell you that much, and I've not ever been married."

Rose instinctively placed herself between Annie and the younger woman. Her palms were damp, but her voice remained calm. "Tressy, if you've something to say, then I'd appreciate your saying it straight out."

Tressy held out a sheet of paper. Managing to sound both spiteful and triumphant, she said, "Here then, is this straight out enough? I come across it accidental when I was looking for a—a piece of paper and a pencil. I reckon now you won't be so high and mighty."

When Rose made no effort to take the letter, Tressy stepped closer and waved it under her nose. "Well, don't say I never done you no favors. He's going to send you packing when he gets back. Know what I bet? I bet he went to fetch the magistrate, to run you off his property."

Rose couldn't help herself. She snatched the letter

and read it. It took only a moment, for there were
very few lines.

My dear sir:
    You will be pleased to know I have annulled
your marriage to Mrs. Augusta R. L. Magruder
as you requested, effective as of the above date.

The rest was blurred by the tears in her eyes.

Chapter Eighteen

I will not beg, I will not, Rose vowed silently as she stood beside the cart Crank had hitched up at her insistence. Pride, even pride that was tattered almost beyond recognition, was all that had carried her through the last hour. She had packed one of Annie's outgrown gowns in with her own, while tears blinded her eyes. She had held her small body, not too tightly, and whispered love messages, then sat her in her crib with all her toys around her. Her own bed was still unmade, and she had left every single black gown she possessed hanging in the wardrobe. They could rot there for all she cared.

"But I don't know nothing about babies," Tressy whined. She had followed her outdoors, a smug look of triumph slowly giving way to one of dismay.

"Crank will show you what to do."

Rose would have taken Annie with her if she'd dared, despite her own uncertain future, but Annie needed a home and Rose didn't have one. Besides, she didn't dare risk a kidnapping charge.

"Remember, now, you're not to give her any meat unless it's freshly cooked, and if her milk smells the least bit sour, open a fresh can. She won't wake during the night, but she'll be soaked when she wakes up in the morning. If her bottom gets red, use Vaseline, otherwise, dust her with cornstarch." There was an edge to her voice that came from trying too hard not to cry and curse and scream out her grief.

"Rosie, listen to me, you got it all wrong," Crank pleaded. He looked ready to weep, himself. If he did, then she would break, too, and she couldn't afford the least show of weakness.

"Another thing, she needs new gowns, larger ones. Ruffles are all right—embroidery, too, but lace scratches. No silk, either."

Crank nodded. "No silk, no lace. Rosie, give the boy a chance to speak his piece."

"He spoke his piece where it counted most, to the lawyer." Her head was high, her eyes dry, but she couldn't quite control the tremor in her voice.

Crank patted her hand awkwardly. "It's all a mistake. I smell Bess's hand in this."

"The letter stated the facts quite clearly, and Bess's name wasn't mentioned."

"Who's Bess?" Tressy put in.

They ignored her as if she weren't even there. "Now remember, I'm counting on you, Crank. Miss Riddle admits she doesn't know the first thing about babies. I'm not at all sure she wants to learn, but she is Annie's aunt. We can't forget that."

"I don't see how you can go off and leave that baby this way, I surely don't," the old man grumbled. Nevertheless, he swung her trunk up into the back of the cart. "It's desertion, that's what it is."

"Crank, don't. It's painful enough without that. Just remember, I'll always love you. And tell Annie, when she's old enough to understand, that wherever I am, I'll always love her, too." She swallowed hard, accepted a boost up onto the seat and took the reins in her hands.

And Matt, she added silently. She loved him enough to forgive him, only not yet. Not while the hurt was so terribly fresh. If he married again—and for Annie's sake, he probably would—then she didn't want to know about it. He might even keep Tressy here. She was certainly pretty enough, and she was Annie's aunt, after all.

Rose still had trouble believing he had ended their marriage without even giving her a chance. He should have told her when she'd confessed her identity. Instead, he had led her on, come to her bed— made her believe he might one day learn to love her. Not in so many words, but certainly by his actions.

Swallowing her tears, she clucked the mule into a torpid walk, praying that Matt would be delayed so that she wouldn't meet him on the road. If that happened, and she knew in her heart that it might, then she could only hope he would have the decency to let her go.

And that she would have the good sense to nod politely instead of hurling herself at him to plead for a second chance.

She mopped her eyes with the back of her hand, braced her shoulders, and told herself this was the only way. She could hardly stay on knowing he'd taken legal steps to get rid of her.

Heat shimmered over the flat sandy road ahead like an ephemeral tide. She knew about mirages. Sometimes it seemed as if her entire life had been a mirage. A house built on shifting sands.

She had lost all sense of how much time had passed when a distant rumble of thunder made her glance up, only to discover that the sky had grown ominously dark.

Oh, Lord, she really didn't need this. "Move, mule, or we'll both be sorry."

Angel continued to plod. The thunder grew louder, more constant. A few minutes later the first few drops of rain fell. "Hurry, Angel!" She had long since lost track of her umbrella, and her waterproof coat, too hot for summer wear, was packed in her trunk.

She could only pray there was a boat at the landing, ready to cast off. She would have to ask someone to carry her trunk aboard and find someone else, perhaps John, to see to Angel and the cart.

At least she had passage money. Crank had insisted on giving her that when he couldn't talk her out of leaving. She had taken it because she had earned it. Matt had promised her a salary, which should have given her some indication of his true feelings, if only she hadn't been so besotted. The fact that he'd never got around to paying her could be either a good sign or a bad one. Either way, it no longer mattered.

There was a sudden flash of lightning, followed almost immediately by a crack of thunder directly overhead. Sand was blowing so that she couldn't look up without being blinded. With her skirts swirling about her knees, she slapped the reins across Angel's rump and shouted, ''Run, you lazy creature, or we'll both be in trouble!''

At the sound of her voice, Angel stopped dead in her tracks.

''Oh, for Heaven's sake, not again,'' Rose wailed. Reins in hand, she leaped down from the high seat and hurried around to see if she could coerce the mule into moving. ''Don't *do* this to me,'' she warned. ''Not again, I won't have it.''

''Twist her ear.''

Dropping the reins, she spun around and slapped a hand over her heart. The mule made a braying noise that sounded remarkably like demented laughter.

''She hates it,'' Matt said calmly. He had ridden up silently, appearing suddenly through the mist of rain and blowing sand. ''You climb back aboard and I'll twist it, but be prepared. She might take off at a gallop.''

She did. Rose hung on, getting thoroughly drenched as the clouds overhead unburdened themselves. Riding beside her, his shoulders hunched against the driving rain, Matt indicated a narrow road that led toward the sound. Rose followed his direction, not daring to admit to herself that she had half expected to meet him again. She had told herself that a clean break was the best way, but the break wasn't clean, it was ragged and hurtful, the kind of wound that took forever to heal.

He pointed to a large shed with a lean-to shelter

off one side. Dismounting, he led both animals under the shelter, then reached up before Rose could move away and swung her down from the cart. Neither of them spoke a word, but as her body slid down past his, she was reminded vividly of the last time he'd lifted her to the ground. Now, as then, no matter how miserable she was, his touch was all it took to set her aflame.

Removing herself from the steadying hands that clasped her shoulders, she drew in a deep, tremulous breath. *Behave yourself, Augusta Rose, don't even think what you're thinking!*

"Come inside, the rain's starting to blow in under the roof."

Not that either of them could get any wetter than they were, but there was hardly enough room for two animals, a cart and a stack of lumber. Besides, it was impossible to remain aloof when she was as aware of his wet clothing as she was of her own. Of the way his shirt, all but transparent now, clung to his body, the intimate details she remembered so well clearly visible. The bronzed skin, the darker nipples, the swirls of hair surrounding them still darker.

Matt sucked in his breath, tugged his wet shirttail from under his belt to hang loose about his hips. Rose plucked her clinging skirts away from her body. "Come inside," he said. Holding the wide door open, he ushered her into a gloomy space that smelled of some spicy wood. "The floor's just sand, but there's a pile of shavings over in the corner. We might as well sit down until it slacks off. You can start by explaining where you were going in such a hurry.''

Rose sat because she wasn't certain how long her knees would support her. But just because she sat, that didn't mean she had to explain. If anyone was owed an explanation, it was she.

He sat beside her—close, but not quite touching. She crossed her arms over her breasts and struggled against feelings of anger, hurt and embarrassment. She was experienced enough to deal with each of those emotions separately, but when they all came together, it made it difficult.

And when they were distorted by sexual awareness, it made it impossible.

Matt moved closer. He leaned over and raised his voice over the sound of the drumming rain. ''You saw the letter, didn't you?''

She didn't reply, didn't have to. He knew.

''I should've brought it with me, either that or taken time to explain, but I wanted to get hold of Dixon and get the paperwork started.''

She turned to stare at him, only to find that he was too close, so close that even in the dim interior she could see the depth of his eyes, the way his mouth shaped itself when he was uncomfortable.

She was uncomfortable, too, and so confused she hardly knew what to say. ''What paperwork? I thought that was all done. Didn't your lawyer handle everything?'' Shivering in her clammy clothes, she tried in vain to ignore the man beside her, but his warmth reached out to envelop her, tempting her to seek shelter in his arms. The elusive scents of salt and sunshine, horses and healthy male sweat, mingled with the fragrance of juniper, were far more intoxicating than any fine perfume.

Robert had favored a heavy cologne, one more reminder, as if she'd needed it, of the many differences between her two husbands. "Rose? I'm sorry you found the letter. I'd like to explain."

"What good would it do? Yes, I read the letter." She refused to implicate Tressy. "The words were perfectly clear. You might have told me before I— that is, before you—"

"Took you as my wife."

"That you did not," she quickly denied.

"That's what I did, Rose, whether you want to believe it or not. It didn't start out that way, I'll admit, because when I first found out you were the woman I'd married, I wanted to make you pay for all the nights I'd lain awake thinking about you in your bed just down the hall. All the times I had to turn away to hide the shape I was in. And then to find out that all along, I'd had every right to want you. You were my wife."

"Then the letter was wrong? Mr. Bagby lied, and you didn't ask him to annul the marriage?"

Matt shifted uncomfortably beside her, his arm brushing against her own. "I did, but like I said, I'd just found out how you deceived me. The trouble is, I'd already started loving you, but since I thought I was married to a woman who had disappeared without a trace, there wasn't one damn thing I could do about it." He shrugged his shoulders and sighed.

"The only excuse I can offer is that I was still mad as hell when I got home."

He had already started loving her?

Her heart swelled in her breast, but Rose had learned to be wary. "Then where does Mr. Dixon fit in? Wasn't Bagby's word good enough for you?"

He grimaced. Even in the dim light that filtered in through the single high window, she could see that much. Lifting her hand from her lap, he began absently stroking her wrist with his thumb. "In case you hadn't noticed, I'm not very good at explaining."

"I'd noticed. You're used to issuing orders and then going about your business, certain you'll be obeyed without question." Her wrist was beginning to tingle, but she didn't withdraw it. She was beginning to tingle in other places, as well.

He had the nerve to grin. "Guilty as charged. But you see, I didn't know if we were married or not until I got the letter. By the time I found out we weren't, I had to do something, fast. You might be— that is, we might have made us a baby, and if that's the case, then the sooner we put this marriage back together, the better."

She made herself take the time to consider his words. "In other words, the first time you married me it was for Annie's sake. Now you want to marry me again for the sake of the baby you think I might be carrying, is that what you're saying?"

They were leaning up against the shed wall, enveloped in the incense-like aura of juniper. The thunder had grown more distant, the blue-white flashes of lightning less frequent. Wind wailed outside, driving walls of water against the outside of the shed.

"It's a good enough reason, isn't it?"

"I'm not sure. I know I agreed to come here and look after Annie so that you could go off again, but…"

"But?" he prompted.

But that was before I learned to love you. Before I learned how not to be seasick so I could go with you wherever you went, and learned how to ride a horse so we could ride together when we came back home for a visit.

"Matt, would you mind explaining why you didn't tell me when I confessed my own sins that you'd had our marriage annulled?"

He grimaced. "Anger. Hurt pride, I guess. I told you, I wanted to make you pay for all my sleepless nights."

"You wanted revenge, in other words." Hurt pride, she could understand, having suffered from it too many times in the past. Anger was a form of passion, and she knew for a fact that Matt was a passionate man.

She also knew that unlike Robert, he had both the strength of character and the maturity to control his emotions.

"You know about Annie, and how I came to have her. Those things happen, Rose, but I've always tried…"

He shook his head, and Rose did her best to remain unaffected by his nearness as he went on to describe his reluctance to take a wife—any wife. And then, when he'd finally overcome his reluctance, his frustration when that wife failed to appear.

"With the lesson of Billy and Murdoch's woman still fresh in my mind, it didn't help when I started noticing Bess's secretary-companion. By noticing, I mean—" He cleared his throat, picked up her hand again and began toying with her fingers. "Once I got to know you better, I—liked you. As a person, I mean. I sort of looked forward to having you around."

"You had an odd way of showing it," she said dryly.

"That's because—well, about the same time I started liking you, you sort of loosened up and I saw you as...well, as a woman."

"I believe that's called lust." She thought he colored then, but in the dim light it was impossible to be certain. "I like you, too," she said quietly. She would admit to that much, but that was as far as she was prepared to go.

His hand slid warmly up under her damp sleeve. He leaned closer to peer into her eyes. "Do you, Rose?"

It took a moment before she could find the breath to answer. "I—you know I do. I would never have..."

"Never have what, Rose? Never have let me make love to you?"

The tension inside was suddenly more powerful than the electrical storm outside. "To be honest, I'm not sure." It seemed imperative to change the subject before she got in any deeper. "Wh-why were you going to see Mr. Dixon?"

He was caressing her upper arm, his fingertips rough on the sensitive skin there. "I told you, to make arrangements to marry you again. And to tell him that if he still wanted me to apply for his job, I'd do it."

She turned so suddenly her nose nearly bumped his. "But—why?"

"Why do I want to marry you again?"

"That, too, but why would you even think of becoming a magistrate now that you've finally got your ship back?"

"You know the answer to the first question. It's also the answer to the second one. Feeling the way I do, I could hardly marry you and then go off and leave you, which means getting a shore job. And Rose, you might as well know everything while we're clearing the air. I had to mortgage the Point, and the job of magistrate doesn't pay much, so we'll never be rich."

She couldn't think of a single thing to say. His hand on her arm grew still. His eyes searched her face, and he said, "Rose, say something. I love you so much it flat-out scares the devil out of me. I can't even look at you without wanting to get under your skirts. Why do you think I've been staying away?"

"You *love* me?" She still couldn't quite believe it.

"Well, hell—you don't think I'd go through all this for anything less, do you?"

"But, Matt—I learned to sail just so I wouldn't

get seasick if you wanted me to go with you. That is, I didn't exactly learn to sail, but at least I can sit in a moving boat without turning myself wrongside out.''

''You did that for me?''

Wordlessly, she nodded. ''If you marry me again, I want us to be together. I don't really care where that is.''

He groaned. And then he said, ''Sweetheart, I don't care, either, as long as there's a bunk. In case you hadn't noticed, my shirttail's been hanging out ever since we got here. Even soaking wet, with your hair hanging in rat's tails down your back, you have that effect on me.'' His voice was tender, amused and tense, all at the same time.

Rose, feeling more confident by the moment, mused aloud, ''Why do you suppose it is that men ended up wearing tight pants and women the long, full skirts?''

''You want to talk about fashion at a time like this?''

''Is there something else you'd rather do while we wait for the rain to slack off?''

''Unless you happen to have a deck of cards, our choices are pretty limited.'' But even as he spoke he was lowering her onto the bed of wood shavings, feeling for the buttons at the front of her dress.

Rose, buoyed by a confidence she had never before known, slid her hands down his chest to his waist, and from there to the impressive ridge pressing against the front of his trousers. When his flesh leaped in response, she closed her eyes and murmured breathlessly, "You'd better tell me now if you don't want me to touch you here. I love the way you feel…the way you make me feel."

"Sweetheart, you can touch me any way you want to, anywhere, anytime, but don't hold me responsible for the consequences."

His eyes widened, his hands suddenly grew still. "Consequences," he repeated. "Rose…do you think—that is, are you—did we make us a baby? Is that why you've been sick?"

"Don't stop now, please," she urged. Between them they had managed to get her drawers down around her knees, her gown up around her waist, his trousers and shirt unbuttoned. It wasn't enough, but it would have to do. "It was the chicken," she gasped. "That and wondering what I'd done wrong. Lift your bottom and let me get your pants off."

"And dust me down with cornstarch?" he growled, laughter threading through the sexual tension.

They laughed together later, too. Having exhausted each other with passion, they lay replete, savoring the sweetness of knowing there was a lifetime of such passion before them.

"There's a demand for inlet pilots, too. Pays some better than magistrate."

"You love the *Black Swan,*" she reminded him.

"I do. But not without you, Rose."

"Do you think Annie would grow up to be like Bess if we raise her aboard the *Swan?*"

"God, I hope not. One Bess is all I can deal with."

"Bess is...different, but she grows on you, once you understand the way her mind works. If it hadn't been for Bess, we'd never have met."

He turned to her then, her bare breasts hot and damp against his naked chest. "Don't you believe it, love. I'm not a superstitious man, but this I know. We'd have come together somewhere, sometime, even without Bess. Some things are meant to be."

* * * * *

Praise for Bronwyn Williams's previous books

BEHOLDEN
"...as welcome as a cool breeze on a scorching day. I can't resist a fast-paced, well-written story."
—*Rendezvous*

ENTWINED
"Her intricately woven story is deftly done, and her depiction of her hero and heroine is masterful."
—*Affaire de Coeur*

SEASPELL
"A terrific read, I loved it!"
—Pamela Morsi

THE PAPER MARRIAGE

Harlequin Historical #524—August 2000

HARLEQUIN®
Makes any time special ™

HARLEQUIN
Duets™

Pick up a Harlequin Duets™ from August-October 2000 and receive $1.00 off the original cover price. *

Experience the "lighter side of love"
in a Harlequin Duets™.
This unbeatable value just became
irresistible with our special introductory
price of $4.99 U.S./$5.99 CAN. for
2 Brand-New, Full-Length
Romantic Comedies.

**Don't miss
an exciting opportunity
to save on the purchase of
Harlequin and Silhouette books!**

Buy any two Harlequin or
Silhouette books and save
$10.00 off future Harlequin
and Silhouette purchases

OR

buy any three
Harlequin or Silhouette books
and save **$20.00 off** future
Harlequin and Silhouette purchases.

*Watch for details
coming in October 2000!*

PHQ400

Romance is just one click away!

online book **serials**

> ➤ *Exclusive* to our web site, get caught up in both the daily and weekly online installments of new romance stories.

> ➤ Try the Writing Round Robin. Contribute a chapter to a story created by our members. Plus, winners will get prizes.

romantic **travel**

> ➤ Want to know where the best place to kiss in New York City is, or which restaurant in Los Angeles is the most romantic? Check out our Romantic Hot Spots for the scoop.

> ➤ Share your travel tips and stories with us on the romantic travel message boards.

romantic reading **library**

> ➤ Relax as you read our collection of Romantic Poetry.

> ➤ Take a peek at the Top 10 Most Romantic Lines!

Visit us online at

www.eHarlequin.com
on Women.com Networks

BRONWYN WILLIAMS

As the daughters of a major-league ballplayer and granddaughters of a sea captain, it's easy to see where the two sisters who write as Bronwyn Williams, Dixie Browning and Mary Williams, get much of their material. The two grew up on the Outer Banks of North Carolina. After years of living away, Dixie, the wife of an electrical engineer, now retired, and Mary, the wife of a Coast Guard officer, also retired, have returned to their roots. As with many of Dixie Browning's nearly seventy contemporaries for Silhouette, most of the sisters' stories written as Bronwyn Williams have been set in northeastern North Carolina, an area rich in history and folklore. The two began writing historicals for Harlequin in 1988, and *The Paper Marriage* marks their return to the line after publishing a number of titles with NAL/Topaz.

HH524IBC